MYSTERY AT
THE STATION HOTEL

By Edward Marston

MYSTERY AT
THE STATION HOTEL

EDWARD MARSTON

Allison & Busby Limited
11 Wardour Mews
London W1F 8AN
allisonandbusby.com

First published in Great Britain by Allison & Busby in 2025.

A CIP catalogue record for this book is available from
the British Library.

First Edition

ISBN 978-0-7490-3124-4

Typeset in 11/16.5 pt Adobe Garamond Pro by
Allison and Busby Ltd.

By choosing this product, you help take care of the world's forests.
Learn more: www.fsc.org.

Printed and bound in the UK using 100% Renewable Electricity at
CPI Group (UK) Ltd, Croydon, CR0 4YY

CHAPTER ONE

Shropshire, 1866

Days began early for Molly Burrage. As owner of the Station Hotel in Shrewsbury, she had to get up at the crack of dawn to unlock the front door so that staff members who lived elsewhere could get in, then she worked through the long list of jobs she had compiled the previous night. Molly was tireless. A stout, bustling, grey-haired widow in her fifties, she was alert, industrious and always smartly dressed. In every way, she set a standard that her employees struggled to match. None of them had her energy and sense of commitment. Nor did they have her natural air of authority.

When she heard the front door open and shut, she did not need to see the newcomer. Molly identified the miscreant at once.

'You're half an hour late, Annie,' she snapped.

'I'm sorry, Mrs Burrage. What happened was this . . .'

'Don't even try to give me one of your excuses. I know them off by heart. There's a penalty for lateness,' said Molly, coming into the corridor to confront the young woman. 'I'll take it off your wages.'

'That's unfair!' cried Annie.

'It's the rules.'

'I didn't do it on purpose.'

'Well, now that you're finally here, make yourself useful. The gentleman in number five asked for an early call because he has a train to catch. Knock on his door and be sure to wait until you hear Mr Lockyer wake up.'

'Yes, Mrs Burrage.'

'Well, don't stand there gawping,' said Molly. 'Do what I told you.'

'I will,' said the other, heading for the stairs.

Annie Garrow was tall, slim, and gangly with a shock of red hair and a freckled face. Now sixteen, she had been overjoyed to land a job at the Station Hotel. The quick turnover of guests meant that she got to meet a whole range of people. Whenever at work, she was conscientious and willing. Her only fault was her bad timekeeping. Given an order, she sought to impress her employer by rushing upstairs to the first floor and trotting to the designated room. Annie rapped on the door with her knuckles. When there was no sound from within, she knocked even harder but there was still no response. She therefore resorted to pounding on the door with her fists. Even if he were fast asleep, the guest was bound to be roused.

Yet she still could not hear any noise from inside the room. It was not the first time it had happened to her. On two previous occasions when she had been told to wake guests up, she had been met by stony silence. In both cases, the gentlemen involved were in a drunken stupor. A brass band playing only feet away could not have woken them up. Had the same thing happened to her again? Annie ran back downstairs to report to her employer.

'I couldn't wake the gentleman up, Mrs Burrage,' she said.

'Then you didn't try hard enough, girl. Mr Lockyer was most insistent. He needs to catch a particular train, and our job is to make sure that he is at the station on time. I'll show you how to wake someone up,' she went on, heading for the stairs with Annie trotting behind her. 'You must be firm. Men of Mr Lockyer's age often have poor hearing. Make allowance for that.'

'I used both fists,' wailed Annie.

'Shut up, girl – and watch me.'

When she reached the room in question, Molly knocked on the door. Eliciting no response from within, she kicked the door hard with her foot a couple of times. Once again, the noise failed to wake up their guest. Seeing the exasperation coming into Molly's face, Annie had the sense to hold her tongue. She watched as the other woman pulled out a key from her pocket and thrust it into the lock. After turning it sharply, Molly tried to open the door, but it would not budge.

'He's bolted himself in,' she complained.

'Then we'll just have to leave him be,' said Annie.

'Don't be ridiculous, girl! If a guest makes a request, we must obey him. Go and fetch Mr Harris and be quick about it!'

'Yes, Mrs Burrage.'

Turning on her heel, Annie raced off downstairs and went into the bar. In less than a minute, she returned with the bulky figure of Wilfred Harris, the resident barman, who had worked at the hotel for years and was used to coping with emergencies. Annie was chattering in his ear. Molly snapped her fingers to shut the girl up then turned to the barman.

'I need to get inside this room, Wilf. It's bolted so there's only one way to open it.'

'Stand back,' he said, grasping the knob and twisting it.

After testing the door with his shoulder, he drew himself back then smashed into it with full force. The bolt flew off immediately and the door swung open. Since the curtains were closed, the room was in shadow. Someone was alone in the bed, apparently asleep. Molly went into the room and pulled back the curtains before crossing to the bed and shaking the guest's shoulder. Julian Lockyer did not respond. When she shook him again, Molly dislodged the bedsheet from his neck and exposed an ugly red wound that stretched from ear to ear. His bare chest was covered with blood.

Harris moved forward to take over, pulling back the bedclothes completely to reveal the fat, ugly, naked body of their guest. Both wrists had been slashed open. Lying beside the man's right hand was a blood-stained knife. Molly was aghast and Annie was retching uncontrollably. Mouth agape, Harris was the first to offer an opinion.

'The poor bugger's gone and killed himself!'

CHAPTER TWO

Superintendent Edward Tallis was known at Scotland Yard for his swift response to a summons. As soon as he read the telegraph, he sent for Robert Colbeck. Within a minute, the inspector was standing in front of his superior's desk.

'Where is it this time, sir?' he asked.

'Shrewsbury. You've been asked for by name.'

'I'll do my best to justify their faith in me.'

'On reflection,' said Tallis, handing him the telegraph, 'you may not need to go there. If it's simply a case of suicide in a railway hotel, I think that the local police can easily deal with it.'

'Then why did they contact us?' said Colbeck, reading the telegraph.

'They didn't. As you can see, the request came from the

stationmaster. The deceased held a position of some importance in the Great Western Railway.'

'I know, sir. Julian Lockyer is a name that I recognise.'

Tallis was surprised. 'Really?'

'He is on the board of directors and is – or was – more than likely to become its next chairman. In other words, he had a very good reason to stay alive. Would a man about to secure a position he has coveted even think about taking his own life?'

'Probably not.'

'Then I have good reason to go to Shrewsbury to investigate.' He handed the telegraph back to the superintendent. 'If you'll excuse me, sir . . .'

'One moment,' said Tallis. 'Before you dash off, would it not be sensible to contact the Borough Constabulary? They will tell you if your journey is necessary.'

'In their eyes, it is not. But for the action of the stationmaster, I would be unaware of what happened in the town. The Shropshire Constabulary and the Borough Constabulary are both based in Shrewsbury. Neither of them feels the need for our assistance. It means that we will be seen as interlopers.' Colbeck smiled. 'It's not the first time we'll have a frosty reception.'

Edward Tallis sat back in his chair and studied the telegraph once more. He inhaled deeply through his nose then looked up at Colbeck. 'What is going on up there in Shrewsbury?'

'There's only one way to find out.'

'I'm very tempted to come with you.'

'That would be foolish, sir,' said Colbeck quickly. 'Your place is here. A captain must not desert his ship.'

'It's the commissioner who is on the bridge at Scotland Yard.'

'Yes, but he has you at his side because he relies so heavily on your advice. Leave this assignment to me and Sergeant Leeming. We'll be in touch from Shrewsbury as soon as we can.' Colbeck headed for the door. 'I don't know why but I have a feeling that it's going to be an interesting case to work on. Goodbye, sir.'

And before Tallis could say another word, Colbeck had left the room.

The three of them were sitting nervously in Molly Burrage's office. Annie Garrow was still trembling, Wilfred Harris was deep in thought and Molly was fearing the impact that the death would have on business at the hotel.

'Nothing like this has ever happened before,' she complained. 'We've never lost a single guest here. What will the other guests think when they realise that they've been sleeping near a dead body? They won't be able to leave quick enough. Who will want to stay here when they hear about Mr Lockyer killing himself in that room?'

'I'll never forget the shock of seeing all that blood,' said Annie. 'It was frightening.'

'Do you feel well enough to stay here?'

'Not really, Mrs Burrage. I'm terrified.'

'Then you'd best go home. I'll expect you back tomorrow – on time.'

Annie nodded gratefully then let herself out of the room. The sound of the door opening and shutting brought Harris out of his reverie. He turned to Molly.

'I've been thinking,' he said.

'What about?'

'Mr Lockyer. When he arrived yesterday, he came into the bar for a drink.'

'So?'

'I poured him a whisky.'

'Nothing wrong in that, is there?'

'He took it from me with his left hand,' recalled the barman. 'And when he paid, he put his left hand into his coat to take out a wallet. Do you see what that means?'

'Yes,' she said, eyes widening. 'He was left-handed.'

'So why was that knife by his right hand? If he meant to cut his throat and wrists, he'd have used the other hand.' His brow furrowed. 'I'll wager that someone else was in that room, someone who made it look as if he'd killed himself. In fact, it wasn't a case of suicide at all,' declared Harris. 'I reckon Mr Lockyer was murdered.'

'That's even worse,' wailed Molly, struggling to keep tears at bay. 'How can we ever let that room to a guest? They'd have nightmares in there. Oh, this is terrible, Wilf! It could finish us off.'

'Let's see what the police have to say. They've been here long enough.'

'At least they had the body removed.'

'Yes,' said Harris. 'That was a blessing.'

'No, it wasn't, Wilf. Having a guest carried out of here on a stretcher by two policemen is an awful thing to see. Tongues will be wagging madly. The hotel will get a bad name.'

'Nothing can damage your reputation,' he assured her. 'Everyone knows that Molly Burrage provides good service for her guests. It's the reason we keep so busy. Nothing will change.'

'I hope so.'

'To be honest, I'm more worried about Annie than about the hotel.'

'Why?'

'She's still young and innocent. The poor girl didn't empty her stomach just because she saw all that blood. It was because it was the first time in her life that she looked at a naked man.' Harris grimaced. 'That sight is going to haunt her for the rest of her days.'

Victor Leeming was accustomed to sudden departures to distant locations. As soon as Colbeck told him that they had to leave London, the sergeant scribbled a note to his wife then reached for the valise that contained all that he needed for nights spent away. Colbeck did the same thing, penning a swift letter and leaving it on his desk beside Leeming's note, confident that both missives would be delivered by hand to their respective wives. Leaving Scotland Yard, they hailed a cab. In what seemed like no time at all, they were climbing into the empty compartment of a train.

'Why are we going to Shrewsbury, sir?' asked Leeming.

'We've been summoned by the stationmaster.'

'He has no warrant to get in touch with us. Why didn't he consult the local police?'

'I suspect that he did just that, Victor. They probably told him that it was none of his business and that we were, in any case, not needed.'

'That means we're going where we're not actually wanted.'

'The stationmaster wants us,' said Colbeck. 'He acted wisely.' He heaved a sigh. 'It's a pity we can't go via the Cotswolds.'

'Why?'

'Because I'd appreciate a word with Stephen Rydall.'

'Do you mean that man we met from Frampton Mansell?'

'Yes, he sits on the board of the Great Western Railway. I'd have been glad to hear his opinion of Julian Lockyer.'

'Who is he?'

'He might well have been the next chairman of the company,' said Colbeck, 'but his corpse was discovered this morning at the Station Hotel in Shrewsbury.'

'Was it a natural death?'

'According to the telegraph, it was a suicide. I disagree. Why would a man about to achieve a position he has yearned for suddenly kill himself? It doesn't make sense.'

'Do you think a rival at the GWR is involved?'

'It wouldn't surprise me, Victor. As we know only too well, railway ownership is a dog-eat-dog world. Competition between companies is fierce and the same goes for rivals among directors. They may beam at each other across the table at board meetings but each one of them is seeking power and influence. Mr Lockyer was not the only candidate for the position of chairman.'

'Would someone kill to achieve such a position?'

'Most certainly.'

'Where will we stay in Shrewsbury?'

'There are three hotels mentioned in Bradshaw,' said Colbeck, flipping through the pages of the handbook he always carried on train journeys. 'Here we are,' he went on as he found what he was looking for. 'The recommended hotels are The Lion, The Raven and The George. I'm sure that any one of them will be ideal for our purposes.'

'What about the Station Hotel itself?'

'It looks as if it may well have been a murder scene. That means the place will be crawling with policemen. I think we deserve more privacy.'

Molly was alone in her office when there was a tap on the door. It opened to reveal the sizeable frame of Detective Inspector Hubert

Crabbe. He was a tall, square-jawed, middle-aged man with a pair of bristling eyebrows meeting to create a bushy hedge that all but concealed his eyes.

'Well?' asked Molly, rising to her feet.

'I do not believe we are dealing with a suicide, Mrs Burrage.'

'Are you quite sure?'

'Oh, yes. I'm certain. Mr Lockyer was murdered by someone who escaped through the window. Before he left, the killer bolted the door. I'd like a list of all the other guests here, please.'

Molly was shaken. 'You're not suggesting that one of them could be the killer, are you?'

'We must explore every possibility.'

'What reason could anyone have to . . . ?'

'I can think of several reasons, Mrs Burrage. The obvious one that comes to mind is theft. Everything of value has disappeared – his wedding ring, wallet, pocket watch, cufflinks and clothing. Even his shoes were stolen. The killer missed nothing. Everything was stuffed into Mr Lockyer's valise and taken.'

'Do you think the killer was a local man?'

'No, I don't,' said Crabbe with emphasis. 'Thanks to us, all the real villains in Shropshire are either dead or in prison. The killer came from somewhere else. I'd put money on it.' He took out his notebook. 'I've taken a full statement from Wilf Harris. Now it's your turn.'

'Yes, of course.'

'And I understand that there's a third person to interview.'

'Annie Garrow. She works here.'

'I'll need to speak to her.'

'Yes, of course. I sent her home, so you'll have to go there. Please be gentle with the girl.'

'Don't tell me how to do my job, Mrs Burrage. Now then,' he said, lowering himself into a seat and producing a pad and pencil, 'at what time did Mr Lockyer arrive here yesterday?'

'Not long after three in the afternoon, I'd say.'

'What was your first impression of him?'

'Well, to be honest, I didn't like him at all. He was so bossy – one of those men who expects to be treated as if he's the only guest in the hotel. Wilf probably told you the same thing. Mr Lockyer walked in here as if he owned the place. Also,' she added, 'I didn't like the look of contempt he gave me. It was as if I was his minion. I won't take that sort of treatment from anybody, Inspector.'

'In his case,' said Crabbe, 'you won't ever have to.'

'He insisted on having a room with a double bed.'

'But he was staying here on his own.'

'He said that he was a restless sleeper.'

Crabbe sniffed. 'Not any more.'

CHAPTER THREE

Victor Leeming hated travelling by train. By way of a defence mechanism, he fell asleep as soon as possible. Colbeck was as immaculately dressed as usual, but the sergeant was now a rumpled heap on the seat opposite, his top hat beside him and his snores hidden beneath the noise of the wheels as they sped along the rails. Looking at his friend, Colbeck gave an affectionate smile. Others might complain about Leeming's spectacular untidiness, but the inspector knew his true worth. Having the sergeant beside him in any investigation was a source of great comfort.

It was not Colbeck's first visit to the county town of Shropshire. He had been there years earlier to meet a man named Donald Underhill, a local solicitor, who was a suspect for the murder of a woman whose body had been found in a shallow grave close to the Newcastle and Carlisle Railway. In fact, Underhill had been innocent of the crime but had nursed more than a fondness for the beautiful young widow in question. Colbeck had warmed to Shrewsbury the moment he saw it, relishing its sense of history and its total lack of major industry. Underhill had told him that the town was known chiefly for its cakes and brawn, jellied loaves that were justifiably popular on market days.

The person he had noticed at Shrewsbury General Station on his first visit was the stationmaster, Simon Biddle, a small, skinny individual of uncertain age who atoned for his lack of physical presence by having a voice like thunder. Even if a train was speeding through the station, the voice could be heard rising effortlessly above the roar. Colbeck hoped that the stationmaster was more subdued in conversation.

Leeming suddenly twitched then sat up abruptly.

'Where are we?' he asked, struggling to open an eye.

'Less than half an hour from Shrewsbury, Victor.'

'Good God! Have I been asleep that long? I'm so sorry.'

'No apology required. You obviously needed a good rest. It's just as well. Once our investigation is under way, neither of us will have much time to enjoy any slumber.'

'Is it going to be a difficult case?'

'I believe so. There was a note of desperation in the stationmaster's telegraph.'

'Why was that?'

'He has no trust in the local constabulary,' said Colbeck. 'That's why he turned to us.'

Word had spread throughout the town like wildfire that something terrible had occurred at the Station Hotel. Hard facts took second place to fevered speculation. On their way to the station, people hung around outside the hotel for a short while, hoping to learn more of what happened during the night. Molly Burrage glanced through the window of her office.

'There must be dozens of them out there,' she protested. 'We've become a peepshow.'

'People are bound to be curious,' said Hubert Crabbe.

'Can't you tell them that the body has been taken away?'

'They'll soon disperse. They all have trains to catch.'

'Yes,' she moaned, 'but as soon as they go, they'll be replaced by another set of ghouls.'

'The stink of death always attracts an audience, Mrs Burrage. It's human nature. If you wish, I'll put a uniformed constable outside to move people on.'

'That would help, Inspector. He could tell them the body is no longer here.'

'Leave it to me,' he said. About to move away, he remembered something. 'I need to give you a word of warning. There'll be a lot of press interest. I'll issue a statement, of course, but that won't keep them at bay. The newspapers will be desperate to speak to you.'

'I don't want publicity!' she cried.

'There's no way that you can avoid it, Mrs Burrage. You were there when the dead body was discovered. And so was Wilf Harris, of course. You're both afraid that people will stay away from here because of what happened. The opposite is likely to happen,' he warned. 'When people stop work at the end of a long day, a lot of them will come into your bar so that they can hear Harris telling them exactly what happened. He's going to have a big audience.'

'That's terrible!'

'It's unavoidable, I'm afraid. You ought to take him aside and tell him to say as little as possible. Otherwise, your bar will turn into a music hall. Crowds will flock in to hear the tale of the blood-covered corpse. You don't want that to happen, do you?'

Shaking visibly, Molly put a hand against the wall for support.

When their train finally arrived at the station, the detectives did not need to search for the stationmaster. The voice of Simon Biddle cut sharply through the hubbub. He had picked Colbeck out by virtue of the latter's striking appearance.

'I'm over here!' he cried, waving an arm.

Spotting him near the exit, they moved towards him with the crowd surging around them. Suddenly, Biddle disappeared. Leeming was worried.

'We've lost him,' he said.

'He's still there, Victor. He is very short. He's probably been standing on something.'

'I've never heard anyone with a voice as loud as that.'

'It's the thing I noticed about him when I first came here.'

As the other passengers began to disperse, the stationmaster came burrowing through the remnants of the crowd. He stopped to marvel at the detectives.

'Thank God you've come!' he said.

'We've responded to your summons,' said Colbeck. 'This is Detective Sergeant Leeming, by the way.' Leeming smiled wearily but Biddle ignored him. 'How did you recognise me?'

'I've followed your career with great interest, Inspector. There were sketches of you in the newspapers.' He pointed a finger. 'My office is over there. Make yourselves comfortable while I dispatch this train.'

'Good idea,' said Colbeck.

He and Leeming walked along the platform until they came to the office. As soon as they entered it, they saw the newspaper cuttings pinned to the notice board. All of them related to their previous cases. Colbeck was praised by name in most of the headlines. There was an occasional mention of Leeming. The office was filled with an amiable clutter of charts, lists, timetables and advertisements. On the large calendar, they noticed, each day had been cancelled with a decisive black cross.

After sending the train on its way, Biddle came into the office and beamed at Colbeck. 'A thousand thanks for coming, Inspector!' he said effusively. 'We need someone of your experience. Inspector Crabbe would never have solved the murder on his own.'

'I thought it was a case of suicide,' said Leeming.

'That's what we were meant to think, Sergeant.'

'What do you mean?'

'If a guest at the hotel had killed himself, all they'd need is two policemen to carry the body out. But a whole posse of them turned up. Mark my words, Detective Inspector Crabbe would only be involved if it was a murder case. He's been in that hotel for hours.'

'I look forward to meeting him,' said Colbeck.

'But I haven't told you about the victim yet. I had a brush with Mr Lockyer when he arrived here yesterday. He was full of himself,' recalled Biddle. 'When he got off the train, he came looking for me and boasted that he was a member of the GWR board. He had the gall to criticise the station and told me that it must be improved.'

'He had no authority to do so, Mr Biddle.'

'Lockyer obviously loved to bully people. That's why I knew he didn't kill himself. He's the kind of man desperate to stay alive so he can give orders to underlings like me.'

'Have you any idea who might have murdered him?' asked Leeming.

'No, Sergeant – but I think there'll be a lot of suspects. He was very easy to hate.'

'The sooner we get involved in the search for the killer,' said Colbeck, 'the better. Before that, we'll need to find some accommodation. Can you recommend a hotel?'

'The Lion will be ideal for you. It's in Wyle Cop – that's at the end of the High Street.'

'What beer do they serve?' asked Leeming.

'The best in the county. Take one of the cabs outside the station.'

'Oh, I think that a walk is in order,' said Colbeck. 'We need to stretch our legs after a long train ride. And it will give us a chance to find our way around.'

'The Lion was good enough for him,' said Biddle, 'so it should suit you as well.'

'Who are you talking about?'

'Charles Dickens, the famous writer. He stayed in Shrewsbury. They say that he wrote parts of them *Pickwick Papers* right here in The Lion.'

'Excellent,' said Colbeck, beaming. 'It sounds like the perfect place for us.'

Hubert Crabbe was thorough. Having questioned the owner and the barman of the hotel, he went to the address given to him by Molly Burrage. He wanted to hear Annie Garrow's version of events. She lived in a tiny house in one of the poorer suburbs. When he knocked on the door, it was opened by the girl's mother, a scrawny woman in her fifties with a servile manner. She was alarmed to hear that a detective inspector wished to question her daughter.

'Annie's a good girl, sir. We brought her up proper. She's not in any trouble, is she?'

'I just want to ask her what happened at the hotel.'

'It fair frightened her to death, sir. When she come back here, Annie was in a terrible state. She's calmed down a bit now but she's still . . . well, shaking like mad.'

'That's understandable, Mrs . . .'

'Winnie Garrow. I'm her mother.' She stood back. 'Please come in.'

'Thank you,' he said, stepping into the house.

The first thing he noticed was an unpleasant smell that seemed to be coming from the little scullery at the rear. As he went into the living room, he was struck by how cramped it was and how battered its furniture appeared to be. Curled up on the sofa was Annie, visibly trembling. When she saw him enter, she leapt up and drew back in alarm. Her mother came into the room.

'This is Inspector Crabbe from the Borough Police,' she explained. 'He wants to speak to you, Annie.'

'What about?' asked her daughter nervously.

'What happened this morning at the hotel.'

'Hello, Annie,' said Crabbe, perching on the edge of an armchair. 'There's nothing to be afraid of. I've taken statements from Mrs Burrage and Mr Harris. They told me that you were the first person to go to Mr Lockyer's room.'

'That's right,' she whispered. 'Mrs Burrage sent me to wake him up.'

'Had you seen the gentleman before?'

'Oh, yes, sir. I was there when he arrived at the hotel yesterday.'

'Describe him in your own words.'

'What?' She looked helplessly towards her mother.

'Just tell the inspector what you saw, Annie,' advised the older woman.

'Well,' said the other, 'he was sort of . . . well, very grand, and he looked very rich to me. When he took his top hat off, I could see that he had no hair. He was rude to Mrs Burrage. I remember that.'

'Did he notice you?'

'Yes, he did, and he frightened me.'

'Why was that?'

'Well, he'd been so nasty to Mrs Burrage,' she explained. 'When he turned round and saw me, I was afraid that he'd do the same to me. But he didn't.'

'How did he talk to you?' prompted Crabbe.

'He didn't say a word, sir. He just stared at me for a long time. It worried me. His eyes were sort of . . . glowing. Then he did something that scared me.'

'And what was that?'

'He smiled at me,' said Annie. 'Only it wasn't a kind smile to show that he liked me. It was a sort of cruel smile. When he looked me up and down, I was shaken. Don't ask me why. I just felt that he was thinking . . .' A blush came into her cheeks. '. . . bad thoughts.'

CHAPTER FOUR

When Detective Constable Alan Hinton got back to Scotland Yard, he discovered that Colbeck and Leeming had been sent off on an assignment. The detective constable knew what he had to do. Letting himself into the inspector's office, he picked up the two letters left on the desk and resolved to deliver them as soon as he could. Hinton was a tall, lithe, handsome man in his thirties who had worked with Colbeck and Leeming several times. Each case had been a learning experience for him. When he left the building, he went first to the inspector's house, where he was admitted by a maidservant. Emerging from the drawing room, Madeleine Colbeck was delighted to see him.

'Come on in, Alan,' she said, having heard his voice in the hall. 'How nice to see you!'

'I only came to deliver a letter.'

Her smile faded. 'Oh dear! Does that mean Robert has gone out of London again?'

'See for yourself,' he said, handing over the missive. 'And I have a letter for Victor's wife as well. I'll have to find time to deliver it.'

'I hope they've not gone too far away.'

'Superintendent Tallis has no concern for his detectives. He'll dispatch them all over the country without a thought for their families. Solving a crime is all that he thinks about.'

'And he's quite right to do so. Robert accepts that – and so does Victor.'

'I'd better deliver his letter to Estelle,' said Hinton, 'or she'll be cooking a meal for him in a couple of hours. Oh,' he added, 'have you seen Lydia recently?'

'No, I haven't, Alan, but I'll hear all her news this evening. She's joining me for dinner, so I'll have company.'

'Please give her my best wishes.'

'You're most welcome to dine with us.'

He shrugged. 'I wish that I could, but I have other plans, I'm afraid.'

'That's a pity. Lydia will be sorry to miss you.'

'The feeling is mutual.'

Madeleine gave an understanding smile. She knew how fond the two friends were of each other, and she wished that they could be closer. But that seemed a forlorn hope. As they moved towards the front door, they heard footsteps descending the stairs. Hinton turned to see Caleb Andrews coming towards them.

'Hello, Mr Andrews,' he said.

'Have you brought good news or bad?' asked the old man.

'We won't know until I open this letter,' said Madeleine, holding it up. 'How is my lovely daughter?'

'She was as good as gold. But then, she always is when her grandfather reads her a story. I have a gift.'

'Stop boasting!'

'I have, Maddy. You ask her. Before you do that,' he suggested, 'why don't you open that letter and see where Robert will be sleeping tonight?'

Opening the letter with some trepidation, Madeleine read it and smiled with relief. 'He's in Shrewsbury. I was afraid he'd be much further away.'

'Why is he there?'

'He's investigating the death of someone on the GWR board.'

'As long as it's not someone from the London and North Western Railway board,' said Andrews. 'Having spent my life driving trains for them, I have the greatest respect for the members. As for Shropshire, four years ago, we took over that line in partnership with the GWR.'

'I thought you hated the company, Mr Andrews,' said Hinton.

'I hate every company except the London and Northwestern Railway. We're the best.'

'You must excuse my father,' said Madeleine. 'He's very prejudiced.'

'I'm being honest, that's all,' claimed Andrews.

'What sort of place is Shrewsbury?' wondered Hinton.

'It's the county capital of Shropshire,' explained Madeleine. 'Robert has been there twice and loved the place. He said that it had some delightful old buildings and a decidedly rural character.'

Andrews grinned. 'It also has a dead member of the GWR board now.'

* * *

Carrying their luggage, Colbeck and Leeming left the station and saw the old castle looming over them, its red sandstone glowing in the sun. The Station Hotel was directly opposite the station, a neat, solid, brick-built establishment that stood out from the half-timbered structures nearby. A uniformed policeman stood outside the front door, moving on anyone who tried to linger there. Shrewsbury was all but surrounded by the serpentine coil of the River Severn. Colbeck led the way down Castle Street until it merged with Pride Hill. They soon turned left into the High Street, which was filled with people going in and out of the motley array of shops, each one displaying their wares outside. Colbeck knew that the street would soon become Wyle Cop because that was where he had visited Donald Underhill during the earlier investigation. Before they got near the solicitor's office, however, they saw The Lion Hotel, one of the oldest in the town, an impressive coaching inn with Doric columns either side of the front door. What struck Leeming was the sculpted lion above the entrance. He thought it so realistic.

When they entered the building, they found themselves in a reception area where a man in his thirties stood behind a counter. Slim and well dressed, he beamed at them.

'How may I help you, gentlemen?' he asked, politely.

'We'd like to book two single rooms, please,' said Colbeck.

'How long will you be staying, sir?'

'We don't yet know, I'm afraid.'

'That's fine with us, sir. The Lion is at your service for as long as you wish.'

'It's a fine old building,' said Leeming.

'In its prime, it was the best hotel in Shrewsbury,' said the man proudly. 'Seven coaches ran daily from here to London, and a further thirteen went to other towns. It's all changed now, of course. Most of our guests come and go by means of the railway. Now, then,' he added, 'let me have your names, please.'

'Is that Charles Dickens?' asked Colbeck, looking at the framed photograph on the wall beside the man. 'We know that he stayed here.'

'We were honoured to have him, sir. Mr Dickens was kind enough to give us the photograph. Over the years, many distinguished people have stayed at The Lion.'

Leeming beamed. 'We're in good company then.'

'What are your names, please?'

'I am Detective Inspector Colbeck from Scotland Yard,' said Colbeck, 'and this is Detective Sergeant Leeming. We are here to investigate a murder that took place at the Station Hotel. That may take time.'

The clerk's jaw dropped.

'Please put our names in your register.'

When the porter delivered the letter to her, Molly was grateful. It was one of many missives sent by the stationmaster. In recent months, Biddle had become a fervent admirer of hers. A lifelong bachelor, he had at last found someone who made the idea of marriage sound faintly appealing. It was the reason that he sent her occasional notes and, from time to time, small gifts. Though she kept him at arm's length, Molly was touched by his attentions. As she opened the envelope, she expected some words of sympathy from Biddle. Instead of that, she read a message that made her sit up with interest. After waiting a few minutes to absorb the shock, she went straight to the bar.

Wilf Harris was behind the counter, cleaning a glass with a

teacloth. He saw the excitement in Molly's face.

'What's happened?' he asked.

'I've just had a letter from Mr Biddle.'

'Oh, is that all?' he said, rolling his eyes. 'I wish he'd stop bothering you like that.'

'He's given me some important news,' said Molly. 'He sent a telegraph to Scotland Yard about Mr Lockyer's death. As a result, they've sent two detectives to investigate the murder – and we now know that it really was a murder and not a suicide.'

'Does he mention any names?' asked Harris.

'Yes, Wilf. The good news is that they're already here. Simon – Mr Biddle, that is – has met them face to face. One is an Inspector Colbeck, and the other is Sergeant Leeming.'

Harris was impressed. 'I've heard of Colbeck,' he said. 'He's famous.'

'And he's come all the way from London.'

'Biddle has done something useful for once.'

'Wilf!' she said in disapproval.

'Well, he usually sends you silly little gifts.'

'It's the thought that counts.'

'Hah!'

'He knows how I must be feeling, and he's done something about it. I appreciate that.'

'Did his letter say that the detectives would be staying here at the hotel?'

'No, it didn't because they've gone to book rooms at The Lion.'

'Pity,' said Harris. 'I've heard good things about Colbeck. It'd be a pleasure to serve him a drink or two. Hey,' he added. 'What about Inspector Crabbe? He's not going to be happy if someone tries to take the case off him.'

'They can work together, Wilf.'

'Fat lot you know about detectives!' he said with a derisive laugh. 'They're very possessive. Crabbe is not going to take orders from somebody who knows nothing at all about Shrewsbury. It's his case and he'll fight like a tiger to keep it that way.'

'Mr Biddle says that Inspector Colbeck is a genius.'

Harris curled his lip. 'Try telling that to Crabbe and the chief constable!'

It was less than six weeks since Colonel Richard Edgell had been appointed as the chief constable of Shropshire. He was still finding his feet. A compact, straight-backed man in his fifties, he had a complexion that suggested time spent in a hot country. In fact, he had applied for the post two years earlier but – despite his sterling qualities – had not been chosen. When the post became vacant again, the county magistrates decided to save the expense of another contest by appointing the man who had impressed them at his earlier interview. His distinguished career in the army had convinced them that he was an ideal choice.

Edgell soon proved that he had the qualities needed for his new role. He was efficient, decisive and wholly committed. Some of the policemen under his command had doubts about his overbearing manner, but all agreed on one thing. Colonel Edgell was a good listener. During the long report about events at the Station Hotel that Inspector Crabbe delivered, the chief constable was attentive. When the recitation ended, he had some questions.

'How certain are you that it was not a case of suicide?' he asked.

'There can be no doubt about it, Colonel,' said Crabbe. 'A left-handed man would never use his right hand to slit his throat and wrists. Also, of course, he had no motive to kill himself. Mr

Lockyer was a successful businessman on the brink of being made chairman of the Great Western Railway. Who would feel the need to take his own life when he was about to fulfil one of his greatest ambitions?'

'A fair point, Inspector.'

'And why choose a place like Shrewsbury when he had a home in London?'

'What exactly was Lockyer doing here?' asked Edgell.

'That's something of a mystery, Colonel.'

'Did he say nothing to the manager?'

'He told Mrs Burrage – she owns the hotel – that he had come to see an old friend.'

'Did anyone see this person?'

'Apparently not,' said Crabbe. 'Mr Lockyer went out to dinner elsewhere, but nobody knows if he dined at another hotel, or if he visited this friend at the person's home.'

'Does anyone remember him returning to the Station Hotel?'

'The owner says that he got back around ten o'clock and went straight to his room.'

'What state was he in?'

'He had obviously been drinking and needed to put a hand against a wall to steady himself. Lockyer asked for an early call because he had a train to catch next morning.'

'And that was the last time anyone saw him alive?'

'Except for the killer, that is.'

They were seated in Edgell's office. It was exceptionally tidy. A framed photograph of the chief constable stood on his desk. It had been taken when he was wearing the uniform of Her Majesty's Bengal Army. As he glanced at it, a feeling of pride surged through him. He shifted his gaze back to Crabbe.

'What conclusion have you reached?' he asked.

'Mr Lockyer was a man of obvious wealth and importance,' said the other. 'I think that someone spotted him on his arrival and decided that he was a tempting target.'

'Is the Station Hotel accustomed to seeing major crimes committed there?'

'Far from it, sir. It has an exemplary record of good behaviour. The only criminals they have encountered were guests who sneaked out without paying the bill. Mrs Burrage has now made that impossible. Guests are now asked to pay on arrival.'

'A sensible decision.'

Before they could continue, there was a tap on the door. It opened to reveal a uniformed constable who was holding a letter. He handed it to the chief constable and left the room. When he read the contents of the letter, he turned to his companion.

'I have distressing news for you, Inspector.'

Crabbe stiffened. 'Really?'

'It looks as if you may have competition,' said Edgell. 'Does the name Inspector Colbeck mean anything to you?'

'Yes, he's a Scotland Yard detective who specialises in crimes related to railways.'

'That explains why he has come to Shrewsbury. This letter is from Simon Biddle, the stationmaster. Without asking for permission to do so, he sent a telegraph to Scotland Yard and asked for help. It seems that Colbeck and a Sergeant Leeming are already here.'

'They've no right to interfere with our investigation,' said Crabbe angrily.

'We should at least see what they have to offer.'

'I disagree strongly, sir.'

'Then how should we proceed?'

'We should put the pair of them on the next train to London, sir,' insisted Crabbe. 'Too many cooks spoil the broth. Too many detectives get in each other's way. Yes,' he went on, 'I know that Inspector Colbeck has a reputation for success, but – unlike us – he has no knowledge whatsoever of this county. In short, he would be useless and likely to distract us.' He tapped his chest. 'I venture to suggest that we are far better placed in every way to solve any murders here in Shropshire!'

CHAPTER FIVE

When the Scotland Yard detectives approached the Station Hotel, the uniformed policeman on duty outside it tried to move them on. It was only when Colbeck explained who they were that the officer stood aside to let them enter the building. They were disappointed to discover that Inspector Crabbe was no longer there, but Molly Burrage gave them a cordial welcome. In the privacy of her office, she delivered a nervous summary of events. They could see how upset she was.

'Nothing like this has ever happened here before,' she explained. 'It's frightening.'

'What state is Mr Lockyer's room in now?' asked Colbeck.

'It's been left exactly as we found it,' she replied. 'The door is locked to keep people out.'

'May we see it, please?'

'Yes, I suppose so, but I must warn you about something. When we went in there first thing this morning, Annie – she's a girl who works here – was so shocked that she was sick over the carpet. Inspector Crabbe told us to leave the room as it was, so the mess is still there.'

'We'll be careful to step around it, Mrs Burrage,' said Colbeck easily. 'We're used to seeing something nasty at a murder scene.'

'How have your other guests reacted?' asked Leeming.

Molly grimaced. 'They grabbed their luggage and left immediately.'

'That's only to be expected,' said Colbeck. 'You have our sympathy. I can see that this hotel is clean, welcoming and well run. Mr Biddle spoke highly of it. You'll soon be as busy as ever.'

'I do hope so, Inspector.'

Opening the door, she led the way to the stairs and went up them with the detectives. When she reached the room where Lockyer had stayed, she unlocked the door. Molly then stood back to let them go in first. They looked around with interest, noting the blood-stained bedsheets on the double bed. Eventually, Colbeck crossed to the open window and looked out. When he turned to Molly, he made a request.

'Could we be left alone for a while, please, Mrs Burrage?'

'Yes, of course,' she replied. 'I'm glad to get out of here. It's so creepy.'

'We'll see you in your office.'

She handed him the key. 'Please lock the door when you leave.'

'Of course.' After ushering her out, he closed the door, then turned to Leeming. 'First thoughts, Victor?'

'We know how the killer got out, sir, but how did he get in here in the first place?'

'You're making a false assumption.'

'Am I?'

'How do you know that it was a man?'

'Who else could it have been?'

'A woman,' said Colbeck. 'Perhaps that's why Mr Lockyer came here in the first place. He might have had an assignation. It would explain why he asked for a double bed.'

'I don't believe a woman could have committed a crime like that.'

'We've arrested more than one woman for poisoning a husband,' Colbeck recalled. 'Not that I'm suggesting Mr Lockyer's wife is involved, mind you. What if he had come here to enjoy the services of a woman who sets a price on her favours?'

'Then she'd have been seen coming into the hotel.'

'Not necessarily. Look out of the window and you'll see how easy it would have been to climb up here. It's only a question of getting onto the roof of a shed directly below.'

Leeming went the window and peered out. 'I see what you mean.'

'If it had been a tryst of some sort, drink would certainly have been involved. Some sort of drug could have been slipped into his glass. It made him drowsy, giving his visitor the advantage. She slit his throat and wrists, stole everything of value and bolted the door before leaving through the window.' Colbeck spread his arms. 'It's one explanation.'

'I'll give you another,' said Leeming. 'Mrs Burrage told us that it was a warm night. The window was likely to have been left open. When he returned from dinner elsewhere, we were told, Mr Lockyer had been drinking. Supposing he just took off his clothes and fell into bed? He'd have been fast asleep when a thief climbed into the room, killed him in the way you described then stole just about everything belonging to his victim.'

'It's something we must consider. A thief might already have been concealed in the room, of course. He waited until Lockyer fell asleep then used a knife to slit the victim's throat and wrists. He put everything into Lockyer's valise and left by means of the window.'

'I'd prefer my version of what happened.'

'Before we speculate any further,' suggested Colbeck, 'we must find out where the body was taken and if there has been a postmortem.'

'The police can tell us that.'

'Then let's go and find Inspector Crabbe, shall we? First, however, we can slip across to the station to send a telegraph. The superintendent needs to know what we've discovered.'

It was late afternoon when Lydia Quayle arrived at the house. Madeleine answered the door herself and welcomed her friend with a kiss. Lydia held up a small parcel.

'I've brought a present for Helena Rose,' she explained.

'You spoil her, Lydia.'

'I'm her honorary aunt, aren't I? That means I have a bounden duty to spoil her.'

Madeleine smiled. 'As long as you don't overdo it,' she warned. 'Take it up, please. She'll be in the nursery with Nanny Hopkins.'

'Good. I won't be a moment.'

Lydia tripped up the stairs on her toes. A slim, well-groomed, attractive woman in her thirties, she had extraordinary grace. It was something that always impressed Madeleine. She soon heard squeals of delight from the nursery, clear evidence that her daughter was delighted to see Lydia and thrilled with her gift. A few minutes later, the visitor came back downstairs. Madeleine took her into the drawing room, and they sat side by side on the sofa.

'Tea?' asked Madeleine.

'All in good time,' said Lydia, face darkening. 'There's something more important first.'

'Whatever is it? Nothing serious, I hope.'

'It could be very serious, Madeleine.'

'Oh dear! I hope that nobody in your family has died.'

'They're all fine, as far as I know,' said Lydia. 'The problem concerns you, I'm afraid.'

'Really?'

'Let me tell you what happened. I was shopping in Oxford Street when I bumped into an old friend. She invited me back to her house for tea. That meant a short stroll through Soho. Margery – that's her name – took me down a street that had all kinds of curious shops in it. One of them sold a delightful mixture of things – antique furniture, crockery, clothing, ornaments and paintings. I happened to glance at the window display and saw something I recognised.'

'What was it?'

'A painting of a railway scene by Madeleine Colbeck.'

'But that's impossible!' declared her friend. 'My paintings are only sold by the art dealer who likes my work. You've met him.'

'I know,' said Lydia.

'You must have been mistaken.'

'That's what I thought at first. But when I left Margery's house, I made a point of going back past that shop and the painting was still there. It's your work, Madeleine – at least, it looks as if it is.'

'What on earth is it doing in what sounds like a junk shop?'

'Heaven knows!'

'Had I signed the painting?'

'Yes, your signature was at the bottom in the right-hand corner.'

'That's where I always put it.'

'And it looked quite genuine,' said Lydia. 'Could it be that the person who bought it decided to sell it to the shop?'

'It sounds unlikely. If someone lost interest in the painting, they'd surely take it back to the Red Gallery where it was bought. Can you describe it, please?'

'Yes, of course. It was a rare country scene. Most of your work features trains in towns or cities. This one showed a locomotive and three carriages steaming past a farm in Devon.'

'Oh,' said Madeleine, 'I remember that painting well. It was on one of the rare occasions when Robert had enough time off for a short holiday. We stayed at the farm in the painting. Helena loved helping to feed the animals. The trains passed within thirty yards of the house, so I set up my easel on the lawn.'

'You showed me the painting when you'd finished it.'

'Then what is it doing in that shop in Soho?'

'There's only one way to find out, Madeleine. Are you free tomorrow morning?'

'I'll make sure that I am,' said her friend, gritting her teeth. 'It sounds to me as if there's fishy business afoot. I want to get to the bottom of this.'

The police station was situated in Swan Hill in the southern part of the town. Colbeck and Leeming arrived there after a brisk walk. When they met the duty sergeant, he disappeared for a few minutes then reappeared to conduct them into the chief constable's office. The newcomers were given a polite welcome by Colonel

Edgell, who introduced them to Hubert Crabbe. While the latter shook hands with the newcomers, he did so half-heartedly, barely able to conceal a scowl. Both men were impressed by Colbeck's appearance, manner and educated voice. Neither Edgell nor Crabbe gave Leeming a second look. When they had all sat down, Colbeck spoke first.

'Congratulations on your appointment,' he said to Edgell. 'How are you finding Shropshire?'

'I'm still at a learning stage,' replied the other, 'and leaning heavily on the inspector. The last thing I need so early during my tenure is what appears to be a murder case.'

'That's exactly what it is, sir. The sergeant and I have visited the scene of the crime and spoken with Mrs Burrage. We've gathered most of the relevant facts.'

'What we need to know,' Leeming interjected, 'is where Mr Lockyer's body was taken and whether or not a postmortem has been carried out.'

'That's private information,' said Crabbe, raising his eyebrows high enough for them to see the resentment in his eyes. 'You are not needed here.'

'We were sent for, Inspector,' said Colbeck.

'By a stationmaster who had no right to summon you.'

'He has reason to take a special interest in the Station Hotel and was right to contact us.'

'Biddle will be spoken to in due course.'

'Well, I hope that he is applauded for what he did. Mrs Burrage was delighted that we offered our services to help in what seems to be an intriguing case.'

'That's for us to judge, Inspector,' said Crabbe.

'Are you rejecting our assistance?'

'We see it as interference.'

'Now, now,' said Edgell, 'let's not be so inhospitable. The inspector and the sergeant have come all the way from London. We should welcome what they have to say.'

'Thank you, sir,' said Colbeck. He turned to Crabbe. 'May I ask how many murders you have handled, Inspector?'

Crabbe thrust out his jaw. 'This one will be my third.'

'Were the killers found and arrested in the two previous cases?'

'No, they weren't,' grunted the other.

'Then you have a record of abject failure.'

'We, on the other hand,' said Leeming, 'have enjoyed great success. You should see the stationmaster's noticeboard. It's like a shrine to our work.'

'Let's go back to the question that brought us here,' said Colbeck. 'Where has Mr Lockyer's body been taken and who has examined it?'

'The corpse was taken to the Royal Salop Infirmary,' said Edgell, 'and is in the hands of Dr Vincent. He is being assisted by Dr William Clement, who is a distinguished physician. He is also the Member of Parliament for Shrewsbury.'

'I admire his versatility.'

'Dr Clement had been visiting the infirmary when the cadaver arrived. His natural curiosity made him wonder what had happened to the victim.'

'Isn't that obvious?' asked Crabbe. 'Mr Lockyer went out for dinner somewhere. One glance at him would have told a thief that he was a man of means. The thief therefore tailed him back to the Station Hotel and found out the number of his room.'

'And how did he do that?' asked Colbeck.

'He went into the hotel and pretended to be a friend of Lockyer.

He must have got the man's room number from a member of staff. While he bided his time, the thief went around to the rear of the hotel and saw how easy it would be to climb up to Mr Lockyer's room. Providentially, it was a warm night and Lockyer had therefore left a window open.'

'Yet according to Mrs Burrage, the gentleman had returned to the hotel having clearly enjoyed a fair amount of alcohol. Would a man in that state even think of opening a window? Or would he have just taken off his clothes, struggled into a nightshirt and fallen into bed?'

'My theory is more likely to be true, Inspector,' said Crabbe.

'Then how do you explain the fact that the victim was stark naked?'

'Quite easily. He must have had one drink too many. Alone is his room, he would have torn off his clothing and fallen into bed. By the time that the thief climbed in, Mr Lockyer was fast asleep.'

'Fast asleep and at the mercy of the intruder,' noted Colbeck. 'That raises an interesting point. Why did the thief feel obliged to kill him? He could simply have gathered up everything of value and fled with it in the valise. In my experience, criminals are highly aware of the penalties they might face. The thief would know that, if caught, he would be sentenced to a long time in prison. Murder, however, carries a more fearful verdict – execution.'

'That's a good point,' said Edgell, turning to Crabbe. 'What's your answer?'

'It's very obvious,' replied Crabbe. 'Lockyer must have woken up and tried to raise the alarm. The thief was forced to kill him.'

'Then why was there no sign of a struggle?' asked Colbeck. 'And why did the thief contrive to make the death look like a case of suicide?'

'Yes,' said Leeming. 'He'd hardly just lie there and let someone slit his throat and slash his wrists open. I don't think that the intruder was only there to steal. He came to kill. Making off with Mr Lockyer's possessions was a bonus.'

Edgell was worried. 'This case is not as straightforward as it first appeared.'

'We'll catch the killer, sir,' promised Crabbe.

'Isn't there a stage before that?' asked Colbeck. 'Mrs Burrage remembers that – when Mr Lockyer first arrived – he was wearing a wedding ring. That suggests he has a wife. Have you taken any steps to inform her of what happened?'

'Of course we have. I contacted the headquarters of the Great Western Railway by telegraph, asking for Lockyer's address.'

'Have you received a reply, Inspector?'

'Not as yet,' admitted Crabbe.

'Then it was just as well that I sent a telegraph to Scotland Yard, asking for the terrible news to be broken to the Lockyer family. They must be wondering where on earth he is.'

Leeming nodded. 'The superintendent will have found out where Mr Lockyer lives and will make sure that his wife and family are made aware of what happened. He has his faults, but he knows how to break news gently in situations like this. That's one thing I will say about Superintendent Tallis.'

Edgell was roused. 'Is that Superintendent Edward Tallis, by any chance?'

'Yes, sir, it is.'

'You look as if you know him,' said Colbeck.

'Oh, I know him only too well,' hissed Edgell. 'We served together in the Bengal Army. Let me just say that he and I did not see eye to eye.'

'I have the same problem with him,' muttered Leeming.

'Superintendent Tallis is a credit to the Metropolitan Police Force,' said Colbeck. 'I'm sad to hear you voicing criticism of him.'

'It's more than criticism,' said Edgell. 'To be frank with you, I hoped that I'd never hear his hateful name again. Tallis, in my opinion, is an absolute menace.'

Unaware that he was being discussed, Edward Tallis stepped out of the cab that had taken him to the house owned by Julian Lockyer. After paying the driver, he studied the building. It was impressively large and reflected the wealth of the murder victim. On receipt of Colbeck's telegraph, Tallis had not only taken steps to find out where Lockyer had lived, he had decided to break the sad news to the man's family in person. After clearing his throat, he rang the bell that hung beside the door. In a matter of seconds, the door was opened by one of the servants, a middle-aged woman with a welcoming smile. When she saw Tallis, her face crumpled.

'Oh,' she said. 'I was hoping that it would be Mr Lockyer. He told us that he'd be back home this afternoon.'

'I am a senior detective from Scotland Yard,' Tallis told her. 'I need to speak to Mrs Lockyer as a matter of urgency.'

'Why – has anything happened?'

'Is the lady at home?'

'Yes, yes, she is,' said the servant. 'She's always at home.'

'Then I wish to speak to her.'

'I can't promise that she'll hear you, sir.' She stood back to allow him to step into the hall.

While the servant closed the front door, Tallis removed his top hat and left it on the hall table. He was then conducted along a corridor and into the spacious living room. Through the window, he could see a woman seated in a wicker chair on the terrace and enjoying the late afternoon sun. When he was led outside by the servant, he realised that the woman had a companion, perched on a bench some yards away. She leapt up immediately.

'Mrs Lockyer?' he asked.

'No,' she replied. 'I'm Mrs Tindall. I look after Mrs Lockyer.'

She indicated the other woman, who was clearly asleep. Beside her chair were two crutches. Still in her fifties, she looked years older. Her face was a mass of wrinkles, and her body was decidedly frail. Tallis realised that she was seriously ill.

'This gentleman is from Scotland Yard,' explained the servant.

'That's true,' he confirmed. 'Is there anyone from the family here?'

'No, sir,' said Mrs Tindall, 'but their son lives quite close. Henrietta, their daughter, moved to Scotland when she married.'

'I need to get in touch with them as soon as possible. I have sad news to pass on about their father.' He looked at Mrs Lockyer. 'It will come as a great blow to his wife.'

'She is in a world of her own, I fear. That's why I need to be with her around the clock to see to her needs. Mrs Lockyer's mind has crumbled. It's a tragedy.'

'Then she will never understand what I am about to tell you, Mrs Tindall. In some ways,' said Tallis, looking at the sleeping woman, 'that may be a source of relief to her. She will be spared news that would have caused her the most intense grief.'

'Her husband is dead?' gasped the woman.

'I'm sorry to tell you that he was murdered in a hotel in Shrewsbury.'

Mrs Lockyer suddenly woke up, twitched violently then went straight back to sleep.

CHAPTER SIX

They had become acutely aware of how hungry they were. Colbeck and Leeming had been so busy since their arrival that they had not even thought about a meal. Both were now suffering the pangs of hunger. They had already booked a table for dinner in the restaurant at The Lion, but it would not be available for hours. Colbeck therefore suggested that they return to the station to visit the refreshment room there.

'I'm starving, sir,' said Leeming. 'I'll eat anywhere.'

'It will give us a chance to have another word with Mr Biddle.'

They walked all the way back to the station and each ordered a light meal. Leeming was more interested in gobbling his food down than in having a conversation. Whenever Colbeck asked him a question, he responded with either a nod or a shake of his head. Soon after they arrived, they heard a train suddenly arrive and squeal to a halt. Doors were heard opening and shutting. Passengers went past the window on their way to the exit. Ten minutes later, they heard a whistle, and the locomotive came back to life again.

When it had left the station, they were joined by an excited Simon Biddle.

'How did you get on with Crabbe?' he asked.

'It was not exactly a meeting of true minds,' said Colbeck. 'The inspector wanted us on the next train to London, but the chief constable was more gracious. He was interested to hear what we had found out.'

'And what was that?'

'Mr Lockyer was deliberately murdered. I will not be at all surprised if it transpires that the killer was hired.'

Biddle was shocked. 'Why?'

'That's what we intend to find out.'

'You are staying, then? I was afraid that the chief constable might send you away.'

'He has no power to do so, Mr Biddle.'

'No,' added Leeming. 'We've been in this position before. When we investigated a murder in York, the police chief tried to get rid of us, so we reported him to our superintendent.'

'What happened?'

'Superintendent Tallis not only came to the city in person, but he carried a letter signed by the Home Secretary, threatening action. That brought the police chief into line.'

'Do you think you'll have to do the same thing here?'

'No,' replied Colbeck, 'I fancy that Colonel Edgell is glad that we offered our help. It's Inspector Crabbe who wants to see the back of us.'

'He's jealous of your success, Inspector. But I'm so glad that

I caught you,' said Biddle. 'There's something I must warn you about.'

'What is it?'

'Reporters from the local newspapers have already been hounding me. They were delighted to hear that you had come to the town. Be warned. They can be very persistent.'

'We've dealt with persistent reporters before, Mr Biddle,' said Leeming. 'We tell them as little as possible. They have a nasty habit of getting in our way.'

'You don't need to tell me that,' said the stationmaster ruefully.

'While you're here,' said Colbeck, 'you may be able to help us. We were told that the body was taken to the infirmary. Where is it?'

'Oh, I can tell you that.'

'We were also surprised to hear that the doctor who was there at the time is actually a Member of Parliament.'

'That's right – Dr Clement. He was elected last year for the Liberal Party. He's in his sixties now,' said Biddle, 'but he's still as hard-working as ever. I thought he was one of the best mayors of the town that we ever had.'

'What is he doing at the infirmary?'

'Once a doctor, always a doctor – that's what he told me. He comes from a medical family. His father – another Dr Clement – worked here for decades, but it was his son who is more famous. He is a practising surgeon and has written learned papers about medicine.'

'I'll be interested in his opinion about Mr Lockyer,' said Colbeck.

'There's something else I must tell you. Inspector Crabbe came here to make use of our telegraph station. He is trying to find out the dead man's address.'

'I did exactly the same thing,' said Colbeck, 'and dispatched a telegraph to someone who will certainly have found details about Mr Lockyer's home by now. In fact, I daresay that Superintendent Tallis has already broken the devastating news to the family.'

Pelham Lockyer was like a younger version of his father. He had the same build, the same posture and the same mannerisms. He was also proud of his ability to remain calm in a crisis, but – when he was told about his father's murder – he discovered that it had limits. On receipt of the news from Edward Tallis, he staggered back a few yards and had to steady himself with a hand on an armchair. The superintendent reacted swiftly. Moving to the little table he had noticed when he first came into the drawing room, he grasped the decanter of brandy, poured a generous amount into a glass then handed it to Lockyer.

'Try this,' he advised. 'It will help.'

'Thank you,' said Lockyer, taking the glass and having a first taste. 'I must sit down.'

'There's nothing better for an emergency than brandy.'

'It's rather more than an emergency, Superintendent. You've just delivered a thunderbolt.' He sank into a chair. 'That's better.' He had a longer sip from the glass. 'I just can't believe it. My father was so careful at looking after himself.'

'My first port of call was at the family house,' said Tallis. 'I was deeply sorry to find your mother in that condition.'

'Watching her decline like that has been agonising.'

'It was a Mrs Tindall who gave me this address.'

'That woman is a saint,' said Lockyer. 'She's dedicated her life to looking after Mother. I don't know how we would have managed without her.'

'You have a sister, I gather.'

'Yes, Henrietta is married and living in Edinburgh. This news will horrify her. I'm eternally grateful that you came here and passed on the grim tidings so gently. You've no need to send word to Henrietta. That's my job.' He realised something. 'Everything is my job now.'

'Did you work with your father?'

'Yes, I entered the family firm when I was sixteen. My father and I have worked side by side for many years. He had a passion for railways.'

'Is it one that you share?'

'I'm afraid not. Railway mania made us rich, but a sizeable amount of our profits disappeared when the bubble burst. Luckily, we've clawed much of that loss back and diversified our investments.'

'That's a sensible course of action, sir.'

'In the face of a threat, one has to make adjustments.'

'Quite so.'

'But I'm sure that you have lots of questions to ask me, Superintendent.'

'The main one is this, sir,' said Tallis. 'What exactly was your father doing in Shrewsbury?'

Pelham Lockyer was startled. 'Shrewsbury?'

'That's where the crime took place, sir.'

'Surely not.'

'I have it on the very best authority.'

'There must be some mistake,' said the other, frowning. 'My father assured me that he was going to spend the night with friends in Kent – in Maidstone, to be exact. What on earth was he doing in Shrewsbury?'

* * *

When they got to the Royal Salop Infirmary, they were impressed by its size and appearance. Four massive stone pillars held up the portico of a building in the Classical style. Built as a subscription hospital, it had clearly profited over the years from benevolent donors. Leeming was struck by the fact that it had five floors and an aura of quiet magnificence.

'I never expected anything like this,' he confessed.

'We're in the county town, remember,' said Colbeck, studying the façade, 'and, according to Bradshaw, over twenty-two thousand people live here. Such a population deserves good medical facilities. Let's see if the interior is on a par with what we see before us.'

They entered the building and doffed their top hats. Colbeck approached a desk behind which a middle-aged man in a white coat was seated. He explained who they were and why they had come to the infirmary. The man was impressed.

'Welcome to Shrewsbury, Inspector,' he said. 'I believe that Dr Clement is still here. If you'd care to go into the waiting room, I'll do my best to find him for you.'

The man headed for a staircase and went briskly up it. Colbeck, meanwhile, took Leeming into the waiting room. Both were impressed by how large and comfortable it was.

'I've never met a Member of Parliament face to face before,' said Leeming.

'He is also a doctor, remember.'

'How can he do both jobs at the same time?'

'I daresay that he will tell us, Victor.'

They did not have long to wait. In a matter of minutes, the man who had gone to fetch Clement brought him into the waiting room and introduced him to the detectives. Clement was a tall, lean man in his sixties with a professorial air about him. With his head cocked to one side, he studied Colbeck and Leeming with interest.

'It's good to meet you both,' he said, 'and reassuring to know that you have been summoned from Scotland Yard. I bid you both a welcome.'

'Why aren't you in the House of Commons?' asked Leeming.

'Parliament is in recess, Sergeant. I've done what I always do at such times and that's to return to my constituency to make myself available to the people I represent – and to deal with my patients, of course.'

'You still work as a doctor?' asked Colbeck in surprise.

'Whenever I can. Medicine is my first love. Luckily, I happened to be in the town when this distressing murder occurred. Dr Vincent, a surgeon here, was kind enough to allow me to help with the postmortem.'

'The cause of death was easy to establish, I daresay.'

'Yes, Inspector. The victim was first drugged then his neck and wrists were slit open.'

'How was the drug administered?'

'We suspect that it was in something that he drank. Dr Vincent is still trying to identify the poison used. It had one virtue, I suppose. When he was killed, Mr Lockyer did not feel a thing. I'm sure that you have lots of questions to put to me,' he went on, indicating the chairs. 'Why don't we make ourselves comfortable?'

As all three of them sat down, the man who had brought Clement into the room let himself out and closed the door behind him. Clement studied his companions through narrowed eyes.

'What do you think of our hospital?' he asked.

'It took our breath away,' said Leeming.

'We are very proud of it, Sergeant. It's almost forty years old now yet it still has a sense of newness about it. We have five floors here. This one contains the board room, dispensary, waiting rooms, admitting rooms and flats for the surgeon and matron. We also have two wards set aside for patients who have had accidents.'

'Mr Lockyer had rather more than an accident,' said Colbeck. 'We were shown the room where he was killed. His death will have serious repercussions.'

'I'll have to leave you to cope with them, Inspector.'

'We'd be grateful if – when it is identified – you could tell us which drug was used.'

'Yes, of course.'

'All we need to do is to find out where Mr Lockyer spent yesterday evening,' said Leeming. 'Someone must have slipped the potion into his drink while he was off guard.'

'The police will be searching for the same thing, surely. Can't you work with them?'

'I fancy that we might make more progress on our own,' said Colbeck. 'One more thing,' he added. 'We were warned about press interest. It's likely to be intense.'

'I can confirm that. If you're not careful, you'll be hounded. The one reporter you can trust is Archie Reeves of the *Shrewsbury Chronicle*. Splendid fellow. He stands out from the crowd.'

'Then we look forward to meeting him.'

Though the meal was excellent, Madeleine Colbeck had little appetite for it. Dinner with Lydia Quayle was usually a treat for her, but she was more interested in gathering information from her friend than in eating food that evening.

'Aren't you hungry, Madeleine?' asked her friend.

'I'm too angry to enjoy dinner.'

'That's my fault. Perhaps I shouldn't have told you what I saw.'

'I'm glad that you did, Lydia. You may well have discovered a crime. Somebody is copying one of my paintings and passing it off as his or her own.'

'What if it really is the one you painted?'

'It can't be. Mine was sold to a retired stockbroker with a passion for trains.'

'Perhaps he fell on hard times and had to sell it?'

'To a junk shop?' asked Madeleine. 'That would be humiliating. It fetched a good price at the Red Gallery.'

'What was the name of the art dealer who handled your work?'

'Mr Sinclair – Francis Sinclair.'

'I remember him now. He had frizzy red hair.'

'He also wanted to help new artists. And that's what I was at the time.'

'Maybe he should be our starting point. We'll go to Mr Sinclair first.'

'No,' said Madeleine firmly. 'Before all else, I want to see this painting. I have a horrible feeling that it's a fake. Someone has stolen my idea and sold it as their own or – even worse – claimed to be Madeleine Colbeck.'

'I'm sure there's an innocent explanation to this mystery.'

'Well, I don't see it, Lydia.'

'Don't let it spoil our evening,' suggested the other. 'Let's talk about something else.'

Madeleine nodded. 'You're right. I'm sorry to go on and on about it.'

'I'd be the same in your place.'

'I doubt it.' She squeezed Lydia's arm. 'Look, I do apologise. My obsession is spoiling the whole evening.'

'There's nothing to apologise for, Madeleine.'

'Oh, I do wish Robert was here! He'd know exactly what I should do.'

'He has problems of his own, by the sound of it.'

'He always gives such good advice.'

'What advice would he give if he were here right now?'

Madeleine laughed. 'He'd tell me that I had to eat my dinner,' she said, 'or I'd wake up hungry in the middle of the night.'

When they got back to The Lion Hotel, Colbeck and Leeming found someone waiting to see them. He was a short, wiry man in his early twenties with a full moustache and a pair of startling blue eyes. Seated in the reception area, he leapt to his feet and shook hands with each of them in turn.

'Welcome to Shrewsbury, Inspector,' he said before turning to Leeming. 'And the same to you, Sergeant. My name is Archie Reeves and it's a pleasure to meet you both.'

'You're from the *Shrewsbury Chronicle*, I gather,' said Colbeck, weighing him up. 'Dr Clement spoke well of you.'

'I'd speak equally well of him. As a doctor and as a politician, he has no equal.'

'If you wish to ask questions, why don't we go through into the bar?'

'An excellent idea,' said Reeves. 'Follow me.'

'How did you know where to find us?' asked Leeming.

'I knew instinctively that you'd choose The Lion. Just to be certain, I had a word with Simon Biddle. He remembered giving you directions to get here.'

'The stationmaster was responsible for bringing us to the town.'

'Yes, he told me that.'

When they entered the bar, they found a table in a corner. Reeves ordered drinks for them. Leeming immediately took a sip from his glass. Colbeck explained that he spent a lot of his time routinely dodging reporters because they tended to hamper him during an investigation. Reeves, he observed, was clearly an exception to the rule, a polite, highly educated man who was bubbling with enthusiasm. Also, guessed Colbeck, he was born in the town so would be a valuable source of information for them.

After sipping his wine, Reeves took out a notebook and pencil. The blue eyes twinkled.

'May I ask what you think of this case?' he said.

'It's fascinating,' said Colbeck. 'I take it that you know who the murder victim was.'

'Yes, of course. Mr Lockyer is – or was – on the board of the GWR.'

'We've yet to establish what he was doing here.'

'He told Mrs Burrage that he had come to see a friend.'

'You've spoken to her?'

'She was my first port of call. The murder has really shaken her. I always thought of her as indomitable, but not anymore.'

'Are the police aware that you are covering this case?'

Reeves grinned. 'They know it was too big a temptation for me to resist. Inspector Crabbe has no time for people like me, but the new chief constable is more approachable.'

'That was my assessment of him,' said Colbeck. 'How did you come to work as a reporter?'

'I suppose that I was lucky. Since the time when I could hold a pen, I'd always been writing something or other. Then I turned to poetry and sent a few of my poems to the editor.'

'Did he like them?' asked Leeming.

'He loved them, Sergeant. He said that they showed great promise. More importantly, he took an interest in me. When I told him that I wanted to be a journalist, he said that I had to master shorthand first. So that's what I did – very quickly, as it happens.'

'Did you have a job at the time?'

'Yes, I was a junior clerk to a hide merchant, but I spent all my spare time scribbling poems and stories. The editor at the *Chronicle* said that I had a gift and offered me a job. I've been doing it ever since.'

'Is that how you see your future?' asked Colbeck. 'Staying with a weekly newspaper?'

'It will suit me for a while,' said Reeves, 'but my real aim is to move to London to work in politics as a parliamentary sketch writer. Dr Clement was kind enough to take me to the House of Commons so that I could get the feel of the place. It was fascinating.' He took another sip of his drink. 'Did you know that the great William Hazlitt once wrote to the *Chronicle*?'

'No, I didn't.'

'He was only thirteen at the time and was living in Shropshire. Hazlitt wrote in 1791 to condemn the riots in Birmingham. His letter was published, and he went on to have an illustrious career as a writer. I hope to follow his example.'

'Well, before you do that,' said Colbeck, 'let's see if you can help us to solve this murder. What are your first thoughts about the crime?'

'You're the detective, sir. My job is to ask questions.'

'Then please fire them at us, Mr Reeves . . .'

Much as she enjoyed her friend's company, Madeleine could not concentrate on her. Instead of chatting at leisure with Lydia over the meal, she kept thinking about the painting of hers that had turned up mysteriously in a shop window in Soho. Lydia sympathised with her plight.

'You can't wait until tomorrow, can you?' she said.

'No, I can't. The delay is agonising.'

'Then let's spare you the anxiety, shall we?'

'What do you mean?'

'Instead of sitting here,' said Lydia, rising to her feet, 'why don't we take a cab to Soho so that you can see for yourself if it really is your painting.'

'It will be too dark.'

'There'll be enough light for you to look in a shop window. Until you do that, you'll be on tenterhooks.'

'Yes, I will,' admitted Madeleine, setting her napkin aside. 'That's a wonderful idea. You're a genius, Lydia.'

'I'm just someone who wants to help a dear friend.'

After getting up to give her a hug of gratitude, Madeleine led her into the hall. Once they'd put on their coats and hats, they left the house in John Islip Street and walked to the cab rank in a matter of minutes. They were soon being driven in the direction of Soho. While Lydia was listening to the clack of the horse's hooves, Madeleine was bracing herself for what she feared would be a nasty shock. The journey made her feel increasingly uncomfortable and forced her to grit her teeth. When they eventually reached their destination, they got out and asked the driver to wait for them. Lydia led the way to the shop window. It was largely in shadow but that did not deter Madeleine. Crouching down, she peered intently at the painting of a train steaming through the countryside. She could just make out her signature in the right-hand bottom corner.

'It's mine,' she decided.

'How can you be so sure in this gloom?'

'I know my work when I see it, Lydia.'

'Oh, dear! I was hoping that it would be a fake.'

'In a sense,' said Madeleine, 'that would be worse. I hate the idea that someone is stealing my ideas for their own benefit.'

'What are we going to do?'

'My instinct is to bang on the door until the owner comes out from the room above it. But I'm trying to keep calm. I'm asking myself what Robert would do in the circumstances.'

'I know the answer to that question,' said Lydia with confidence.

'Do you?'

'Yes, he'd come back in the morning when he could see the painting in daylight.'

CHAPTER SEVEN

Archibald Reeves was an engaging companion. He had a pleasant manner, an obvious intelligence and the true instincts of a reporter. The questions he fired at the two detectives kept them on their toes. Having filled several pages of his notebook with their answers, he sat back in his chair.

'Now it's your turn to ask me whatever you wish,' he invited.

'Did you put the same questions to Inspector Crabbe?' asked Colbeck.

'Yes, I did.'

'And did you get satisfactory answers?'

'I certainly didn't,' recalled Reeves. 'In fact, I got no answers of real substance. Unlike you, the inspector kept me at arm's length. You and the sergeant were far more honest.'

'It's no more than you deserve.'

'Who do you think did murder Mr Lockyer?' asked Leeming.

'I don't know the killer's name, Sergeant, but I could hazard a guess at his occupation.'

'What was it?'

'The man was a porter.'

'How do you know that?'

'Because I spoke to the staff at the Station Hotel,' said Reeves, 'the ones completely ignored by Inspector Crabbe. There was a maid who does all the odd jobs and a lad who helps in the kitchen. They both saw him.'

'When was this?' said Colbeck.

'It would be soon after Mr Lockyer returned last night. Each of them spotted a porter from the station, flitting around the hotel.'

'Is that unusual?'

'It's very unusual.'

'Don't some of them call in for a drink at the bar?'

Reeves laughed. 'Do you realise how much porters get paid?' he asked. 'They can't afford to go drinking if they have families to support. Also, they like to keep out of the stationmaster's way. They see enough of Biddle at work – and he drinks at the Station Hotel regularly.'

'Did anyone describe this porter to you?' asked Leeming.

'They tried but neither of them had more than a glimpse. What they did agree on was that he was short, slim and very quick.'

'Where exactly was he spotted?'

'Running upstairs.'

'Was this after Mr Lockyer returned to the hotel last night?'

'It sounds as if it was very soon after, Inspector.'

'That could just be a coincidence. Then again . . .'

Colbeck brooded for the best part of a minute then thanked

Reeves for the information. The reporter had opened a new line of enquiry for them. Leeming had another question.

'Mr Lockyer went out yesterday to see "a friend". If that so-called friend had to be paid for her services, where in the town might she live?'

Reeves smiled. 'I'm not an expert on the brothels of Shrewsbury,' he said, 'but they do exist. Mr Lockyer was patently a wealthy man. He could afford to be selective.'

'So where would he go?'

'I can give you a couple of addresses, if you wish.'

Leeming took out his notepad and pencil. 'Please do so, Mr Reeves.'

'We'll visit both places in the morning,' said Colbeck. 'If we went tonight, our interest might be misinterpreted and that could be embarrassing for all parties.'

Reeves laughed. 'I couldn't have put it better myself, Inspector.'

'And while the sergeant has his notepad out, I'd be grateful if you could give us the names of the two people at the hotel who caught sight of that porter last night.'

'I'd be glad to do so.'

When they returned to the house, Madeleine and Lydia finished the remains of their dinner. Though she had promised not to mention the painting they had seen, Madeleine was unable to dismiss it from her mind. It had taken years for her to acquire the skills needed for an artist and her earliest paintings had been summarily rejected by art dealers. When she had finally sold something, it had boosted her confidence. A regular income soon followed. The thought that a painting of hers had turned up in a shop in Soho at a price that was embarrassingly low had hurt her deeply.

Lydia read her mind. 'Try not to think about it,' she advised.

'I wish that I could.'

'All will become clear in the morning.'

'Will it?' asked Madeleine. 'What if the owner of the shop refuses to tell me how that painting came into his hands? Why is he asking so little for it? How much did he pay the person who sold it to him? If it's not really mine, why did someone go to the trouble of copying it?'

'The scene obviously appealed to him.'

'How do you know that it was a man? Women can paint equally well.'

'You're living proof of that, Madeleine.'

'Oh, I don't flatter myself that I'm a real artist.'

'But that's exactly what you are.'

'No, Lydia, I'm just someone with enough talent to sell my work. I've had no formal training. That's why I'm so surprised that someone might have tried to copy a painting of mine. Why not choose a more famous artist to copy? According to Robert, there are people producing fake copies of masterpieces all the time. Some of them are sold for ridiculously high prices,' said Madeleine. 'That could never happen to any painting of mine.'

'Well, I think that all of your paintings are masterpieces,' said Lydia loyally. 'But they're not the kind that end up in famous art galleries.'

'Thank God for that!' They laughed together. 'Oh, I'm so sorry to bore you with my problem, Lydia. You probably regret even telling me about that shop in Soho.'

'Would you have preferred that I didn't mention it?'

'Not at all. I'm very grateful to you.'

'In that case, I'll ask you a favour.'

'What is it?'

'When you go back there in the morning,' said Lydia, 'please take me with you.'

Madeleine smiled. 'I wouldn't dream of going without you.'

Dinner at the Lion Hotel gave them an opportunity to review their day. During an excellent meal, Colbeck first asked a question about their new source of information.

'What did you make of Archie Reeves?'

'I liked him,' said Leeming. 'He knows everything there is to know about Shrewsbury.'

'Everything except the name of the killer.'

'Do you think it could be that porter he mentioned?'

'It's a possibility, Victor. If nothing else, we must find out what the porter was doing at the hotel last night. The stationmaster might be able to shed some light on that. As for Reeves, I thought he was an interesting young man with a questing intelligence. I was fascinated by the way that he had befriended Charles Dickens, who had also started his writing career as a reporter.'

'What about that other writer he mentioned – Guzzlit?'

'Hazlitt,' corrected Colbeck with a grin. 'William Hazlitt. He's long dead now but he left behind an impressive list of books, essays, lectures and a biography of Napoleon. I seem to remember that his father was a Unitarian minister. I wonder if he approved of his son becoming a major literary figure.'

'Is that what Mr Reeves hopes to become?'

'I doubt it, Victor. I sense that he has set his sights lower. Since he has an interest in politics, his ideal job would be as a contributor to a satirical magazine like *Punch*.'

'Isn't that the one that poked fun at Superintendent Tallis in a cartoon?'

'Yes – he's never forgiven the editor.'

'That's another mystery we have to solve,' said Leeming.

'What is?'

'Why does the chief constable hate the superintendent?'

'Who knows? You'd have thought that being in the same regiment in India would have forged strong bonds between them, but judging by what the chief constable said, the pair of them are bitter enemies. We must bear that in mind.'

'Why?' asked Leeming.

'Because it's important to keep the two of them apart. We must ensure that Superintendent Tallis stays well away from Shrewsbury. Otherwise, we'll have another problem on our hands,' warned Colbeck. 'They'll start barking at each other like a pair of over-excited dogs.'

Edward Tallis was seated at his desk in Scotland Yard, smoking a cigar and reading the copious notes he had made during his visit to the murder victim's son. The interview with Pelham Lockyer had been a revelation. Tallis had had no idea how wide the father's business interests had stretched. While the man's primary concern had been a major railway company, he had invested heavily elsewhere. As a result, his son stood to inherit a substantial amount of money. Tallis felt bound to ask a question. Might that be a motive for murder?

Working by the light of a lamp, Tallis grew increasingly weary. It was time to leave the building and go home. As he closed his notebook, however, his eye fell on the latest telegraph from Colbeck. It had contained the news that the chief constable of

Shropshire was no less a person than his sworn enemy, Colonel Richard John Edgell. After grinding his cigar into the ashtray, he picked up the telegraph and tore it into shreds before dropping the pieces into the wastepaper basket.

At the end of a working day, Colonel Edgell was reviewing the case that was demanding their full attention. He was in his office with Inspector Crabbe, who had delivered his report with a mingled disappointment and rancour. Edgell was unimpressed.

'In other words,' he said, 'you have made virtually no progress.'

'That's unfair, sir,' replied the other. 'Our investigation has been thorough and wide-ranging.'

'But you have been unable to identify the killer.'

'We believe that Mr Lockyer was seen returning to the Station Hotel when he was clearly the worse for wear. His appearance would have confirmed that he was a man of some importance and therefore had obvious wealth. He was followed to the hotel by someone who sensed rich pickings. The man spoke to a member of the hotel staff to find out the number of Mr Lockyer's room, then he went to the rear of the building to identify the room and to see if it was possible to gain entry through a window that had been left ajar on a warm night. After allowing his target some time to fall asleep, he climbed up to the room and saw that Mr Lockyer was on the bed, completely naked and fast asleep. He moved in for the kill.'

'Yet no violence was necessary,' Edgell reminded him. 'If Mr Lockyer was deeply asleep, the thief could have taken whatever he liked and left with the spoils. I incline to Sergeant Leeming's suggestion. The interloper was an assassin. He had been paid to kill. Stealing whatever he wanted was second nature to him.'

'With respect, sir, that's pure guesswork.'

'It makes more sense than your theory. I believe that he had been given a good description of Mr Lockyer. He probably travelled here on the same train as him. After watching Lockyer enter the Station Hotel, the assassin bided his time.'

'But how did he know that Mr Lockyer was coming here in the first place?'

'His paymaster must have told him.'

'That means the murder was planned by someone in London.'

'Yes,' agreed Edgell, 'and the person who devised the plan was someone who was probably a member of his social circle. Perhaps he was a rival for the position of chairman of the GWR or had a strong urge to want Mr Lockyer dead. He may even have insisted that the murder was made to look like a case of suicide.' Edgell lowered his voice. 'Can you hear what I'm telling you, Inspector?'

'I think so, sir.'

'The answers you seek are not here in Shrewsbury. They are far more likely to be in London.'

Crabbe curled a lip. 'That's Inspector Colbeck's territory.'

'Exactly,' snapped Edgell. 'It's the reason you must learn to work together rather than in competition with him.'

'But that would mean he got all the credit for solving the murder.'

'Colbeck struck me as an honest, decent man who would never deprive anyone of his due share of recognition. I know that you and he are not exactly birds of a feather, but you must put your hostile feelings towards him aside. Let me be brutally honest,' said Edgell. 'Without his help, you stand no chance whatsoever of finding and arresting the killer. By working alongside him, however, you will get your fair share of glory and learn something from a master of his art.'

'But I loathe the very sight of the man,' snarled Crabbe.

'I loathed the sight of Edward Tallis,' confided Edgell, 'but I was able to work perfectly well alongside the man in the Bengal Army. In fact, I freely admit that he taught me a lot.'

When she opened the front door to leave the house the next morning, Madeleine Colbeck saw her father walking towards her. Since he was not expected until later, she was surprised.

'Why are you here so early?' she asked.

'Is that a complaint?'

'No, of course it isn't. You can come and go as you please.'

'Thank you. Where are you off to, Maddy?'

'It's a long story . . .'

'Give it to me in a few words,' said Andrews.

Madeleine told him about the painting of hers that had appeared in a shop window in Soho. Andrews was duly horrified on her behalf. He immediately volunteered to go with her.

'There's no need, Father. Lydia is meeting me at the shop.'

'Then you need some protection. Shopkeepers in Soho can get very aggressive. Their language is disgusting. I'll come along to make sure that the man who runs that shop behaves himself.'

Over breakfast, Colbeck and Leeming discussed the case once more. The sergeant was uncharacteristically depressed. When he had swallowed the last of his bacon, he pulled a face.

'The only way that we could find out where Mr Lockyer went that evening is to set up a house-to-house search – but we don't have the resources.'

'The local police do, Victor. I hope that they have the sense to set a search in motion.'

'If they do, they're unlikely to tells us the results.'

'Inspector Crabbe will not cooperate, but I fancy that the chief constable would.'

'I disagree. He'd see it as helping Superintendent Tallis, and – for reasons unknown to us – that's the last thing he wants to do.'

'I think that your suggestion is the best one,' said Colbeck. 'Mr Lockyer was not killed by a thief who happened to spot him returning to his hotel. He was murdered by a hired assassin who probably followed him here from London.'

'Then we'll have to search for him there.'

'All in good time, Victor. We still have some clues right here. One of them concerns that porter seen on the night of the murder at the hotel.'

'That will mean talking to the two people who work there.'

'Before we do that, we'll speak to the stationmaster. He might be able to guess exactly which member of his staff it must have been.'

'What if he wasn't a porter at all?' asked Leeming. 'He was the killer in disguise.'

'That thought crossed my mind.'

'He might have stolen the clothes from a real porter.'

'It's possible. Then he slipped into the hotel soon after he saw Mr Lockyer staggering in through the front door.'

'My guess is that he followed him to the house of the friend whom Mr Lockyer had come to see and then trailed him back to the hotel. He would have seen the state that the man was in and realised that he would soon fall asleep and be unable to defend himself.'

'Who hired him in the first place?' asked Leeming.

'Someone with good reason to hate him.'

'An angry husband whose wife had been seduced by Mr Lockyer?'

'A business rival would be more likely. We still have much to do here, Victor.'

'Does that include talking to the police?'

'Yes, of course,' said Colbeck. 'They will have gathered information that could be valuable. But I'd also like to question Archie Reeves again. He is far more of a detective than Inspector Crabbe. That's not a complaint about Crabbe. Within his limits, he is a conscientious man. His problem is that he's a well-meaning plodder. Reeves, by contrast, has imagination. He also has a job that involves sniffing around for information. He's one of nature's bloodhounds and – unlike the inspector – he's keen to help us.'

When their cab dropped them off in Soho, Madeleine and her father saw that Lydia was already there, standing beside her cab. She was looking in the window of a dress shop. Delighted to see them, she embraced Madeleine and shook hands with Caleb Andrews.

'I see that you've brought reinforcements,' she said.

'When Maddy told me about this painting of hers,' said Andrews, 'I offered to come along as a sort of bodyguard.'

'The more, the merrier,' said Lydia.

'Where is it?' he asked. 'I'm dying to see it.'

'Then we'll have to cross the road,' said his daughter, leading the way.

They crossed together and looked through the window of the shop. In broad daylight, the painting of the locomotive in a country scene looked very different. Certain that it was his daughter's work, Andrews became truculent.

'I'll demand to know who sold it,' he promised. 'And its price ought to be three times higher.'

'It's a delightful scene,' said Lydia. 'You're so clever, Madeleine.'

Her friend shook her head. 'You're being misled, I'm afraid.'

'What do you mean?'

'Well,' said Madeleine, 'now that I see it properly, I can give a proper assessment of it. Yes, it's very similar to my painting but it is, in fact, a fake.'

'Are you sure?' asked her father.

'I'm certain that it is. It's nothing but a clever copy.'

When they got to the railway station, the first thing that the detectives did was to visit the telegraph office there. As he had hoped, there was word from Superintendent Tallis. Among other things, Colbeck was told that Julian Lockyer had lied to his son about where he was spending the previous night. Colbeck was bound to wonder why.

'What does he say?' asked Leeming.

'He passed on the grim news to Lockyer's son.'

'That was good of him.'

'And he sends a warning to both of us, Victor.'

'What is it?'

'I quote his own words,' said Colbeck. '"Do not mention my name to Colonel Edgell."'

'It's too late. We've already done that.'

After handing the telegraph to Leeming so that he could read it for himself, Colbeck led the way to the stationmaster's office. Delighted to see them, Biddle leapt to his feet.

'Anything I can do for you, Inspector?' he asked.

'Yes, there is,' said Colbeck. 'You told us that when Mr Lockyer first arrived here, he made a point of speaking to you.'

'It's true – except that he didn't speak to me, he spoke at me.'

'We've got someone at Scotland Yard who does that,' said Leeming.

'While you were talking to him,' said Colbeck, 'most of the passengers who alighted from the train must have left the station.'

'Yes, they had,' confirmed Biddle. 'They streamed past me.'

'Did you notice anyone else who lingered until Mr Lockyer had left the station?'

Biddle removed his hat so that he could scratch his head. 'As a matter of fact, I did,' he recalled as a memory surfaced. 'I was still too angry at Mr Lockyer's complaints about my station to pay much attention to him. But this man did hang around for some time.'

'Can you describe him?' prompted Leeming.

'Not really, Sergeant. I only had a glimpse of him. He was about your height and build, and he was well dressed. He carried a small valise.'

'What age would he be?' asked Colbeck.

'I'd put him in his thirties.'

'Did he say anything to you?'

'Yes, he did,' said Biddle. 'He asked me the time of the earliest train to London the following morning. I knew that's where he came from because he had a sort of London voice.'

'Do you mean that he was a Cockney?'

'Yes, that's the word. He was a proper Cockney. You'd never think of it to look at him. He seemed a proper gentleman, but he was common. That's about all I can tell you.'

'You've been very helpful,' said Colbeck. 'Thank you, Mr Biddle.

There's a strong chance that the man you spoke to had come here to kill Mr Lockyer.'

'Good heavens!'

'We also know that he stayed the night in Shrewsbury. If we can track down which hotel he chose, we can get even more details about him.'

'It won't have been far from the station,' decided Biddle.

'Quite so. Moving on to another matter,' said Colbeck, 'were you, by any chance, at the Station Hotel on the night of the murder?'

'Yes, I was, as it happens, Inspector. It was the end of a long day. I called in for a drink and a few words with Molly . . . Mrs Burrage, that is. Why do you ask?'

'Two people reported having seen one of your porters there.'

'That's news to me,' said Biddle. 'The porters usually drink at the Dog and Badger. The beer is cheaper there and they like the atmosphere. I can't think of anyone likely to go to the Station Hotel. Do you have a description of this porter?'

'All we know is that he was short and moved very quickly.'

'You've just described half-a-dozen members of my staff.'

'Then we'll trouble you no further,' said Colbeck. 'We'll bid you goodbye and start our search of the hotels. Thanks to your telegraph station we've just learnt an interesting piece of news.'

'Yes,' said Leeming. 'Mr Lockyer was not supposed to be anywhere near Shrewsbury.'

'He told his son that he was going to somewhere in Kent.'

Biddle was mystified. 'Why on earth did he do that?'

As Madeleine, her father and Lydia entered the shop, the owner came out of a room at the back. He was a big, broad-shouldered man in his fifties with watchful eyes that flicked from one to the others as he assessed the trio. A smile appeared on his face.

'Good day to you,' he said, 'and welcome to my shop. How may I help you?'

'We've come about that painting featuring a train in the countryside,' said Madeleine. 'We'd like to know the name of the artist.'

'Her name is on the painting,' said the man.

'But the painting is a fake,' declared Caleb Andrews. 'My daughter here is Madeleine Colbeck and that painting in your window is a copy of the one that she painted.'

'It was sold at the Red Gallery,' added Lydia, 'and fetched a lot more than the one you have.'

'What we'd like,' said Madeleine, 'is the name of this so-called "artist".'

Anger brought a deeper colour into the man's cheeks. He put his hands on his hips.

'Who the devil are you?' he demanded.

'My name is Caleb Andrews,' he said, 'and I have a special interest in that painting because I was an engine driver for many years. When my daughter was young, I took her to see the trains at Euston and she fell in love with them. That's why she started to paint railway scenes. And before you start to get angry,' he warned, seeing the look in the man's eye, 'I should warn you that her husband is a detective inspector at Scotland Yard.

'Oh, I see,' said the man, controlling his rage.

'Who sold that painting to you?' asked Lydia.

'She said her name was Madeleine Colbeck.'

'She lied to you,' said Madeleine, eyes flashing. 'You've been tricked, Mr . . .'

'Davies,' said the other. 'Solomon Davies.'

'My version of the same scene sold for many times more than the price you've put on it.'

'How do I know that?'

'Go to the Red Gallery. My paintings have all been sold there by Mr Sinclair.'

'Give us the address of this other artist,' demanded Andrews.

'I don't have an address,' said Davies.

'Then how do you keep in touch with her?'

'She comes in from time to time to see if the painting has been sold. There's been a lot of interest in it – but we've had no offers.'

'Take it out of the window. It's a fake.'

'Don't tell me what I can and can't sell,' warned Davies. 'It's pure coincidence that it looks a bit like a scene that your daughter claims to have painted.'

'It's an exact copy,' argued Madeleine.

'I can vouch for that,' added Lydia.

'The other artist not only stole my daughter's idea,' said Andrews, wagging a finger, 'she stole her name as well. You've been tricked, Mr Davies.'

'I think it's time you left my shop,' said the shopkeeper, pointing to the door. 'Get out!'

'Not until you take that fake out of your window.'

'Come on, Father,' said Madeleine, taking him by the arm. 'There's no point in arguing. This is a job for the police. I'll speak to my husband.'

'Get out!' yelled Davies, going to the door and opening it wide. 'And don't come back!'

When the three of them left, he slammed the door behind them then glared.

They took a last glance at the painting in the window, then got into their respective cabs and were driven away. Andrews was delighted. He turned to his daughter.

'That was fun, wasn't it?' he said, cackling. 'I put the fear of death into him!'

After leaving the stationmaster, Colbeck decided that they should split up. He sent Leeming back to the Station Hotel to the speak to the two members of staff who saw the porter on the night of the murder. He himself went off to meet Archie Reeves. When he approached the offices of the *Shrewsbury Chronicle*, he saw the young reporter stepping out into the street. After they had exchanged greetings, Reeves took him down an alley.

'There's something I've been asking myself,' he said.

'What is it?'

'How did Mr Lockyer know where to go that night?'

'I've no idea,' said Colbeck.

'He must have been to Shrewsbury before.'

'Not necessarily – he might have been given an address by a friend.'

'Given what we know about him,' argued Reeves, 'that seems unlikely. Mr Lockyer seemed to have been a decisive and overbearing man. I can't imagine him discussing the whereabouts of a brothel with anyone.'

'We can't be certain that that is where he went on the night of the murder,' said Colbeck. 'The so-called friend he mentioned may well have been a man. I just want to cover all the options and see parts of the town that are off the beaten track. Experience has taught me not to have exaggerated hopes,' he added. 'Detective work is full of disappointments.'

'I sense that we could be lucky.'

'Let's find out, shall we?'

Reeves led him through a veritable maze of streets, lanes and alleys until they reached a sizeable house that stood on the corner of a wide road. Colbeck glanced up at it in surprise. During his early days in the Metropolitan Police Force, he had taken part in raids on brothels. They had always been squalid places, hidden away in narrow lanes in seedier parts of the city. The one outside which they had stopped was a detached house in good condition.

'Are you sure that this is the right place?' he asked.

'Don't be deceived by appearances, Inspector,' said Reeves. 'By day, this is a respectable house owned by a middle-aged lady named Sarah Wellborne. At night – I am reliably informed – she changes her name to Dorothea Quinn and provides a service to trusted clients.'

'At a considerable charge, I suspect,' said Colbeck, looking up at the house.

'Shall we see if the lady is at home?' asked Reeves.

'Yes, please.'

The reporter rang the bell beside the door then stood back. Almost immediately, the door opened to reveal a middle-aged man with the look of a sailor about him. Stocky and with darting eyes, he was inhospitable.

'What d'you want?' he demanded.

'We wish to speak to Mrs Wellborne,' said Colbeck politely. 'Is she at home?'

'No,' said the man. 'Good day to you.'

He tried to close the door, but Colbeck got a foot to it to keep it open.

'You heard me,' warned the man, 'or you'll be sorry.'

'You're speaking to a detective inspector,' said Reeves, 'so show some respect.'

'We've already had police sniffing around. I'll tell you what I told them. Leave us alone. We can't help you.'

'I'd still like to speak with Mrs Wellborne,' said Colbeck firmly.

'Well, you can't.'

'Let them in, James!' called a female voice. 'Show them into the drawing room.'

Clearly dismayed by the instruction, the man opened the door wide with obvious reluctance. Colbeck stepped past him and was followed by Reeves. When the front door was shut, the man led them into a drawing room that was tastefully furnished. The first thing that Colbeck noticed was the crucifix on the mantelpiece. After giving each of them a hostile stare, the man left them alone. They had only seconds to take stock of their surroundings because Sarah Wellborne sailed into the room with a beatific smile on her face.

'Do sit down, gentlemen,' she said.

She lowered herself into an armchair and studied them in turn. She was a fleshy woman in a beautiful dress and had a decided air of respectability about her. Both visitors noticed that she had kept much of her youthful prettiness into middle age. The smile never left her face.

'How may I help you?' she asked.

'If the police have already been here,' said Colbeck, 'they will have told you about a murder that occurred at the Station Hotel two nights ago.'

'What has that got to do with me?' she asked.

'It's possible that the murder victim came to this town in search of pleasure.'

'Well, he never sought it here. I can assure you of that. We had a group of friends here two nights ago to celebrate my birthday. Why should I invite a stranger into my home?'

'The man's name was Julian Lockyer.'

'I've never heard of him, Inspector.'

'It may be that he used an alias to conceal his identity.'

'Whatever name he used,' she insisted, 'he would never have been allowed through my door. When confronted by an unwanted visitor, James will get rid of him at once.'

'He tried to get rid of us,' noted Reeves.

'That was before you explained who you were.' Her smile broadened. 'It's been a pleasure to meet you both,' she went on, 'but I have other commitments to attend to so you will have to excuse me. I am always more than willing to assist the police but – in this case – that is not possible.' She rose to her feet. 'I wish you the best of luck in your search, gentlemen. James will show you out.'

When she indicated the door, it opened immediately and the man they had already met stepped into the room. He had clearly been listening to their conversation.

'This way,' he said with a sly grin. 'It was good to meet you.'

Victor Leeming's interview with Clarrie Venables was equally unproductive. She was the maid at the Station Hotel who had noticed a porter climbing the stairs on the night of the murder. A nervous young woman, Clarrie asked if the hotel owner could be present and, throughout the interview, she kept looking at Molly Burrage for approval.

'Just tell the sergeant what you saw,' advised Molly.

'It was over so quickly,' said the girl. 'As I was coming out of the laundry room, I saw this porter running upstairs. He disappeared in a flash.'

'What time was this?' asked Leeming.

'It was not long after Mr Lockyer came back to the hotel so he would have been up in his room. That's all I can tell you.'

'Well done, Clarrie,' said her employer. 'You can go now.' The girl scurried thankfully out of the room. Molly turned to Leeming. 'I'm sorry, Sergeant. All that she got was a mere glimpse. My staff are trained to do their jobs, not to watch guests come and go.'

'But this porter she spotted was not a guest,' said Leeming. 'Someone must have invited him into his room.'

'It's possible,' she said, 'but it was not Mr Lockyer. He could barely walk up the stairs. Once in his room, he would probably have torn off his clothes and gone to bed.'

'We'd still like to find out who this porter was and why he came here.'

'Have you spoken to Simon . . . Mr Biddle, that is?'

'Yes, he told us that porters always go to a pub called the Dog and Badger.'

'It is unusual to see one here.'

'That means he came for a special reason,' said Leeming. 'Right, let me speak to this young man who works in the kitchen. Maybe he had a better look at this mysterious porter. I'm sorry to take up so much of your time, Mrs Burrage. I'm sure that you have lots to do.'

'Nothing is more important than finding the killer,' she said. 'Until you do that, I won't be able to have a moment's sleep. I'll fetch the lad at once . . .'

Colbeck's second visit to the home of a high-class prostitute was even shorter. They did not even get to meet Venetia Osborne. When they arrived, a doctor was leaving the premises. He explained that he had been treating Mrs Osborne for a disease that had already kept her in bed for a week.

'I'm sorry to have wasted your time, Inspector,' said Reeves as they walked away.

'Not at all,' said Colbeck. 'We've had a pleasant walk, and I've learnt something about this town that I found extremely interesting. I think it's clear that Mr Lockyer did not come here for the purposes of visiting either of the ladies who put a high price on their services. No matter,' he went on. 'There are more avenues to explore. Before long, I promise you, we will find the trail that leads directly to the killer.'

The first thing that Leeming noticed about Rodney Grant was that he brought a strong smell of fish into the room. He was a stringy young man with traces of flour on his apron. Unlike Clarrie Venables, he was full of confidence.

'Sorry about the stink,' he said with a grin. 'We've had a delivery from the fishmonger.'

'Just answer the sergeant's questions,' ordered Molly.

'Yes, Mrs Burrage.'

'Tell me about the porter who was here on the night of the murder,' said Leeming.

'What happened was this,' replied Grant, keen to help. 'I was working in the kitchen when the chef sent me with a message for Mrs Burrage. As I stepped into the corridor, I saw this porter coming into the hotel and going past me towards the stairs. Clarrie must have seen him as well because she came into the corridor near the bottom of the stairs.'

'Describe the porter, please.'

'Well, he was short and slight and ran up the stairs as if he was in a hurry. I thought no more about him at the time,' said Grant, 'but, given what happened, I've been thinking.'

'Go on.'

'He was dressed like a porter, but his coat was far too big for him, and he had baggy trousers. I know that the stationmaster is very fussy about the appearance of his staff because my brother works for him, and Ted is always getting told off about the way he dresses.' Grant tapped his chest with his finger. 'I got this idea, see.'

'What is it?' asked Leeming.

'Well, I'm not sure that he was a real porter at all. He was only pretending, see. I fancy that he might have got hold of a uniform somehow and used it as a disguise. And there's another thing . . .'

'Spit it out, Rodney,' said Molly.

'Well, I wondered if it wasn't a man at all.' His eyes widened. 'What if it was a woman?'

Leeming forgave him for stinking of fish.

CHAPTER EIGHT

After their visit to Soho, they considered their next move. Caleb Andrews suggested that they should forget about the painting and return home. Madeleine felt that that would be akin to admitting failure, and she wanted the truth. She therefore persuaded her father to go with her to the Red Gallery. When the cab dropped them off, she looked up at the building with a profound sense of gratitude. Several oil paintings were on display in the window. Andrews peered at the selection.

'Nothing of yours is here, Maddy,' he observed.

'That's a good sign. It means that they've all been sold.'

'This place is so much better than that junk shop. Let's go in.'

He opened the door so that Madeleine could enter the shop. After following her inside, he shut the door behind him. Francis Sinclair, a tall, thin, cultured man with ginger hair was thrilled to see one of his favourite artists. He came out from behind the counter to welcome them.

'What a lovely surprise!' he said.

'It's good to see you again, Mr Sinclair.'

'Your paintings continue to find new customers, Mrs Colbeck.'

'That's very gratifying.'

'Tell him about that crime, Maddy!' urged her father.

'Crime?' repeated Sinclair in alarm.

'We've just come from a shop in Soho,' she explained. 'They had a copy of one of my paintings in the window. It was a complete fake.'

Sinclair was roused. 'Then they have no right to put it on sale.'

'We want the artist who stole Maddy's idea to be thrown into gaol,' said Andrews.

'Who owns the shop?'

'It's a nasty man by the name of Solomon Davies,' replied Madeleine. 'He more or less threw us out of his shop.'

'Did he say who brought in the painting?'

'Yes – Madeleine Colbeck.'

'That obviously wasn't her real name,' claimed Andrews. 'She stole it from my daughter and tried to pass it off as one of her own paintings.'

'The other artist might not even have been a woman,' said Sinclair.

'He or she is breaking the law.'

'Unfortunately, there's a lot of fraud in the art world. In a way, I suppose, it's a compliment to Mrs Colbeck that someone wanted to copy one of her paintings. But it does make my blood boil. In my opinion, fake artists are bare-faced thieves.'

'We wondered if you could help us, Mr Sinclair,' said Madeleine. 'When the painting was on display in your window, did you notice anyone taking a close interest in it?'

'A lot of people stopped to stare at it,' said Sinclair, 'and quite rightly. It's such a lovely painting. More than one person came into the shop to ask what it cost. They were not only delighted by the scene. They were amazed that a woman had painted it.'

'Maddy can do anything,' boasted Andrews.

'Someone must have studied it for a long time in order to copy it,' she said. 'Did you ever see a woman with a sketch pad outside your shop, Mr Sinclair?'

'I can't say that I did,' he replied. 'But a woman did buy a print of that painting.'

'Did she give a name?'

'No, she didn't.'

'Can you describe her, please?'

'Well, she was a smartly dressed woman of middle years, and she was well spoken. She was impressed by your work. No,' he went, shaking his head, 'I can't believe that she was in any way connected to the fake copy. She was a real lady.'

'Real ladies sometimes commit crimes,' said Andrews.

'Did she leave an address?' asked Madeleine.

Sinclair shook his head. 'No – she just bought the print on impulse.'

'The man who actually bought my painting of that scene was a stockbroker, wasn't he?'

'That's right, Mrs Colbeck. He's a great admirer of your work.'

'Does he still have it, I wonder?'

'I'm sure that he does. He bought three or four of your paintings.'

Madeleine's eyebrows lifted. 'I don't suppose that you have his address, do you?'

When they met up at The Lion Hotel, they compared notes. Leeming explained that the two people who had seen a porter enter the Station Hotel described him in identical terms.

'There was one thing, though,' he added.

'What is it, Victor?'

'Well, the lad from the kitchen wondered if it wasn't a man at all – but a woman in disguise.'

'That's an interesting possibility,' said Colbeck. 'Might she have been going up to Mr Lockyer's room?'

'Who knows?'

'Why else would a woman who is not a guest go upstairs in the first place?'

'Rodney didn't have an answer to that, sir.'

'He's given us a new version of events.'

'It was only a random guess.'

'We should nevertheless be grateful. I'm sorry if you had to put up with the stink of fish but your suffering had adequate recompense.'

'What about you?' asked Leeming. 'How did you get on?'

'We had the pleasure of meeting one of the town's more illustrious women. She lives a double life. By day, she is a pillar of respectability. By night, she entertains a sequence of male guests. I liked the contented smile she wore.'

'Was Lockyer a client of hers on the night of the murder?'

'I'm certain that he was not.'

'In other words, you learnt nothing of real use to us.'

'I was interested to see the two establishments to which Archie took me, but they had no connection with the murder. My time, however, was not wasted. When I told him about the man described to us by the stationmaster, he picked out the hotel where the visitor must have stayed. It was close to the railway station and the guest chose a room that looked out on the Station Hotel.'

'Did you get his name?'

'No, Victor. When he signed in, I fancy, he used an alias – Jack Brown. The description that the manager gave of him matched the one that Mr Biddle gave. He went out somewhere on the night he stayed here, but they had no idea where it was. On the following day, he caught the first train to London. I think,' said Colbeck, 'that he's a far more likely killer than someone in a porter's uniform that was far too big for him.'

'Too big for her,' corrected Leeming. 'The lad thought it might be a woman, remember.'

'Then we can rule her out, I fancy.'

'Why would a woman sneak into the hotel and go upstairs?'

'She might have had an arrangement with one of the guests.'

'Mr Lockyer?'

'I doubt it. If he came here for female company, he would surely enjoy it somewhere more appealing than in the Railway Hotel.'

'Unless he came here for a very different reason,' warned Leeming.

'I'm inclined to think that he did.'

'How do we find out what brought him to Shrewsbury?'

'We use our imagination.'

'I do that best with a glass of beer.'

Colbeck smiled. 'Then perhaps we should look at the luncheon menu.'

* * *

Archibald Reeves was hard at work. Seated at his desk in the offices of the *Shrewsbury Chronicle*, he read through the reports in the national newspapers of the murder at the Station Hotel. Only one shop in the town had the national editions on sale every morning, and he had bought a copy of every newspaper so that he missed no detail. Because of his links to the GWR, the victim was portrayed as a man with great ambitions for the future of railway travel. Those ambitions had been snuffed out during his stay in the town. Speculation was rife. Was the murder connected to Lockyer's passion for train travel? Or was he killed by someone with a deep-seated grudge against him? One journalist argued that an assassin employed by a rival railway company might conceivably have been involved. Other suggestions were even more bizarre.

Reeves had the advantage of seeing the case through Colbeck's eyes. He applauded the way that the inspector was looking at the possibilities one by one and slowly eliminating them. What nobody could say with certainty was what Lockyer was doing in Shropshire. London reporters had contacted Pelham Lockyer for a comment and been told that even the son was unable to explain the reason for the visit. Reeves noted that articles in the national press were based largely on speculation rather than on hard facts. Unlike him, no reporter was working beside a famous detective from Scotland Yard. He was grateful to be able to assist in the investigation as it unfolded. It would give his forthcoming article in the *Shrewsbury Chronicle* an authenticity that no other newspaper could match. He felt empowered.

Neville Henderson was a retired stockbroker in his late sixties, a pot-bellied, silver-haired gentleman who was rich enough to buy what he wished and who basked in his good fortune. When they entered his house, Madeleine and her father thought that they were in a glorified antique shop. Exquisite furniture, beautiful decorative objects and gilt-framed paintings were everywhere. The one disappointment for Madeleine was that she could see nothing that she had painted. Henderson was aware of her dismay.

'Your work lights up my study,' he explained. 'I love steam locomotives and only Madeleine Colbeck can bring them truly to life.'

'My father must take some credit,' she said. 'He taught me to revere steam engines.'

Leading them into the drawing room, Henderson indicated a sofa, and they sat down on it. He, meanwhile, lowered himself with some difficulty into a leather armchair. They saw him wince.

'Old age is catching up with me,' he explained. 'I'm beginning to creak.'

'I know the feeling,' said Andrews.

'Oh, this is such an unexpected delight! It's a real joy to meet you at last, Mrs Colbeck.'

'It's a pleasure to meet you, Mr Henderson. I'm eternally grateful for the interest you've taken in my work. The Red Gallery has been my salvation. Mr Sinclair sends his regards.'

'He's sent something far more interesting than that – one of his most talented artists.'

'This is not a social visit,' she warned.

'How disappointing!'

'We came for some advice.'

'Yes,' said Andrews. 'It's because you like my daughter's paintings so much. One of them shows a steam engine going past a little farmhouse.'

'It's a delightful scene. I never tire of looking at it.'

'If you go to a shop in Soho,' said Madeleine, 'you can see it again. The identical painting is for sale. There's one problem. I was not the artist.'

Henderson was aghast. 'Someone copied it?'

'They tried to. It fooled me at first.'

'The moment I saw it,' insisted Andrews, 'I knew it was a fake.'

'It must have been so distressing for you,' said Henderson. 'I sympathise, of course, but I can't see how I can help you.'

'Oh, I'm not here to ask for help,' said Madeleine. 'I just wondered if it was possible for me to see my original painting. That's why we asked Mr Sinclair for your address. If I could study every detail of that scene, I could relive the experience of painting it. Is it too much to ask of you?'

'Not at all, Mrs Colbeck. I'm delighted to be of help.'

Rising slowly to his feet, he led them out of the drawing room and along a corridor. When he opened the door of his study, he stood back so that Madeleine could enter the room first. She found herself in a miniature art gallery with paintings on all four walls. Pride of place went to the very painting they had been talking about. It brought back happy memories of the holiday on a farm where she had worked outdoors in the sun and produced one of her finest oil paintings.

'If I'd been the engine driver,' said Andrews, 'I'd have gone past as slowly as possible so that my daughter had plenty of time to get a good look at us.'

'I think that she saw more than enough,' argued Henderson. 'Every detail is a delight. I've had so much pleasure admiring your skill, Mrs Colbeck. That's why I simply had to add it to my collection.' Seeing how entranced Madeleine was by her own work, he nudged Andrews then led him out of the study. 'We're in the way,' he said. 'Let the artist feast her eyes on it for as long as she wishes.'

Pelham Lockyer was also in his study, but he had no interest in studying an oil painting. He was too busy reading his father's obituary in *The Times*. It was long and detailed. Julian Lockyer had been praised for his success as a businessman and for his work as a member of the board of the GWR. The only jarring note was in the last line. It asked what the man had been doing in Shrewsbury on the night of his murder. Scrunching up the newspaper, his son flung it angrily aside.

When they left the dining room at the Lion Hotel, they came into the reception area. There was a letter waiting for Colbeck. He opened it to find a scribbled note from the stationmaster. It asked him to call on Biddle as soon as possible. With Leeming beside him, Colbeck set off at a brisk pace. His companion soon had a complaint.

'Must we really walk so fast?' asked Leeming.

'Yes, Victor.'

'We've just had a big meal.'

'All the more reason for some strenuous activity. Mr Biddle has news for us. I don't want to keep him waiting a moment longer. If it's too much effort,' he added, 'go at your own pace.'

'I can manage,' said Leeming, lengthening his stride.

By the time they reached the station, he was panting from his exertion. He put a hand against a wall to steady himself and suggested – between gasps – that Colbeck go on ahead. The inspector headed straight for the stationmaster's office. When Biddle saw him entering, he rose to his feet.

'You got my message, then.'

'Thank you for summoning me,' said Colbeck.

'I've learnt something that might interest you, Inspector.'

'What is it?'

'I had a visit from Betty Rees earlier on,' said Biddle. 'She's married to Gwyn Rees, one of my porters. Her husband is ill and off work. When we had fine weather a few days ago, Betty decided to wash his clothes and hang them out to dry.'

'It was very sensible of her.'

'That's what she thought – but there was a problem.'

'Oh?'

'When she looked through the window, she saw that his shirt, jacket and trousers had disappeared. Gwyn's hat had also vanished. Betty thought that they must have been blown off the line but, when she went into the garden, there was no sign of them. She thought that someone had stolen them.'

'In fact,' said Colbeck, 'someone had simply borrowed them.'

'How did you guess?'

'That porter who went into the Station Hotel on the night of the murder was possibly a woman in a man's clothing. I daresay that she put it all back.'

'That was what startled Betty. When she looked through the window next morning, the coat, shirt and trousers were back on the washing line – but not in the order she'd hung them there.'

'Did she get a glimpse of the thief?'

'No, she didn't. Gwyn was outraged. He wanted to tear the thief to pieces. Well,' said Biddle, 'you know what the Welsh are like. They're hot-blooded beggars.'

'Thank you for the information,' said Colbeck. 'I'm certain that the person who borrowed the porter's clothing handled them with care. Only one question remains. What exactly was he – or she – doing in the hotel on the night in question?'

During their cab ride back to John Islip Street, they had ample time to discuss their visit. Madeleine had been delighted to see her painting once more and grateful to the retired stockbroker for letting her study it for as long as she wished. It had brought back precious memories.

'I so enjoyed working on it,' she said.

'Why did this other woman choose to copy that painting?'

'I've no idea, Father.'

'It's nothing short of robbery!'

'I agree.'

'And how many others is she going to steal from you?'

'We've got to stop her.'

'Then she needs to be found and arrested,' said Andrews. 'If it was left to me, she'd serve a life sentence in London's worst prison.'

'I'd just like to meet her and stop her from stealing my ideas. At the same time,' said Madeleine, 'I can't help feeling flattered. This woman really loves my work.'

'That doesn't give her the right to copy it.'

'I agree, Father. Oh, I do wish that Robert was here. He'd know what to do. We've picked up a trail, but the truth is that we are amateurs. What we need is a real detective.'

'I think I know just the man,' he said, 'and I'm sure he'd love to help us.'

'Who are you talking about?'

'Detective Constable Alan Hinton.'

'Of course!' cried Madeleine, laughing. 'Why didn't I think of him?'

'I bet that he'd love to help us. Just tell him that Lydia is involved in the search for this woman, and Alan will be here like a shot.'

When Colbeck and Leeming went to police headquarters in Swan Hill, they were taken immediately to the chief constable's office. They were pleased that Inspector Crabbe was there even though he gave them a guarded welcome. Colbeck and Leeming were invited to sit.

'I wondered when we would see you again,' said Edgell.

'Like you, sir,' replied Colbeck, 'we have been extremely busy. We've also been dodging the hordes of reporters who have been sent here by national newspapers.'

'They get in our way,' grumbled Crabbe. 'And we have enough problems as it is.'

'In other words,' said Leeming, 'you have made no arrests.'

'We have a suspect in mind, Sergeant.'

'So do we.'

'It's the reason we are here,' explained Colbeck. 'We feel that it's time to share information instead of hoarding it selfishly. Our belief is that Mr Lockyer was followed here by a man hired to kill him. He used the alias of Jack Brown. We found the hotel in which he stayed. Early on the following day, he caught the first train to London.' He saw them exchange a look of surprise. 'I see that you have not been able to identify this individual as the killer.'

'I'm not sure that there was such a person,' said Crabbe. 'We explored other avenues.'

'To no effect,' said Leeming under his breath.

'If you are so sure of this man's guilt, why didn't you arrest him?'

'It was because he had already fled the town,' said Colbeck, 'and gone back to London. Our search for him will continue there.'

Crabbe's eyes lit up. 'Does that mean you are leaving Shrewsbury?'

'All in good time. We have other business to conclude here.'

'Really?'

'Among other things,' said Colbeck, 'we would like to find the person who sneaked into the Station Hotel shortly after Mr Lockyer returned there that night. There's a possibility that it was a woman disguised as a railway porter. She was seen going upstairs.'

'Did you know about this person?' asked Edgell, turning to Crabbe.

'No, sir,' admitted the inspector.

'I spoke to two people who worked at the hotel,' said Leeming. 'Both of them remember a porter slipping into the hotel that night and wearing baggy clothing.'

'It had been stolen from the home of a real porter,' said Colbeck. 'I'm fairly convinced that the thief was a woman.'

'Have you spoken to Annie Garrow?' asked Crabbe.

'No, we haven't. Who is she?'

'A young woman who worked at the hotel and who was present when the corpse was discovered. She was so upset that Mrs Burrage told her to go home until she felt well enough to return.' Crabbe straightened his back. 'On the principle of leaving no stone unturned, I interviewed the girl at her home, and she told me something about Mr Lockyer that may be relevant.'

'What was it?' asked Colbeck.

'The girl was young and ignorant of the ways of the world, Inspector. She was therefore distressed when Lockyer looked at her with an evil glint in his eye. It made her shudder. The girl must be almost forty years younger than Lockyer, but that didn't matter to him. He was a lecher,' said Crabbe, 'and he lusted after her. The girl was still badly shaken by the experience.'

'I'm sorry that she had to endure such discomfort.'

'Put Annie Garrow's evidence next to what Sergeant Leeming told us about the woman disguised as a porter and we have an explanation of what happened. There was no assassin from London,' argued Crabbe. 'Lockyer had hired a prostitute that night and she came disguised as a porter. Evidently, they shared some alcohol, then she slipped a drug into it. When he was unable to defend himself, she either killed him or opened the window so that a male accomplice could climb in. The man then slit his throat and cut his wrists to suggest that Lockyer had killed himself. He stole everything of value before bolting the door and climbing out of the window with the woman.' He smiled defiantly. 'That's my theory, anyway.'

'It's ingenious,' said Colbeck, 'but it is also fatally flawed.'

'I disagree.'

'If Mr Lockyer had a fondness for young girls, he would surely have gone to an establishment that could provide him with one. It would also have offered him anonymity. Can you really imagine him luring a woman into the hotel and advising her to come in disguise as a porter? No, of course not,' said Colbeck. 'It would be far too dangerous. Whatever reason brought him here, I refuse to believe that it was an assignation with a woman who had to steal a porter's uniform so that she could share a bed with him. If he had a predilection for girls of a tender age, he could have visited one of the many brothels in London that cater for clients with such depraved tastes.'

'I'm inclined to agree with Inspector Colbeck,' said Edgell.

'I stand by my version of events,' declared Crabbe. 'I met Annie

Garrow, remember. She told me that Lockyer was thinking bad things when he looked at her.'

'How old was this girl?'

'Fifteen or sixteen at most, sir. Lockyer frightened her.'

'I have sympathy for the girl,' said Colbeck, 'and I'm interested to hear that there was a more sinister side to Mr Lockyer. Be that as it may, we must remember that he is the victim in this case.' He turned to the chief constable. 'May I ask if you got hold of his address in London?'

'Yes, we did,' said Edgell. 'I've written to his family to acquaint them with the dreadful news of Mr Lockyer's murder.'

'It's information they have already received.'

'Yes,' said Leeming, 'it was delivered in person by Superintendent Tallis.'

Edgell winced.

'He felt that they deserved to hear as soon as possible.'

'Mr Lockyer's son will by now have been in touch with his sister, who lives in Scotland,' explained Colbeck. 'Obituaries of Mr Lockyer have already started to appear in national newspapers so members of the GWR board of directors will all be aware of his untimely death.'

'Quite so,' said Edgell. 'We are grateful that you have shared new information about your investigation, Inspector. I am still of the view that an assassin was employed and that the young woman in a porter's uniform went to the hotel at the behest of another guest altogether. This man, Jack Brown – or whatever his real name is – must be considered our prime suspect.'

'I'm glad that we agree on something, sir.'

Crabbe was unrepentant. 'I stand by my earlier version of events.'

'That's your prerogative,' said Colbeck. 'This case would be far easier to solve if we knew what brought Mr Lockyer here in the first place. He claimed that he was here to see a friend and he went out that evening to do so. Only house-to-house enquiries would have identified that friend.'

'They have so far been disappointing,' admitted Edgell. 'Officers have knocked on almost every door in the town. Nobody has even heard of Julian Lockyer, let alone confessed that they are the mysterious friend he came here to see.'

'Our search will continue,' promised Crabbe.

'So will ours, sir.'

'I thank you for coming here today,' said Edgell.

'We are on the same side,' Colbeck reminded him. 'I think we should remember that.'

Edgell nodded in agreement, but Inspector Crabbe simply glowered.

Detective Constable Alan Hinton had picked up the message when he arrived at Scotland Yard, but it was late afternoon before he was able to call on Madeleine Colbeck. She took him into the drawing room and explained the situation in full. He was complimentary.

'You did all the right things,' he told her. 'You confronted the man who owned the shop, then you tracked down the painting at the home of the person who actually bought it.'

'I just wanted the reassurance of seeing the original,' explained Madeleine. 'Mr Henderson had it on display in his study. As I looked at it in detail, I could see how many mistakes the person who copied it had made.'

'It was good of Lydia to warn you about the fake.'

'At first, she thought it might be genuine. It even fooled me for a while.'

'Then you saw it properly in daylight.'

'We confronted Mr Davies, who owns the shop, and he was very rude to us. I was glad that my father was with me – as well as Lydia, of course.'

'What I can't understand is how the other so-called artist was able to copy your painting. Did she make a sketch of it when it was on display in the window at the gallery?'

'Mr Sinclair had the answer to that,' replied Madeleine. 'He had sold a print to a woman.'

'Was he able to give you her name and address?'

'No, Alan. It just caught her eye, so she went into the gallery and bought it.'

'In order to copy it, I daresay.'

'We can't be certain of that.'

'No other female artist has your passion for railways, Madeleine,' he said. 'They're more likely to paint country scenes or portraits of children.'

'That's unfair,' she complained. 'If you go to any major gallery, you'll find that women can tackle a whole range of subjects.'

'I stand corrected. To be honest, art is a closed book to me.'

'It's given me so much pleasure and pride. That's why I'm horrified that something I created has been stolen and put on sale by another artist.'

'Yet she had the gall to use your name, Madeleine.'

'That was what hurt me the most.'

Hinton was sympathetic. He could see how wounded she was. Ordinarily, she could complain to her husband about the outrage, but he was investigating a murder in Shropshire. Keen to help,

Hinton was not entirely sure what steps to take.

'I'll tackle Solomon Davies first,' he decided. 'There are laws to protect artists from having their paintings copied and sold. Also, he won't be able to threaten me – not unless he wants to be arrested, that is.'

'Can I make a suggestion?'

'Please do.'

'Well, it was Lydia who discovered that shop in Soho. But for her warning, I'd never had known what was going on. I'm sure that she'd love to be there when you confront Mr Davies.'

'What a wonderful idea!' he said, beaming.

'I thought it might appeal to you.'

'I'll get in touch with her at once.'

'Lydia will be delighted to hear from you.'

After leaving the police station in Shrewsbury, the detectives returned to The Lion Hotel. As soon as he saw them come in, the man on duty behind the counter picked up an envelope.

'This arrived for you, Inspector,' he said.

'Thank you,' said Colbeck, taking it from him and glancing at it. 'Oh, I was hoping that it was from my wife, but it clearly isn't.'

'A message from the superintendent?' guessed Leeming.

'No, Victor. I've no idea who sent it.' He opened the letter then smiled as he read it. 'Good news at last.'

'Who is it from?'

'Mr Lockyer's son.'

'What does he want?'

'Even as we speak,' replied Colbeck, 'he's on his way to Shrewsbury. He's asked me to book a room for him here at The

Lion Hotel. That's heartening. It looks as if we're going to have him all to ourselves.'

Leeming frowned. 'Why is he coming?'

'Wouldn't you in his position?'

'I don't think so. My father died peacefully in his bed years ago.'

'Mr Lockyer's son is behaving as I had hoped,' said Colbeck. 'He will be able to provide us with the answers we need. He will also be able to tell us about his father's work on the board of the GWR.'

'What time is his train arriving?'

Colbeck glanced at the clock on the wall. 'In less than half an hour, I fancy. We'll book a room for him first, then we can stroll to the station to give him a proper welcome.'

Pelham Lockyer sat in a first-class compartment and once more read through the obituaries of his father in a succession of newspapers. While he was pleased with the praise lavished upon him, he was irritated by the speculation about who would replace his father as the favourite to become the next chairman of the GWR board. Since the news of the murder had been made public, he had received many letters of condolence. Some had been sent by the very people named in the newspapers.

His father had been proud of his work for the GWR and confident that he would be elected to the position he had coveted for years. While he had prided himself on having firm friends on the board, he had also been aware of having enemies. Had one of them been involved in some way in the murder? If so, how had they known that Julian Lockyer would be staying at the Station Hotel in Shrewsbury on a particular night? It was more than the son had known and raised the possibility that his father had been watched and tracked by an assassin of some kind.

Who had paid for the murder? And what was the motive behind the crime? He knew only too well that his father had his faults because he had been at the mercy of them throughout his life. On the credit side was the fact that Lockyer had been wedded to his work, tireless in pursuing fresh ways to increase his income and generous to his children. The problem was that, as Julian Lockyer's fortunes had risen, those of his friends and associates had fallen away – disastrously, in some cases. Was it simply envy that had made someone hate him enough to feel impelled to contrive his death? Or was there a more personal reason behind the murder?

What distressed him most was the fact that he had no idea why his father had lied to him about going to Kent when he had, in fact, decided to go to Shropshire. And what possessed him to stay in a station hotel? Whenever he had travelled somewhere before, Julian Lockyer had always stayed at the most expensive hotel. It was an act of faith with him. Why make so much money without enjoying the full benefits of it? Pelham had agreed with that argument wholeheartedly. Yet his father had ended his life in a small, functional hotel that catered almost exclusively for railway passengers. It was beneath him.

The shock of the dreadful news had left him paralysed. Sleep was impossible and there was a steady throb of pain inside his head. It made him confused and desperate. The one saving grace was that the news of his father's murder had been passed on to him by Edward Tallis. The latter's long experience of confiding grim intelligence had taught the superintendent how to soften a blow that would otherwise have been devastating. Pelham Lockyer was grateful to him and given some comfort by the fact that the investigation of the murder was in the hands of the most experienced detective inspector at Scotland Yard.

Inspector Colbeck, he believed, would find out the full truth of what happened. Pelham was convinced of that. There was only one problem. Would he have the strength to cope with it?

CHAPTER NINE

Lydia Quayle was in her drawing room when she heard the tinkle of the doorbell. She looked up from the novel she was reading and wondered who the visitor could be. When her maidservant opened the front door, Lydia heard a man's voice. It made her put the book quickly aside and hurry into the hall. She was in time to see the girl admitting Alan Hinton into the house.

'Thank you, Betty,' said Lydia. 'I'll take over now.'

After closing the front door, the maid went off towards the kitchen, leaving Alan and Lydia standing there yards apart and just staring at each other.

'Hello, Lydia,' he said, smiling.

'It's lovely to see you, Alan.'

When she took a step towards him, he responded by reaching out to place a kiss on her hand. Lydia was glowing with pleasure.

'I'm not interrupting anything, am I?' he asked.

'No, of course not. You're always welcome, Alan.'

'That's a comforting thought,' he said. 'Actually, I've come on serious business. I've been talking to Madeleine about this business with her painting.'

'Yes, it's dreadfully upsetting for her.'

'She told me that you had suggested that she approach me.'

'It's true,' said Lydia, 'but let's not stand out here in the hall. Come into the drawing room.'

'I will.'

She led the way into the adjoining room and sat on the sofa. Hinton lowered himself into the chair opposite and simply enjoyed the pleasure of looking at her. Eventually, he remembered why he had come to the house. After giving a gesture of apology, he became serious.

'Madeleine told me that you spotted the painting in a shop window in Soho.'

'Yes, it gave me quite a shock.'

'But it hadn't actually been painted by her.'

'Someone had copied the original – a woman, we were told.'

'What did the owner of the shop say?'

'He refused to accept that it was a copy of Madeleine's painting and became quite aggressive, to be honest. We decided that the best thing was to get out of there. Madeleine's father was ready to take him on, but we didn't want Mr Andrews to be hurt. We left quickly.'

'That was probably the sensible thing to do, Lydia.'

'I'm not sure that it was. In hindsight, I wish that we had stood up to the man. He was daring to sell something that had been copied from one of Madeleine's paintings.'

'She told me how distressing it was.'

'It's tantamount to bare-faced robbery,' she said. 'The artist was wrong to steal someone else's idea, and the shopkeeper was wrong to offer it for sale. Isn't there some way that they can both be prosecuted?'

'They can certainly be stopped in their tracks. And if the shopkeeper behaves in the way that he did when you confronted him, I'll be happy to arrest him.' He smiled. 'Madeleine hoped that you might be interested in coming to Soho with me.'

'I'd love to, Alan!'

He stood up. 'Then let's go, shall we?'

'Right this minute?'

'Sooner, if possible.'

She laughed. 'I'll get my coat and hat.'

When the train came into the station, Colbeck and Leeming were waiting on the platform. Clouds of steam and smoke obscured their view. As soon as the train came to a halt, doors were opened, and passengers streamed onto the platform. Leeming was alarmed.

'We'll never pick him out in this crowd,' he complained.

'We may not need to,' said Colbeck. 'Hopefully, Mr Lockyer will recognise us. I daresay that he will have travelled first class. Let's head for the passengers alighting from those carriages.'

They picked their way through the mass of bodies until they reached a carriage from which a corpulent young man was stepping out. One glance told Colbeck that it was Pelham Lockyer. He waved a hand to catch the man's attention. Lockyer was relieved to see them.

'I wasn't expecting a welcome,' he said.

'It was the least we could do,' said Colbeck, offering his hand. 'Your letter told us the exact time of your arrival. I am Detective

Inspector Colbeck. And,' he went on, indicating his companion, 'this is Detective Sergeant Leeming.'

'It's good to meet you, Sergeant,' said Lockyer, shaking hands with each of them in turn.

'May I take your valise?' offered Leeming.

'Oh, that's very good of you,' said Lockyer, handing it over. 'I'm not sure how long I'll be staying but I packed for three nights, just in case.'

'Let's take you to the hotel,' suggested Colbeck. 'We can talk properly there.'

'Good idea.'

The three of them headed for the exit but they did not get far. Simon Biddle stepped out of the crowd and stared in amazement at Lockyer.

'You gave me such a shock, sir!' he apologised. 'You're the spitting image of your father.'

'This is Mr Biddle,' explained Colbeck. 'He was kind enough to send the telegraph that made us aware of a murder here. We owe him profound thanks.'

'We do,' agreed Lockyer, shaking hands with the stationmaster. 'Thank you.'

'Welcome to Shrewsbury, sir.'

Biddle stood aside to let the trio pass. Colbeck led the way to the exit then the three of them emerged and Lockyer got his first view of the Station Hotel. He was unimpressed.

'Is that really the place where my father stayed?' he asked.

'Yes, sir,' said Colbeck. 'He wanted the hotel close to the railway station, it seems.'

'The Lion is much better,' Leeming put in. 'It won't take us long to get there.'

'I'll want to take a closer look at the Station Hotel at some point,' said Lockyer. 'It's one of the reasons I decided to come. I intend to see everything.'

After staring ruefully at the building for the best part of a minute, he fell in beside the detectives and they set off downhill.

During the cab ride to Soho, they hardly said a word. Alan Hinton and Lydia Quayle were so happy with their shoulders rubbing against each other that they enjoyed the rare moment of togetherness. They did not feel the slightest discomfort when the wheels rattled over cobblestones, nor did they hear any of the pandemonium in the streets through which they went. When the cab finally came to a halt in Soho, they were so disappointed that they heaved a sigh in unison. Hinton got out first so that he could help Lydia down into the street. Having asked the cab driver to wait for them, they walked to the shop window where Lydia had first seen what she believed was a painting by Madeleine Colbeck. A shock awaited them. It was no longer there.

'It's gone,' she said. 'Has somebody bought it?'

'Let's go and find out,' he suggested.

Hinton opened the door so that she could step into the shop first. Solomon Davies emerged from behind a curtain. When he saw Lydia, his face hardened.

'What are you doing here?' he demanded.

'I've brought Detective Constable Hinton with me to show him the painting that has been copied from one by Madeleine Colbeck.'

'It's not here,' said Davies, eyeing the detective cautiously.

'Then where is it?' asked Hinton.

'The artist reclaimed it this morning.'

'Why did she do that?'

'You'll have to ask her.'

'But you wouldn't even tell us her name,' recalled Lydia, 'let alone give us her address.'

'We had a business arrangement,' said Davies. 'I promised to put it on display for a month in the hope of finding a buyer. Nobody liked it enough to make an offer, so the artist took it back.'

'Why did you offer to sell it in the first place?'

'I thought it might make some money for the two of us.'

'What was the woman's name?' asked Hinton.

Davies shrugged. 'Madeleine Colbeck. That's what she told me.'

'Where does she live?'

'I've no idea.'

'It's a funny way to do business, Mr Davies. A strange woman, claiming to be an artist, walks into your shop and asks if you can sell her painting, yet she doesn't even tell you how you can get in touch with her.'

'That didn't worry me.'

'Did it never occur to you that the painting was a fake?'

'Why should it?'

'Because it's a copy of one by a real artist,' said Lydia. 'Madeleine Colbeck.'

'Whose husband happens to work with me at Scotland Yard,' added Hinton.

'So what?'

'It means that you are liable to arrest, sir.'

'On what grounds?' demanded Davies. 'I accepted the painting in good faith and did my best to sell it for the artist.'

'You were aiding and abetting a fraudster.'

'How was I to know that?'

'A man of your experience should have realised that you were dealing with someone who could not be trusted.'

'All I saw was a painting that would fetch a decent price. I came to an arrangement with the artist herself.'

'Didn't you ask her for proof that it really was her work?' said Lydia.

'Yes, of course. She gave me her word.'

'What did she say when you returned it to her?'

'She said that she would try to sell it somewhere else.'

'Please describe this woman to us,' said Hinton.

'Well,' said Davies, 'she was not the sort of person who usually comes into my shop. She was far too grand. I'd put her in her fifties. She was very well dressed. When she showed me her painting, I could see that she had real talent. And it was unusual to find a woman who had painted a picture of a train.'

'It was a copy of another woman's painting' Lydia reminded him.

'How was I to know that?'

'It was because the real Madeleine Colbeck came here to tell you.'

'I once had the pleasure of arresting someone who copied a painting,' recalled Hinton. 'He made the mistake of choosing a famous Flemish artist, Rubens. An art expert spotted that it was a fake straight away. I remember attending the trial. The man had made a living by producing fake copies of the works of Old Masters. He won't come out of prison for another six years.'

'I hope that the same thing happens to the woman in this case,' said Lydia.

'And I hope you've learnt your lesson,' said Hinton, staring at

Davies. 'There's something I forgot to mention. The dealer who tried to sell that fake painting also went to prison.'

A look of fear came into the shopkeeper's eyes.

Pelham Lockyer was pleased with the accommodation. When he had checked into The Lion Hotel and left his valise in his room, he joined the detectives in the bar. They sat at a table in the corner and ordered their drinks.

'I not only came to see how the investigation was going,' said Lockyer, 'I'm here to deal with the practicalities. As soon as my father's body is released, I need to arrange for it to be taken back to London. I've already engaged a funeral director.'

'Then you can instruct him to come as soon as he is able,' Colbeck told him. 'I had word from the hospital that the body is now available.'

'I would like to speak to the surgeon who performed the postmortem.'

'I'll take you to the infirmary myself, Mr Lockyer.'

'Thank you.'

'Superintendent Tallis sent word of his visit to you,' said Leeming. 'He told us that you were shocked to hear where the crime had occurred.'

'I was, indeed, Sergeant.'

'Was your father in the habit of deceiving you?'

'Not at all,' replied Lockyer. 'He was remarkably truthful. I don't ever remember him telling me a downright lie.'

'Then why did he do so on this occasion?'

'I wish that I knew.'

'He must have had a reason to come to Shrewsbury,' said Colbeck. 'Have you any idea what it might have been?'

'I'm afraid not. The shock for me was that he chose the Station Hotel. Frankly, I'd have thought that it was beneath him.'

'Then why did he opt to spend a night there?'

'I was hoping that you might be able to answer that question, Inspector.'

'We are still trying to find that answer,' said Colbeck. 'What I can tell you is that the hotel is much more comfortable than its exterior would suggest. We've both been inside it and found its owner, Mrs Burrage, to be extremely helpful. She and two members of her staff discovered the body. They sent at once for the police.'

'Luckily,' said Leeming, 'the stationmaster felt that we might be of more use. That's why he contacted us.'

'We are, of course, working with the police and sharing any information gathered. If you would prefer to deal with them, I can put you in touch with the chief constable.'

'No, no,' said Lockyer firmly. 'My father was a wealthy man who always believed in having what was best on offer. That's why I'm relieved that you responded to the stationmaster's appeal. A provincial police force will not be able to compete with you. When I met him, your superintendent told me that you were the best detectives at Scotland Yard.'

'He doesn't always treat us as if we were,' muttered Leeming.

'Feel free to ask us anything you wish,' invited Colbeck.

'Then my first question is this,' replied Lockyer. 'Have you established the motive behind the murder?'

'We are still at the stage of speculation, I'm afraid. But there is something you need to know. When the killer left the scene, he took your father's valuables, including his wedding ring. That suggests he intended to sell them. But there is a more worrying aspect, I fear.'

'What is it?'

'He also stole the key to the family home and, I daresay, the key to his desk.'

'The desk was always kept securely locked. I know that because I tried to open it myself in the hope of finding something that explained why my father came here.'

'The killer would have access to whatever was kept in the desk.'

Lockyer was alarmed. 'And he also has the key to the house.'

'Did your father employ a manservant?'

'Yes, he did, Inspector. Peter Rigby – a good man, utterly reliable.'

'Then we need to contact him at once,' said Colbeck. 'We can send a telegraph to alert Superintendent Tallis to the danger. He will send someone to the house to warn the manservant to have the front door lock changed immediately.'

'That's excellent advice,' said Lockyer.

'It's a sensible precaution – and it will help to still your fears.'

'Does the killer know where the family house is?'

'I'm afraid so, sir. He stole your father's wallet. I daresay that Mr Lockyer kept some business cards in it?'

'Yes, he did.'

'Then sooner or later the killer will try to let himself into the house.'

The man strolled down the avenue between rows of large, impressive, detached houses set well back from the road. When he came to the address in which he was interested, he pretended to give it a casual glance. Instead, however, he was noting its salient features. By the time he was well past the house, he allowed himself a broad smile. He would be back.

On the cab ride back, Lydia told Hinton how impressed she was with the way that he had behaved.

'You put the fear of God into him, Alan,' she said.

'He deserved it.'

'Did you really arrest an artist who copied famous paintings?'

'No,' he confessed with a grin, 'but I wanted to give Davies a shock. He'll think twice about trying to sell a fake painting in the future.'

She laughed. 'You sounded so honest.'

'I hope it hasn't changed your opinion of me, Lydia.'

'On the contrary, I can see now that it was clever of you. It shook him.'

'That was the idea.' He turned to her. 'How do you think Madeleine will react?'

'I don't follow.'

'Will she be shocked that I told a bare-faced lie?'

'Yes – but she'll be very glad that you scared the shopkeeper.'

'It was the least I could do.'

'What happens next?' she asked.

'We'll have to wait until the fake Madeleine Colbeck turns up on sale elsewhere.'

'Are you going to tell the owner of the next shop the same lie?'

'No,' he said with a broad grin. 'I'll invent a much bigger one so that I can watch him suffer.'

Lydia laughed and squeezed his arm affectionately. 'I'm seeing a whole new side to you, Detective Constable Hinton.'

'Is that good or bad?'

'You terrified that awful man,' she said. 'I can't tell you how delighted I was.'

* * *

When they got to the infirmary, they discovered that Dr Vincent was not there, but that Dr Clement was available. Colbeck and Lockyer were conducted to the waiting room. It was not long before Clement arrived. After being introduced to Lockyer, he offered his sympathies then assured the son that his father would not have suffered any pain.

'Dr Vincent and I are not expert toxicologists,' he explained, 'but we were able to identify traces of substances like henbane that would have sent him deeply to sleep.' He studied Lockyer. 'I must say that you bear an uncanny resemblance to your father.'

'You are not the first person to observe that, Doctor,' said Lockyer with a wan smile. 'The inspector tells me that you are also a Member of Parliament.'

'It is only one of my achievements. I am also an honorary fellow of the Royal College of Surgeons, a fellow of the Society of Apothecaries and surgeon to the first battalion of the Shropshire Rifle Volunteers. In short,' he told them, 'I love to keep busy.'

'You are an example to us all, Dr Clement,' said Colbeck.

'I'm just very glad to be of help in this instance.'

'Is it possible for Mr Lockyer to view the body?'

'It's his right as a member of the family.'

'Thank you,' said Lockyer. 'I would like to take advantage of that right, please.'

Clement rose to his feet. 'I'll take you there immediately.'

When the telegraph reached him, Edward Tallis responded at once. Instead of sending a warning to the Lockyer household, he made a point of visiting the house again. He was admitted by Peter Rigby, a strapping, middle-aged man who had worked for the family for many years.

'It's good to see you again, sir,' said Rigby.

'This is only a flying visit,' warned Tallis. 'I've been reminded by a telegraph that the man who murdered Mr Lockyer also stole all his possessions. They include the key to the front door and the one that opens his desk. I would suggest that you change the front door lock as a matter of priority or, if it can't be done today, make sure that you bolt the front door before you retire to bed.'

'I always do, sir.'

'I should have given you a warning on my first visit.'

'It was kind of you to alert us.'

'The family has suffered enough. The last thing it needs after an untimely death is a burglary. At a time like this, what it wants most is the time to mourn in private.'

'I'll make sure that that's what it gets,' promised Rigby, straightening his shoulders.

When he came back to the waiting room after viewing the body of his father, Pelham Lockyer was subdued. The experience had had a profound effect on him. Colbeck remained silent as he took the grieving son out of the infirmary. The fresh air seemed to make Lockyer aware that he had a companion beside him.

'I do apologise,' he said. 'It was very rude of me to ignore you like that.'

'No apology is needed,' replied Colbeck. 'When you came back from such a testing experience, you were bound to be preoccupied.'

'I kept asking myself the same question again and again. What on earth drew my father to this part of the world? I've never even heard him mention Shrewsbury, yet the town clearly had a special meaning for him.'

'Your father must have had an appointments diary,' said Colbeck.

'He did, Inspector. When I searched his study, there was no sign of it.'

'Then he must have travelled with it in his valise.'

'It was probably stolen by the man who killed him.'

'I hope that he still has it in his possession when we catch up with him.'

'You sound confident of arresting this man.'

'I am very confident. Bear in mind that the occupants of the house have by now been warned to be on the alert. It is not only because they will change the lock on the front door. It's because the superintendent will have taken an extra precaution.'

'And what is that?'

'If I know him, he will put detectives in a house adjacent to that of your father's to keep it under surveillance throughout the night. If the killer turns up – and I'm sure that he will – the man will be arrested and dragged off in handcuffs.'

'That's very reassuring.'

'If the killer still has the appointments book, then we can solve the problem that is vexing you and complicating our investigation. Why choose Shrewsbury?'

'And why lie to me about where he was going?' said Lockyer. 'We were close, Inspector. My father was, by nature, an extremely honest man. Why tell me that he was going to Kent when he was heading in a totally different direction?'

'We all want to know the answer to that question, sir.'

As they left the infirmary, Lockyer fell silent again. They walked side by side in the direction of The Lion Hotel. Without warning, Lockyer came to a sudden halt and turned to Colbeck.

'I must ask you a favour,' he said.

'What is it?'

'Take me to the Station Hotel. I wish to see where my father's life was so abruptly ended.'

When they gave Madeleine a full account of what had happened in Soho, she was at once surprised and puzzled. She was amazed that Alan Hinton had told a blatant lie to shock the truculent owner of the shop, but she understood his reason for doing so.

The three of them were in the drawing room of the Colbeck residence.

'I can't thank you enough,' said Madeleine, looking from one to the other.

'I ought to be thanking you,' said Hinton. 'It was an interesting encounter – all the more so because Lydia was beside me.'

'You really shook that appalling man, Alan,' she told him.

'He needed shaking.'

'I knew that you would make a good team,' said Madeleine. 'Lydia had already been to that shop and so she knew what to expect. As a detective, Alan had the authority needed to confront that shopkeeper. Mr Davies probably regrets ever agreeing to put that painting on sale.'

'Did we ever discover the real name of the artist?' asked Hinton.

'According to Mr Sinclair at the Red Gallery, she is a middle-aged woman who refused to give her name. He remembered selling her a print of my painting. She obviously copied that,' said Madeleine. 'Or, at least, she tried to copy it. I spotted several mistakes.'

'How do we find this woman?'

'I suspect that you may have to leave it to us, Alan.'

'Why on earth should I do that?'

'It's because I think that you are needed elsewhere,' said

Madeleine, picking up the envelope beside her. 'While you were out, this was delivered by hand. It's from Superintendent Tallis. I recognised his handwriting immediately.'

'How ever did he know that he could reach me here?' asked Hinton.

'Read the letter and you may find out.'

He took the envelope from her and opened it. As he read the message inside, his eyes widened, and he gave a sigh of resignation.

'I'm supposed to be off duty,' he said. 'The superintendent is aware that I often deliver letters here so he hoped that he might be able to contact me at this address. He wants to me return to Scotland Yard at once to take part in what he calls *special operations.*'

'What does that mean?' asked Lydia.

'It means that I'll have to answer his summons,' he said, getting up from his seat.

'You could always tell him that you never received his letter.'

'That would be lying!' he protested.

'You're good at that,' she reminded him. All three of them grinned.

'I'm sorry but I must go. It may well be that I'm going to be sent to Shrewsbury to work with the inspector and Victor Leeming. I'd hate to miss a chance to do that.'

'If you do see Robert,' said Madeleine, 'give him my love and tell him how you gave that man in Soho a terrible scare. I told my husband about the fake painting in my last letter to him.'

'We're sorry to see you go, Alan,' said Lydia, rising to her feet.

'I'm sorry to leave,' he replied, squeezing her hands, 'but duty calls.'

She smiled fondly. 'I'll be here when you get back.'

* * *

Pelham Lockyer was pleasantly surprised. After seeing the interior of the Station Hotel, he apologised for the way that he had earlier dismissed it as being unsuitable accommodation for his father. It was clean, well-furnished and patently comfortable. Introduced to Molly Burrage, he was impressed by her appearance and by her readiness to help him all she could. He listened intently to her description of the discovery of the dead body of his father and thanked her for summoning the police.

'Has anyone used that room since?' he asked.

'No, sir,' she answered. 'We didn't think it would be right to put a new guest in there. It needs to be thoroughly cleaned before we can even consider it. Wilf – my barman – has offered to redecorate it completely.'

'That's very wise,' said Colbeck.

'May I see the room, please?' asked Lockyer.

Molly was shocked. 'Do you really want to, sir?'

'Yes, I do.'

'If you give me the key,' volunteered Colbeck, 'I'll take him up.'

'That's very kind of you,' she said. 'I'd rather not go in there myself.'

She handed Colbeck the key and let them out of her office. Colbeck led the way upstairs and paused outside the room. He warned Lockyer that they were about to enter a crime scene and that it was bound to have a searing effect on him.

'I still wish to go in there,' said Lockyer firmly. 'Alone, please.'

'Yes, of course.'

Colbeck handed the key over then stepped back. Lockyer opened the door and entered the room, walking slowly around it then going to the window to look out. Colbeck waited patiently. It was several minutes before Lockyer came out again, his face now ashen. He handed the key to Colbeck, who locked the door before leading the way downstairs. At the very moment when they stepped into the corridor below, Annie Garrow, now back at work, came through a door. She took one look at Pelham Lockyer and screamed in horror.

'You're back!' she exclaimed.

Moving quickly, Colbeck caught her before she hit the floor.

Archibald Reeves called at The Lion Hotel in the hope of catching the detectives there. Victor Leeming was alone in the bar, reading through the notes he had made in his pad. Reeves crossed eagerly over to him, and they exchanged greetings.

'I just wondered if there'd been any developments,' said Reeves.

'Yes,' replied Leeming. 'We have news for you.'

'What's happened?'

'We had an unexpected visitor.'

'Oh? Who was it?'

'Mr Lockyer's son,' said Leeming. 'He wrote to tell us that he was on his way, and we were able to meet him off the train.'

'What state was he in?'

'He'd obviously been brooding about . . . what happened to his father.'

'Where is he staying?'

'Right here in The Lion.'

'That's wonderful,' said Reeves, sensing a scoop. 'Is he up in his room?'

'No, he went off to the infirmary with the Inspector. Young Mr Lockyer wanted to arrange the transfer of his father's body to London. He and the inspector will be back soon.'

'I obviously came at the perfect time. This deserves a drink, Sergeant.'

'I'm not supposed to drink when I'm on duty, sir,' said Leeming with a grin, 'but in your case, I'll make an exception.'

Alan Hinton returned to Scotland Yard in a cab and hurried to the superintendent's office. The idea that he might join the murder investigation led by Colbeck had given him an anticipatory delight. He could not wait to board a train to Shrewsbury. After tapping on the office door, he opened it to find Tallis going through a pile of paperwork. The superintendent looked up at him.

'Excellent!' he said. 'I was hoping to reach you. That's why I sent a letter both to the house where you live and to the one owned by the inspector.'

'I read your message at the latter, sir.'

'And you responded promptly.'

'It was an urgent summons.'

'I've had word from Inspector Colbeck. A problem has arisen.'

Hinton smiled. 'Does he need additional help in Shrewsbury?'

'He has requested additional help,' replied Tallis, 'but he needs it here in London. After he had murdered Mr Lockyer, the killer stole everything of value. It included the key to his house and possibly a key to his desk. I'm sure that he means to make use of them.'

'I'm certain that he does, sir.'

'When I passed on the warning to the manservant in the house, I took the trouble to go across to the house opposite to explain the situation. The owner was only too glad to help. As a result, I want you and Detective Constable Boyce to move into that house and keep Mr Lockyer's property under surveillance during the night.'

'Yes, sir,' said Hinton, unable to hide his disappointment.

'I know that you would prefer to be in Shrewsbury but it's

unlikely that the killer is still there. There's a good chance that he will already have visited the Lockyer residence to have a good look at it. When night falls, he may well decide to make use of the stolen house key.'

'I'll get over there at once, sir.'

'Here are directions to the house,' said Tallis, handing him a piece of paper. 'The one opposite is owned by a Mr Jeremy Hull, a retired lawyer. He and Mr Lockyer were good friends. That's why Mr Hull was so pleased to help us. He offered to provide you and Boyce with a vantage point from which to watch the house opposite, and he has promised to make sure that his cook keeps the pair of you well fed.'

'That's kind of him, sir.'

'There's something else you should know.'

'What is it?'

'I've already spoken to Boyce and told him that you will be in charge. He was quick to accept that you are more experienced than him. In short, you will make all the decisions.'

'Thank you, sir.'

'Don't thank me. I was acting on Inspector Colbeck's advice.'

Hinton brightened. 'That was very kind of him.'

'Get out there,' ordered Tallis, 'and prove that our confidence in you is not misplaced.'

CHAPTER TEN

During their stroll back to the hotel, Colbeck had been honest, telling Pelham Lockyer that he had little faith in the local police's ability to track and apprehend the killer. He also warned him that there were reporters from national newspapers in the town.

'The only reporter we choose to trust,' he told Lockyer, 'is from the *Shrewsbury Chronicle*.'

'Is that a daily newspaper?'

'No, it's a weekly periodical.'

'What is the reporter's name?'

'Archibald Reeves – but he answers to the name of Archie among friends. One of these friends is a man you recently met – Dr Clement. I found his judgement of Reeves to be sound.'

'Then I look forward to meeting this reporter.'

'He is certain to pop up soon at The Lion. Archie told me that

Charles Dickens has stayed at the hotel on two occasions. He was able to befriend the great writer.'

'That's quite an achievement. By report, Mr Dickens is notoriously busy.'

'He took a liking to a fellow reporter,' said Colbeck. 'That's why a Dickens novel is always so realistic. He gathered his facts with such care.'

'Some of the things written about my father were not gathered with care,' said Lockyer sharply. 'In the newspapers I read on the way here, a false impression was given of him by most of the obituaries.'

'His work with the GWR meant a lot to him, didn't it?'

'Yes, Inspector. It was his passion.'

'How did he get on with the other members of the board?'

'He won most of them over, but my father was inclined to be outspoken. That made him enemies as well. And before you ask me,' he went on, 'no, I don't believe that the killer was hired by another member of the board. Even those who hated him would never go that far.'

'I take your word for it, Mr Lockyer.'

The Lion Hotel came in sight. Standing outside the front door was Archibald Reeves.

'There's our young reporter,' said Colbeck. 'I told you that he'd be keen to meet you.'

Lydia Quayle was still seated in the drawing room with Madeleine Colbeck. Sad that Alan Hinton had left so abruptly, they talked about him at length.

'The way he stood up to that man in Soho was a treat to watch,' said Lydia.

'Mr Davies was such a bully.'

'He was careful what he said in front of someone from Scotland Yard.'

'I'm glad that I sent the two of you there together.'

'It was wicked of you, Madeleine,' said her friend. 'And if I hadn't enjoyed it so much, I'd be very cross with you.'

'But for you, I'd never have heard about a fake copy of one of my paintings.'

'But for you, I'd never have shared a cab with Alan Hinton.'

'I had the feeling the pair of you would get on.'

Lydia laughed. 'You're very naughty,' she said. 'On a more serious note, how do we find the woman who copied a painting of yours?'

'We have to trawl through shops that might have agreed to accept it for sale.'

'That would take ages.'

'Yes, but it would be worth it. If this phantom artist gets away with copying one of my paintings, she'll be certain to do so again.'

'What we really need is the help of a detective.'

'I'm married to one,' said Madeleine, 'but I can't expect him to abandon a murder investigation in order to trace a woman who copied a painting of mine.'

'There's always Alan to step into the breach.'

'Oh, I don't think so, Lydia. My guess is that he's no longer in London. You're forgetting that summons he had from Superintendent Tallis. It could mean only one thing. Alan is on his way to Shrewsbury to join in the hunt for a killer.'

When they were dropped off by the cab at the address Hinton had been given, he paid the driver then looked up and down the tree-lined avenue.

'Do you think we could ever afford to live in an area like this?' he asked.

'On police pay?' said Eric Boyce. 'Never!'

'Then we must enjoy staying here for one night at someone else's expense.'

'I agree.'

Hinton was glad to have Boyce as a partner. The other detective was tall, angular and almost boyish. What Hinton liked about him was that Boyce was a man of few words. The latter never indulged in pointless conversation. That suited Hinton. Some of the other detectives with whom he had worked hardly ever stopped talking. Boyce did something more important. He listened.

After spending some minutes staring at the Lockyer house on the opposite side of the road, they turned to find that their host was watching them. Jeremy Hull was a gaunt man in his seventies, bald, wrinkled and wearing a pair of spectacles. Standing on his doorstep, he beckoned them over.

'A warm welcome to you, gentlemen,' he said in a reedy voice. 'I'm so glad to be able to help. Julian Lockyer was a good friend and neighbour. I'm as keen as you must be that his killer is caught and hanged.'

'Thank you, Mr Hull,' said Hinton. 'I am Detective Constable Hinton, and this is Detective Constable Boyce.' They shook hands in turn with Hull. 'We are very grateful for your assistance.'

'Come into the house and see where I'll put you.'

'Thank you, sir.'

'Yes,' added Boyce. 'We're grateful.'

When they stepped into the hall, the retired lawyer closed the front door before heading for the stairs. He had the rounded shoulders of someone who had spent the bulk of his life bending over a desk. The detectives also noted that he had a slight limp. Hull led them up to the first floor then opened a door that took them up to the attic. Through the window, they had a good view of the house opposite.

'This will suit us very well,' said Hinton.

'Yes,' agreed Boyce.

'There's only one defect.'

'Really?' asked their host. 'What is it?'

'Well, sir, if the man we're after does turn up, it will take us some time to get down two flights of stairs. It would have been better if we'd been on the ground floor.'

Boyce pointed a finger. 'That tree.'

'I agree, Eric,' said Hinton. 'Good suggestion.'

'What do you mean?' asked Hull.

'If one of us is up here, he'll have an excellent view. If the killer turns up, he can signal to whichever of us is lurking behind that tree. When the man tries to let himself into the house, he can be apprehended.' He turned to Boyce. 'We'll take it in turns to be down there.'

'I'll be first,' volunteered Boyce.

'You must sort it out between you,' decided Hull. 'Meanwhile, I daresay that both of you would appreciate a meal of some sort if you are going to be on duty for so long. I'll see what our cook can rustle up for you, shall I?'

'Yes, please,' said Hinton.

Boyce settled for a nod of gratitude.

Since he knew how keen Reeves would be to meet the murder victim's son, Colbeck introduced them then left them to go into the bar together. He went upstairs and knocked on the door of Leeming's room. The sergeant's head popped out almost immediately.

'Ah,' he said, 'you're back. How did you get on?'

'If you let me in for a moment, I'll tell you.'

'Oh, of course . . .'

Leeming stood back to allow Colbeck to step into the room. He then closed the door. While the inspector chose a chair, Leeming sat on the edge of the bed.

'When I told Archie who was here,' he said, 'he was delighted. I came up here so that the two of them had time together.'

'That's why I left them alone, Victor. I'm sure they'll get on very well.'

'What happened at the infirmary?'

'Mr Lockyer viewed the body then told them he would like his father transferred to London tomorrow. He intends to go with it.'

'What a gruesome way to travel!' said Leeming. 'I could never sit beside a dead body.'

'I daresay that it will be in the guard's van. Mr Lockyer will be in first class.'

'You've been gone longer than I expected.'

'That was because he was keen to visit the Station Hotel.'

'Brave man!'

'I admired his thoroughness. He wanted to know the truth about his father's death, even if it would be something of an ordeal for him. As we came downstairs, Annie Garrow came into the corridor. She was the girl who went into Lockyer's room with Mrs Burrage and found the dead body. The sight of the dead man's son made her hysterical. She thought it was Julian Lockyer himself, back from the dead. I was lucky to catch her when she fainted.'

'Poor girl! It must have been a terrible shock.'

'She'll recover, I'm sure. Any word from the telegraph station?'

'Not yet, sir. If something does arrive for you, I'm sure that the stationmaster will send it here. I hope that the superintendent did what I suggested.'

'He usually does,' said Leeming. 'It's only when I come up with an idea that he dismisses it without even bothering to consider it.'

'Alan Hinton will be a good choice for the assignment.'

'What if the killer doesn't turn up?'

'Oh, I don't think there's any doubt about that. He has a key to the house, remember. That gives him an opportunity to steal money and anything of value that he can sell. My interest is less in him than in the person who employed him.'

'What do you mean?'

'Jack Brown – or whatever his real name is – tailed Mr Lockyer here and bided his time before seizing the opportunity to kill him. But he was not acting on his own initiative. I'm certain that he was a hired killer. We also need to catch the man who employed him.'

'That will take us back to London.'

'Eventually,' said Colbeck. 'It will give you the opportunity to solve another mystery.'

'What is it?'

'Why do the chief constable and Superintendent Tallis hate each other?' asked Colbeck.

'I'll be interested to know the reason behind their mutual enmity.'

Archibald Reeves took full advantage his good luck. As he and Pelham Lockyer sat together in the bar, the reporter elicited a lot of new information about the man's father. It emerged that Julian Lockyer had been a generous donor to all manner of causes. His principal interest had been in a children's home. He had visited it regularly.

'Will you continue to support the place?' asked Reeves.

'Yes, of course – though I daresay that my father will have made provision for the home in his Will. He always gave the impression of being rather tight-fisted. In fact,' said Lockyer, 'he was one the kindest men I ever met.'

'Am I allowed to say that in my article about him?'

'I'll be disappointed if you don't, Mr Reeves.'

'Thank you,' said the reporter, closing his notepad. 'You've answered all my questions with refreshing honesty. Is there anything you wish to ask me?'

'Yes, there is – what manner of man is the chief constable?'

'He's been a breath of fresh air. When he first applied for the post, he was turned down. Instead of moping, he went off to study the way that the Essex Constabulary was run. It was an invaluable education for him.'

'I gather that he had a distinguished career in the Bengal Army.'

'He also won a medal for service in Afghanistan. Colonel Edgell must find Shropshire a rather quiet place after being in the army. When he took office, he realised that the constabulary was deplorably small in numbers. He also noted that it possessed only fifty-four cutlasses so that over half of the constables under his control lacked the weapon that is vital during elections when passions tend to run high.'

'Did he complain?'

'He certainly did. As a result, he was given permission to buy an additional thirty-six cutlasses. They were sorely needed. There was a lot of armed interference with the police, especially during elections. The colonel was determined to confront it.'

'I admire him for doing that,' said Lockyer, 'but I'm worried that he has never had to deal with a murder case like this one.'

'He'll do his best. That's all one can ask. Besides, you have someone else who is involved in the pursuit of your father's killer – Inspector Colbeck. In my view, he is an outstanding detective. I have complete faith in him to find and arrest anyone directly involved in the murder.'

When they had eaten the dinner prepared for them, they saw that light was fading from the sky. Eric Boyce left the building and crossed the road so that he could hide behind a tree near the house. It had been agreed that Hinton and he would change places every couple of hours. They had kept vigil on houses together before. Seated beside the window in the attic, Hinton looked down at the Lockyer residence. There was no sign of Boyce. He was completely hidden. They had accepted that the killer might not turn up that night, but it did not dismay them because they knew that they were at least giving the occupants of the Lockyer house a feeling of security. Besides, their meal had been very tasty. A second day under Jeremy Hull's roof would be a treat.

Nevertheless, Hinton would still have preferred to be in Shropshire.

After coming off duty, Simon Biddle strolled across to the Station Hotel. He found Molly Burrage alone in her office. He gave her an affectionate smile.

'I've got some news for you,' he said.

'What is it?'

'Mr Lockyer's son has turned up.'

'Yes, I know,' she replied. 'He came here and asked to be let into the room where his father was killed. Inspector Colbeck took him up there. When they came down again, Annie happened to step into the corridor. At the sight of young Mr Lockyer, the poor girl fainted.'

'I had the same shock when I saw the son. He's the image of his father.'

'It was very brave of him to go into that room alone. I certainly wouldn't have done it.'

'Have you stopped offering it to guests?'

'Yes, of course,' she replied. 'Not that we've had all that many bookings.'

'The word must have spread,' said Biddle. 'This is the hotel that had a murder.'

'Don't rub it in, Simon.'

'I'm sorry. There is better news coming, though.'

'I don't see it,' she moaned.

'Take heart, Molly. It's only a matter of time before Inspector Colbeck solves the crime. People will realise it's safe to book a room here again. Business will be back to normal.'

'That will never happen,' she said. 'We're going to struggle.'

'Then I'll have to start booking a room here myself,' he said with a grin. 'And I know which room it will be.'

She laughed. 'You are silly, Simon Biddle!'

He put a hand on her arm. 'It would be a real treat to sleep closer to you.'

'Behave yourself,' she warned, pushing him gently away.

'I'm doing my best to help the investigation,' said Biddle. 'When I leave here, I'm going to The Lion Hotel to pass on some information to the inspector.'

'What sort of information?'

'Do you remember that "porter" who sneaked in here on the night of the murder?'

'The inspector thinks it was a woman in disguise.'

'It was, Molly – and I know her name. I also know that she had nothing to do with Mr Lockyer. The room she went into was on the top floor.'

'How ever did you find that out?'

'There's very little that escapes my eyes and ears,' he boasted.

'Then who was this woman who slipped into my hotel that night?'

He smiled. 'Do I get a kiss if I tell you?'

Since the arrival of Pelham Lockyer in the town was an important event, Colbeck felt obliged to take him to police headquarters so that he could meet Colonel Edgell and Inspector Crabbe. The two of them plied him with questions and assured him that their investigation would soon produce positive results. They also thanked Colbeck for bringing the murder victim's son to see them. As the two of them left the building, Lockyer was frank.

'I got the impression that they were floundering,' he said.

'They're doing their best with inadequate resources,' explained Colbeck.

'I put my faith in you and the sergeant.'

'That's very gratifying, sir, but it's a complex case.'

'You've dealt with far worse, Inspector.'

'That's true,' admitted Colbeck. 'Our secret is unremitting hard work. Luckily, your arrival has given us an important new option.'

'I don't follow,' said Lockyer.

'There's one way to delve more deeply into your father's life and that is to read his Will. I daresay a copy of it will be in a safe in his study. If you could find access to it, I fancy that it will explain a lot about your father's wishes.'

'I don't know the combination to his safe, I'm afraid.'

'Then his solicitor will have a copy of the Will.'

'I'll get in touch with him as soon as I return to London.'

'Prepare yourself for a surprise, Mr Lockyer.'

'There's no need,' said the other confidently. 'My father kept no secrets from me.'

'Then why did he tell you he was going to see a friend in Kent when he came here instead?'

Lockyer was stunned into silence.

When Hinton replaced his colleague behind the tree near the Lockyer house, there were still some hours of daylight to go. Boyce had experimented with a series of hiding places from which he could watch the house. Hinton was impressed with the one that Boyce had finally chosen. It provided good cover and was very close to the house.

'Your turn up in the attic,' said Hinton.

'Thank you.'

'I'll see you in a couple of hours, Eric.'

'Right.'

'You were almost invisible from up there.'

'Good.'

'If he does turn up, it won't be for hours.'

'I can be patient.'

'I'm on duty here,' said Hinton. 'You have a rest – but keep one eye on the house.'

'I will. Promise.'

Without saying another word, Boyce walked quickly away.

When Colbeck and Lockyer strolled back to their hotel, they found that Archibald Reeves had left. Lockyer excused himself to go up to his room to prepare for dinner, leaving Colbeck alone with Victor Leeming. The inspector sensed that his colleague had important news to pass on. As they sat down together in the bar, he gave Leeming his cue.

'Something has happened, hasn't it?'

'Yes,' replied Leeming. 'While you were gone, I had a visitor.'

'Who was it?'

'The stationmaster. He's discovered something.'

'What is it?'

'We were right to think that the porter who entered the hotel that night was a woman. Mr Biddle has discovered her name.'

'How on earth did he do that?'

'He has eyes everywhere,' said Leeming. 'A friend of his who came to Shrewsbury that day spotted a woman he recognised. Her name is Betsy Dale. She's well known to the police in Wellington. That's where she lives, but she does pop over here by train if a client requests it. Somebody must have done just that.'

'Mr Lockyer?' asked Colbeck.

'I don't think so. He was a toff and beyond her reach. When she came here that night, she stole a porter's uniform – I daresay she'd use the word "borrowed" – so that she could slip into the hotel in disguise. Betsy wasn't there for Mr Lockyer's benefit. She came to share a bed with one of the other guests at the hotel.'

'How does the stationmaster know this?'

'His friend from Wellington came back here late this afternoon,' said Leeming. 'He'd read the newspapers and seen reports of the murder at the Station Hotel. He was certain that Betsy Dale was there to offer her services to someone other than Lockyer. Mr Biddle didn't say this, but I got the impression that his friend had done business with this woman himself. The man knew the way she worked and the sort of clients she attracted.'

'Was she in the habit of stealing clothes off somebody's line?'

'Betsy has had convictions for theft but never – oddly enough – for selling her body.'

'I wish I'd been here when Mr Biddle called,' said Colbeck. 'This information exonerates the woman in a porter's uniform. We don't need to waste any more time considering her as a part to the murder investigation. The stationmaster has done us another favour.'

'I bought him a drink to thank him.'

'I'd have done the same, Victor.'

'He's the reason we're here, after all.'

'If we eliminate a prostitute, we come back to your theory of a lone assassin who was using the name of Jack Brown.'

'He's the person we need to arrest.'

'And that may happen sooner rather than later,' said Colbeck. 'Superintendent Tallis will have realised that the killer may well use Lockyer's key to gain entry to his house. I'm sure that there will be officers keeping an eye on the property.'

Light was fading at the end of Alan Hinton's stint close to the house. He'd varied his position during the two hours on duty, standing behind a tree, crouching behind some bushes or leaning in shadow against the side of the house itself. When Boyce came to relieve him, Hinton was back behind the tree.

'How have you got on?' asked Boyce.

'I had a false alarm.'

'Oh?'

'Someone approached the house,' said Hinton, 'and kept looking around. When he got close, he suddenly slipped behind the bushes. I leapt up from behind the tree and challenged him.'

'What happened?'

'It wasn't the man we're after. He was desperate for a piss, so he stepped out of sight.' Boyce grinned. 'It's not funny, Eric. I thought I'd caught the man we're after. Unfortunately, I can't arrest someone for relieving himself. I told him he was on private property and sent him on his way.'

'My turn on duty again,' said Boyce. 'Off you go.'

'I'll be back in two hours.'

'Thanks.'

Seated in the dining room at The Lion Hotel, the detectives were halfway through a meal with Pelham Lockyer. Colbeck decided to tell him about the new information passed on to them by the stationmaster. Lockyer was horrified.

'You thought my father had paid for a prostitute?' he said with evident disgust.

'We had to consider every possibility,' said Colbeck.

'He was a deeply Christian man, Inspector. He often went to church twice on a Sunday. It would never have crossed his mind to . . .'

'You knew him, sir. We didn't.'

'I feel insulted on his behalf,' said Lockyer. 'My father was philanthropic. I told you about his donations to a children's home. What I didn't mention was the money he gave to the church.'

'That was very commendable of him.'

'I'm surprised that you even imagined such a thing about him.'

'Have another glass of wine,' suggested Leeming, reaching for the bottle.

'I'm too shocked to drink anything – shocked and appalled.'

'We've been shocked and appalled from time to time, sir. I once arrested a man for the attempted rape of a young female parishioner. He was a retired vicar.'

'Why don't we change the subject?' suggested Colbeck.

'Good idea,' said Lockyer, still flushed.

'When will your father's body be transferred to London?'

'Tomorrow. We'll travel on the same train.'

'Don't forget your promise to contact his lawyer.'

'I'm as keen to see Father's Will as you seem to be, Inspector.'

'Please forgive my curiosity,' said Colbeck, 'but it may contain clauses that are relevant to this investigation.'

'I think that highly unlikely.'

'You may well be right, sir.'

'I certainly will be,' insisted Lockyer, tossing his napkin aside and rising to his feet. 'I'm feeling tired so I will bid you both farewell until morning.'

Without another word, he sailed out of the room.

Leeming rolled his eyes. 'We seem to have upset him.'

'There may be worse to come, Victor.'

'What do you mean?'

'When a man leaves a last Will and testament,' said Colbeck, 'he exposes his true self. I suspect that Mr Lockyer's son may be dismayed by what he discovers.'

'I'm sorry that he flounced off like that. He insisted on buying dinner for us, but he hasn't even touched his wine. Everything left in the bottle,' said Leeming with a grin, 'is ours.'

Madeleine was having dinner with her father that evening. She tried to join in idle conversation with him, but Caleb Andrews could see that she was preoccupied. He was sympathetic.

'You're still thinking about that painting of yours, aren't you?'

'It's at the forefront of my mind,' she admitted.

'I'll help you to track down this fake artist.'

'I detest the woman for what she's done but I must concede that she does possess a degree of artistic talent. Why waste it by copying someone else's work?'

'She sees it as a way to make money, Maddy.'

'Yes, but not very much money. Mr Davies had it on sale for a very modest amount. If the woman painted something that was entirely her own work, she might attract the interest of an art dealer like Mr Sinclair.'

'What do we know about this woman?'

'Very little, Father. Mr Davies described her as "very grand". She was certainly no down-at-heel artist.'

'I could say the same about you,' said Andrews proudly.

She laughed. 'Don't be silly! I'm just ordinary – and glad to be so.'

'You're a far better artist than this woman.'

'I like to think so.'

'You are, Maddy. Don't be so modest. I've never met anyone who can conjure up a scene involving trains the way that you do.'

'You had something to do with it because you taught me how to love railways.'

'Yes,' said Andrews, chuckling. 'I first sneaked you onto the footplate when you were only five. Your mother was very angry with me.'

'That was because I went home with coal dust on my clothes.'

'It didn't put you off steam engines.' He speared a potato and put it into his mouth. 'What will you do next?'

'Lydia and I have a plan of action. We're starting first thing tomorrow morning. We're going to the Red Gallery to ask for Mr Sinclair's advice. He may know where someone may offer it for sale.'

'It deserves to be tossed on the scrap heap.'

'Be fair,' said Madeleine. 'The artist does have more than a glimmer of talent. That's why I'll be so interested to meet her – however grand she is.'

'Will you have Alan Hinton with you?'

'I'm afraid not. He's been given a more important assignment.'

He was coming to the end of his second stint outside the Lockyer residence. It was now dark and there was limited visibility. Hinton glanced up at the attic window in the house opposite, hoping that Eric Boyce was still awake and ready to change places with him very soon. There was no sense of danger. If the man they knew as Jack Brown came to the house, Hinton believed, it would be in the dead of night when he could be certain that everyone inside was fast asleep. There was a new problem. It started to rain. Hinton turned up his collar and pulled down his hat. As he did so, he caught a brief glimpse of someone moving stealthily towards the house in the darkness.

His first assumption was that Boyce had come to relieve him, but the newcomer did not head for the tree behind which Hinton was hiding. After checking that he was completely alone, he instead moved to the front door of the house and took something from his pocket. Hinton acted instinctively. He came out from behind the tree and trotted silently towards the house. Since he had the advantage of surprise, he was confident that he could overpower and arrest the man. Blood racing, he dived on the killer's back, forcing him to bang his head against the door. Hinton pulled out his handcuffs and tried to force the man's hands behind his back.

But he had reckoned without the killer's strength. The man suddenly swung round and delivered a punch to Hinton's stomach that made him stagger backwards. It was followed by two punches to the face. Recovering quickly, the detective parried the relay of blows thrown at him then shook the man with a punch of his own to the chin. Enraged by the pain, the killer pulled out a knife and lunged at Hinton, but the latter got a firm hold on the man's wrist, twisting it sharply so that he dropped the weapon. Hurling himself at the detective, the man got him in a bear hug and squeezed hard, gaining the advantage at last. Before he could exert full pressure, however, he became aware of footsteps racing across the road. He looked up to see a figure emerging from the darkness. Eric Boyce had come to the rescue.

When he got close, however, he was unable to get a grip on the intruder because Hinton was thrown bodily at him. By the time the detectives untangled themselves, the man had raced off down the road. Both detectives ran after him, but they eventually lost him and abandoned the chase.

'Thank God you came when you did,' said Hinton, breathing heavily. 'He was a handful.'

'Was he armed?'

'Yes, he had a knife. It's on the ground somewhere because I managed to twist it out of his grasp. Let's go back and find it.'

'We made a mistake,' said Boyce.

'Mistake?'

'We should have been down here on duty together.'

'You could be right.'

'We must do that tomorrow night.'

'There's no point,' said Hinton.

'Why not?'

'It's because he tried to let himself into the house and failed. The front door was bolted. Then he discovered that someone was on guard here,' said Hinton. 'Would you be stupid enough to come back for a second attempt?'

'No, I wouldn't.'

'That means we can go back to the attic. Apart from anything else, I can lick my wounds.'

'Sorry I didn't come down earlier.'

'It's too late to worry about that now,' said Hinton. 'Let's go back to Lockyer's house and find that knife dropped near there.' He put a hand on Boyce's shoulder. 'You saved me, Eric. I'll always remember that.'

'How do you feel now?'

'I've got bruises everywhere – but the worst is yet to come.'

'The worst?'

'Facing the superintendent tomorrow and confessing that I missed the chance to arrest the man who killed Mr Lockyer and stole the key to his front door.'

CHAPTER ELEVEN

They began their search next morning. Madeleine decided against asking her father to join them and went off alone with Lydia Quayle. The cab took them first to the Red Gallery where they were given a warm welcome by the proprietor, Francis Sinclair.

'Have you managed to trace the artist posing as Madeleine Colbeck?' he asked.

'I'm afraid not,' said Madeleine. 'It's the reason we came back here.'

'How can I help?'

'Well, I'm sure that you know the names of all the art dealers in the city, but what about the shops that sell paintings along with a variety of other things?'

'Legitimate art dealers tend to operate in parts of London where people are more likely to be interested in buying a painting.

If my shop was in Soho, for instance, I would struggle to make a living. People there are looking for bargains and not for art of real quality to hang on their walls.'

'Yet it was in Soho that I found that fake painting,' noted Lydia. 'Do you think it might have been offered to genuine art dealers before it ended up in Mr Davies's shop?'

'I think that it probably was. Because it was a poor version of an existing work, no dealer would have taken it. And of course,' Sinclair went on, 'the so-called artist didn't bring it here because she knew that I would recognise it as a fake immediately.'

'If only she had given you her address,' said Madeleine.

'When she bought a print of your work, she was careful to keep it from me – and now we know why.'

'Yes, she wanted to guard her privacy.'

'Solomon Davies believed that she was called Madeleine Colbeck,' recalled Lydia. 'That's whom she claimed to be. She is probably doing the same with other shopkeepers.'

'How do we find them?' asked Madeleine.

'Yes – where else might this woman go?'

'I may be able to help you there,' said Sinclair, reaching under the counter for a book and leafing through the pages. 'I've got a list of shops that are off the beaten track, but which do sell occasional paintings. They certainly have a better standard of items than the man in Soho.' He stopped at a page. 'Would you like me to jot down some of them?'

'Yes, please,' said Madeleine.

'It will point us in the right direction,' added Lydia.

'We'd be very grateful, Mr Sinclair.'

Reaching for a quill pen, he began to jot down some of the addresses from the list.

'If you want a major art dealer,' he told them, 'you will need to go to somewhere like Bond Street or in that area. These addresses are in less salubrious parts of the city.'

They waited patiently until he had finished. When he handed over the list, Madeleine ran her eye over it with growing excitement. The visit to the Red Gallery had delivered a bonus. They now knew where they could begin the search.

It was not until morning that Alan Hinton realised how badly he'd been wounded in the scuffle. Bruises had come out all over his body and, when he looked in the bathroom mirror, he saw that he had a black eye and a livid scratch down one cheek. Their host, Jeremy Hull, was shocked by the sight of him and disappointed that they had been unable to arrest anyone. After a hearty breakfast, the detectives thanked him for his help and headed back to Scotland Yard in a cab.

Since he was nominally in charge of the operation, Hinton chose to face the superintendent alone. As he stood outside the door of his office, he took a deep breath before tapping gently.

'Come in!' yelled Tallis.

Hinton opened the door gingerly and stepped into the room. Tallis gaped at him.

'What, in the name of God, happened to you?' he demanded.

'He got away, sir,' admitted Hinton. 'When I tackled him, he fought back. We had quite a tussle. At one point, he pulled this on me,' he explained, putting the knife on the desk. 'I managed to get it off him before he could use it.'

'Where was Boyce when all this was happening?'

'On his way to relieve me and take my place. Eric came in time to save me because my attacker took to his heels. We chased him but he got away in the dark.'

'In other words, you bungled your chance to catch him.'

'I did my best, Superintendent.'

'It was not good enough, Hinton. And why weren't the pair of you guarding the house together? That would have given you a much better chance of an arrest.'

'I realise that now, sir.'

'Sit down, man. You look as if you're about to collapse.'

'Thank you,' said Hinton, lowering himself carefully into a chair. 'The main thing is that he was not able to get into the house. He tried the key in the lock, but it didn't open the front door. I saw my chance and pounced on him.'

'It looks as if he pounced on you.'

'He fought back, sir. I came off worse.'

'You're still alive, thank God.' Tallis picked up the knife. 'He could have cut you to shreds with this. You should have been armed yourself.'

'I realise that now, sir.'

'And you should have had Boyce with you.'

'It was my idea that we each had two-hour shifts.'

'Your safety should have been the prime consideration. The pair of you could have arrested the man, deprived him of his weapon and taken him to the nearest police station. Instead of that, you bungled everything and ended up looking as if you'd been knocked out in a prize fight.'

'It could have been worse, sir.'

'Yes,' said Tallis, 'you could have finished up dead.'

'I feel as if I am,' confessed Hinton.

The superintendent gave a hollow laugh then offered a morsel of sympathy. He asked Hinton if he felt well enough to be back on duty, and the latter assured him that he was. When he heard a full report of the incident, Tallis was pleased to discover that the man would not be back to burgle the house again because he had discovered that his key would not let him in, and because he had learnt that the place was being guarded.

'The occupants of the house can sleep in safety now, sir,' said Hinton.

'That's a relief, I suppose.'

'May I ask what's happening in Shrewsbury?'

'Inspector Colbeck and Sergeant Leeming are continuing their investigation. And before you volunteer to help them,' he went on, 'the answer is that I would never let you go there in that state. You'd frighten the horses and terrify the women.'

A man from the funeral home in London had arrived in Shrewsbury early that morning. He was dressed in mourning attire and was travelling with an expensive casket. Pelham Lockyer met him at the railway station, and watched as the casket was loaded onto the horse-drawn cart he had hired. As the cart was driven to the infirmary, the two men followed in a cab. Lockyer helped to carry the casket into the building and was deeply moved when his father's body was lifted gently into it. The body of Julian Lockyer was taken at a deliberately slow pace to the railway station, where Colbeck and Leeming were waiting to lend their help. Lifted onto a trolley, the casket was wheeled by porters to the edge of the platform. Hat held in his hand, the stationmaster watched respectfully. When the train arrived, the casket was loaded with reverential care into the guard's van. After seeing it safely stowed, Lockyer turned to Colbeck.

'Thank you for everything you have done, Inspector,' he said.

'Our work is not yet finished, sir,' Colbeck pointed out.

'What you have achieved so far has given me great comfort.'

'The only comfort I seek lies in the arrest of the person or persons involved in the murder. To that end, we will continue to work tirelessly.'

Lockyer shook hands with him and with Victor Leeming before getting into a first-class compartment. The man from the funeral home was travelling in the guard's van with the casket. As the train began to move, Biddle replaced his hat. Leeming turned to Colbeck.

'That was very considerate of you, sir,' he said. 'You didn't mention the telegraph that you got from the superintendent this morning.'

'Mr Lockyer has enough grief to contend with. That's why I didn't tell him that last night's attempt to catch the killer outside his father's house had, unfortunately, failed.'

'How does that affect us?'

'We move back to London and hunt the man down,' said Colbeck.

When they met in his office, the grey-haired old man with the walking stick was surprised by his friend's appearance. He used the stick to point at the visitor's face.

'How did you get that bruise?' he asked in concern.

'Somebody was waiting for me outside the house,' replied the other.

'How could they possibly know that you'd be there at night?'

'They must have realised I'd stolen his key to the front door. Not that it was any use to me,' said the visitor bitterly. 'The door was bolted. Then, out of the blue, someone grabbed hold of me.'

'Who was it?'

'A policeman, I reckon. He was young and strong. We had a real tussle.'

'How did you escape?'

'With a struggle,' said the man. 'He wasn't alone. A friend of his came running to help so I left as fast as I could. They chased me until they ran out of breath.'

'Thank goodness!'

'Anyway, I've come for the money you promised me.'

'I've already paid you for killing Lockyer,' said the older man sharply.

'You told me there'd be more if I got inside the house.'

'But you didn't.'

'That's not my fault,' protested the other. 'I obeyed my orders to the letter.'

'Yes, and you almost got arrested while doing it.'

'How was I to know there'd be someone on guard outside the house?'

'You should have checked when you first got there,' said the other sternly. 'You were recommended to me because you always got results. This time, you failed.'

'That's unfair,' roared the other. 'I killed a man you hated, and I got away with it.'

'You were handsomely paid for that – or had you forgotten?'

'It wasn't enough. Because of what I did for you, I've got the Shropshire Constabulary and detectives from Scotland Yard on my tail. They'll hunt me for the rest of my life.'

'That's your problem.'

'I need more money,' demanded the killer, moving to stand over the other man, 'and I'm staying here until I get it.'

'All right, all right,' said the older man, holding up the palms of his hands. 'You'll get what you deserve, I promise.'

Using the stick to move across the room, he stopped beside a safe in the wall and turned the tumblers to insert the correct code. When the door was finally pulled open, he reached inside and took something out before swinging around to face his visitor. In his hand was a gun. The tables had been turned. The killer backed away.

'Look, I'm sorry,' he apologised. 'I shouldn't have made demands. You paid me well.'

'I turned to you because you had a reputation.'

'Yes, I did – and I lived up to it.'

'Only to some degree,' argued the older man. 'Yes, you rid the world of a loathsome man, but you failed to get the vital information I was after.'

'I tried to follow him, but he took a cab. I had to wait until he walked back to the hotel.'

'You failed – then you dare to come here and make demands.'

'That was a mistake. I see that now.'

'You get paid for results – not for failures.' He lowered the gun. 'You'll have to get into the house in some other way. There's information in his study that I simply must have.'

'I'll do my best to get it, I promise.'

'If you don't,' warned the other, 'I'll hire someone else.'

'What happens to me?'

'I'll have you killed. I can't abide failure. Do you understand?'

The man was utterly cowed. 'Yes, sir. I understand.'

The first address on their list was on a street off Charing Cross Road. It sold a variety of items, including a couple of paintings.

Madeleine and Lydia went into the shop together. There was an even larger display of goods inside. They looked in vain for the fake painting by the woman who had stolen both Madeleine's name and an example of her work. The proprietor of the shop was a dapper individual of middle years in a dark suit. Unlike Solomon Davies, he was excessively polite.

'Welcome to my emporium, ladies,' he said, beaming at them. 'Are you looking for anything in particular?'

'As a matter of fact,' said Lydia, 'we are. It's a painting by Madeleine Colbeck of a train steaming past a small farm.'

'I'm sorry to disappoint you but we have nothing like that here, I'm afraid.'

'Have you been offered such a painting?'

'No, we haven't,' he said. 'May I ask why you are so interested in it?'

'It's because it is a fake version of the work of my friend here, Madeleine Colbeck. Her version was sold by the Red Gallery, and someone bought a print of it so that she could copy it and pass it off as her own.'

'That's dreadful!' exclaimed the man. 'It's both shocking and downright illegal.' He turned to Madeleine. 'I've heard of the Red Gallery. They sell paintings of real quality. I'm delighted to meet one of its artists.'

'Thank you,' said Madeleine. 'The other version was spotted in the window of a shop in Soho. When we pointed out that it was a fake, the owner became very truculent.'

'Yes,' added Lydia. 'On our second visit, we took a Scotland Yard detective with us for protection. The owner told us that the "artist" had withdrawn it and was intending to find someone else to sell it.'

'Well,' said the man, 'she didn't come here. More's the pity! After so many years in the trade, I can usually spot people trying to unload stolen goods on me – and the same goes for those who use false names.' He turned to Madeleine. 'You have my sympathy. I hope you find this fake artist.'

'So do we,' she replied. 'If we fail, it won't be for lack of trying.'

'I admire your spirit, ladies, and I wish you well in your search.'

'Thank you.'

'If, by chance, this woman does try to sell me a painting, she will be asked to leave the premises at once.' He reached for a pen. 'I'll be happy to inform you of her visit. Is there an address where I might contact you?'

'Yes, of course,' said Madeleine, taking the pen from him and writing her address on a pad. 'We'd be most grateful.'

'I'm only too glad to help.' He took his business card from a drawer and handed it to Lydia. 'Everything sold here is above board.'

'We could see that at a glance,' Lydia told him.

'It's kind of you to say so.' He looked at the name on the pad. 'I've realised that your name rings a bell. Isn't there a famous Inspector Colbeck?' he said.

'Yes,' said Madeleine, smiling, 'there is, and he happens to be my husband. He deals with murders and other serious crimes. I can't expect him to go looking for a woman who copies my paintings. I can do that myself.'

Before they left Shrewsbury, the detectives made a series of calls. The first was to Archibald Reeves to thank him for his help and to ask that a copy of his forthcoming article about the death of Julian Lockyer was sent to them. The next visit was to the chief constable, whom they found alone in his office. Though he was polite and grateful for their help, they could see that he was glad they were returning to London and handing over the murder investigation in the town to them. Before they left, Colbeck could not resist asking Colonel Edgell a question.

'Do you have a message for Superintendent Tallis?'

'Yes, I do,' replied Edgell darkly. 'Stay away from Shropshire!'

'I'm sure that he has good reason to do so, Colonel.'

Their third and last visit was to Molly Burrage, assuring her that they would track down the man who committed the murder at the Station Hotel, and thanking her for the help she had given them during their stay. Overcome with emotion, she embraced each of them in turn. Stepping out of the hotel, they headed for the station.

'That warm hug was more than we got from the chief constable,' said Leeming. 'It made me feel that we were wanted here. I'd be happy to come back.'

'There's unfinished business to attend to first,' Colbeck reminded him. 'I can't wait to begin the search in London.'

Eric Boyce could not resist staring at his companion. When they were having lunch together, he kept looking at his face. Alan Hinton began to feel embarrassed.

'It will get better in time, Eric,' he told Boyce.

'It looks even worse than it did first thing this morning.'

'Don't rub it in.'

'I'm sorry, Alan. It was partly my fault. I should have come earlier.'

'Turning up like that saved me from having a worse beating,' admitted Hinton. 'I'll always be grateful to you for that.'

Boyce studied his face. 'Can you actually see through that black eye?'

'I couldn't when it first happened.'

'You probably wished you'd been in Shrewsbury with Inspector Colbeck.'

'No, I didn't. I knew that I had the chance to capture the man and that excited me. Before I could get the handcuffs on him, he attacked me. I wouldn't dare to show you the bruises on my body. He punched me everywhere.'

'I'm sure that you fought back, Alan.'

'Oh, I did, and I had the satisfaction of hearing him squeal with pain when I punched him. All I want now is the chance to tackle him once again.'

'That's very brave of you,' said Boyce, 'but you need to be armed next time – and have someone like me backing you up. When will Inspector Colbeck return to London?'

'My guess is that he's already on his way here. The superintendent will have sent him a telegraph that confirms that the killer is now in London.'

'What is he going to say when he sees your face?'

'Stop staring at my black eye!' complained Hinton.

'I was staring at that ugly scratch down your cheek. It makes you look like a pirate.'

Still smarting from his encounter with the man who had employed him, the killer was back at the house owned by Julian Lockyer. He was viewing it from all angles, trying to work out how best to get into it. Trees and bushes gave him plenty of cover to carry out his survey. What interested him most was the rear entry of the property. An old lady was sleeping outdoors in a wheelchair. A woman was bending solicitously over her. Breaking into the house from the rear would not be difficult. He had burgled houses that were far better protected.

Having annoyed his paymaster, he did not wish to repeat the experience. The last thing that he had expected was to have a gun aimed at him. It had jolted him and taught him not to make demands on the man who had hired him. He prided himself on having committed a murder then fled to the comparative safety of London. The fact that he had nearly been arrested the night before made him realise that the police were on his tail. It was unsettling. The capital was no longer the safe hiding place he had assumed. He would have to move on with as much money as he could get from the old man with the walking stick.

As he reflected on what had happened so far, he asked himself questions that he had not dared to put to the person who ordered the assassination. Who was the man? Why did he want Julian Lockyer murdered? What was he supposed to steal from Lockyer's study? Would the old man honour his promise to pay more money? There was a more chilling possibility.

Would he really dispose of the killer if he failed again?

The second address to which they were taken by cab was in Baker Street. At first glance it looked as if it specialised in only one thing. Its window was filled with tennis rackets, golf bags, croquet mallets, fishing tackle, cricket bats and other sporting paraphernalia. Since the address was on the list, they nevertheless went into the shop. The first thing they saw was a collection of shotguns, locked in a display cabinet. A handsome, fair-haired young man with a neat moustache was on duty behind the counter. Although he gave them a welcoming smile, he was clearly surprised that they should come into the shop. His raised eyebrows asked the question.

'This place was recommended to us,' explained Lydia.

'By whom, may I ask?'

'By the proprietor of the Red Gallery. Mr Sinclair told us that you occasionally sold paintings.'

'That's quite true. Most of them tend to be sporting scenes, but we do occasionally have landscapes for sale.'

'We wondered if you might have been approached to sell a painting that featured a small train passing a farm.'

'It doesn't sound like our kind of thing, I'm afraid. Why do you ask?'

'The painting was a fake,' said Lydia. 'We are desperate to find the woman posing as Madeleine and copying one of her paintings.'

'That sounds like a job for the police,' he argued.

'We want the satisfaction of finding this person ourselves,' said Madeleine. 'The painting was on sale in a shop in Soho but was withdrawn when it failed to attract a buyer.'

'This bogus artist did not offer it to us,' said the man. 'Even if we had liked it, we would have needed cast-iron proof that she really was the artist. You mention the Red Gallery. It's a reputable establishment.'

'All my paintings are sold there,' Madeleine told him.

'And the proprietor suggested that you came here, did he?'

'Yours is only one of a number of shops he recommended.'

'Might I see this list?' he asked. 'It's possible that I may be able to help you. There are, alas, shops that accept anything they can sell regardless of its origin. I suspect that you may have more luck visiting one of them.'

'That would be so kind of you,' said Madeleine, taking the list from her reticule and passing it over to him. 'You might save us a lot of wasted time.'

He smiled at her. 'I'll do my best.'

It wasn't until their train was halfway to London that the detectives had the luxury of an empty second-class compartment. Until that point, there had always been other passengers seated with them, making any discussion of the case impossible.

'Young Mr Lockyer travelled in first class,' said Leeming.

'He's rich,' said Colbeck. 'We have to operate on a more limited budget.'

'I'm glad. I feel more at home in second class.'

'Then let's take full advantage of the fact that we are alone to discuss the case. I am sorry to leave Shrewsbury, but I believe that we will have to return there before long.'

'Why is that?'

'The search began there, Victor, and it must end there.'

'I don't understand.'

'What took Mr Lockyer there in the first place? It was something extremely important – so much so that he lied to his son about his destination.'

'I still wonder if a woman is somehow involved.'

'There's nothing we've gleaned about him that suggests immorality of any kind,' said Colbeck. 'Recall what his son told us about him. The father was a decent, upstanding, church-going man who supported good causes. He had led what appears to be a good life in every sense.'

'You've forgotten that girl at the hotel – Annie Garrow.'

'What about her?'

'According to Inspector Crabbe, she told him that the way Mr Lockyer stared at her was frightening. It made her flinch. That's not what a true gentleman would do to a young woman.'

'You have to remember the state she was in,' reminded Colbeck. 'The poor girl had been there when they discovered the naked, blood-covered body of the murder victim. Such a hideous sight must have upset her deeply. When Crabbe interviewed her, she was probably still in shock.'

'It may explain why she fainted when she saw the son and believed that Lockyer had come back from the dead. There was a strong resemblance between young Mr Lockyer and his father.'

'There was obviously a deep affection between the two of them.'

'I feel sorry for the son. This whole business has knocked the stuffing out of him.'

'He may have to endure other shocks before too long.'

'Why do you say that?'

'Young Mr Lockyer will have to read his father's Will,' said Colbeck. 'I suspect that it will be a revelation for him. He may well learn things that Julian Lockyer strove to hide from his son.'

'Such as?'

'The real reason he had to go to Shrewsbury.'

Seated behind the desk in his office, the grey-haired old man studied a photograph. It had been taken at a GWR board meeting and showed a group of directors smiling at the camera. At the centre of the group was Julian Lockyer, beaming happily. Beside him was the grey-haired old man. After looking at the photograph for some time, he reached for his pen and used it to obliterate Lockyer's face with a series of crosses.

Replacing his pen, he sat back to study the photograph with relish.

Madeleine and Lydia headed for their third shop with renewed hope. When they'd showed their list to the young man at the previous shop, he had picked out an address near Euston, telling them that it always had a selection of paintings for sale. Madeleine was unable to control a feeling of optimism, but Lydia was more realistic.

'It may take us a dozen or more visits before we find the right shop,' she said.

'But there are only ten names on our list,' Madeleine pointed out.

'I know that, but remember how helpful that young man was at the last shop. If we draw a blank wherever we go, we can ask the individual proprietors to recommend a place that is not on Mr Sinclair's list.'

'I never thought of that, Lydia.'

'That's why you need me with you. Oh,' she went on, 'isn't this exciting? It's real detective work. Robert will be proud of the way you decided to track down the false Madeleine Colbeck.'

'I might find her,' said Madeleine, 'but only a police officer can arrest her. Someone like Detective Constable Hinton, for instance.'

'He'll be preoccupied with real crimes.'

'This is a real crime,' said Madeleine indignantly. 'What is worse than having my name stolen by a bogus artist who has copied a painting of mine? It's a horrible experience, Lydia.'

'I know and I do sympathise with you.' The cab began to slow down. 'Ah, it looks as if we're almost there. Fingers crossed.'

They climbed out onto the pavement and asked the driver to wait for them. Then they took a first look at the shop beside them. It had far too many items on display, jostling for position in the window. Amongst them, however, was a series of paintings. Madeleine ran an excited eye over them before sighing with disappointment.

'Perhaps it's on display inside,' suggested Lydia. 'Let's go in.'

Leading the way, she opened the door and went into the shop with Madeleine following in her wake. On the back wall was another collection of paintings but none featured a train. Madeleine's earlier hopes waned. When the proprietor came through a door at the rear of the shop, they were both taken aback to see that it was a striking, well-dressed, middle-aged woman with a warm smile.

'Welcome, ladies,' she said, spreading her arms. 'I'm Victoria Dowling and this is my shop. Please feel free to look around.'

'Actually,' explained Lydia, 'we're searching for a particular painting. The artist's name is Madeleine Colbeck.'

'Heavens!' exclaimed the woman. 'You should have come yesterday because that was when she brought the painting in. You could have met the artist herself.'

'I'm very keen to do so,' said Madeleine, 'because that painting was copied from one of my own that was originally sold by the Red Gallery.'

The proprietor was shocked. 'What are you telling me?'

'The artist lied to you, I'm afraid. I am Madeleine Colbeck, and I am keen to find the woman who has not only stolen my name but copied a painting of mine that is very special to me.'

'Can this be true?'

'Yes,' confirmed Lydia. 'I chanced to see it on sale in a shop in

Soho. The owner was very unpleasant to us when we pointed out that he was trying to sell a fake. When we went back to the shop again, we took a detective constable with us for protection. As it turned out, he was not needed because the so-called artist had reclaimed her painting to sell elsewhere.'

'And yours is the shop she chose,' said Madeleine. 'She didn't give her address to the previous owner who put the painting on display, and I daresay that she did the same to you.'

'Well, yes,' conceded the woman. 'It did seem odd. I had no means of getting in touch with her when the painting was sold. She told me that she would pop in regularly to see if anyone had been interested.'

'Someone is very interested – me. I resent the fact that my work has been stolen by someone trying to pass it off as her own.'

'I don't blame you, Miss Colbeck.'

'Mrs Colbeck,' corrected Madeleine.

'Her husband is a detective inspector at Scotland Yard,' explained Lydia, 'so we know that we have the law on our side. If you offer it for sale, you will be liable to arrest.'

'That's dreadful,' cried the woman. 'I took it in good faith, I promise you.'

'I'm sure that you did,' said Madeleine.

'Something like this has never happened before. I can usually spot people who are trying to sell me things that are not strictly theirs. In this case, the woman was so convincing. She told me that she had been on holiday at a small farm with a railway close by. That was where she got the idea of the painting. It meant a great deal to her.'

'It means even more to me,' said Madeleine.

'What must I do?'

'Find out what her real name is and where she lives.'

'It will be in one of the more lucrative parts of the city,' replied the woman. 'She was beautifully dressed and had a sort of dignity about her.'

'What else can you tell us about her?'

'How convincing she was. She really made me believe that the painting was her work.'

'Did she name a price she hoped it would sell for?' asked Lydia.

'Yes, she did, and it was surprisingly modest. I'm not an expert on paintings, but I could see that it was worth far more than she suggested.'

'What was her motive?' said Madeleine. 'If she was not hoping to make money out of it, why did she go to the trouble of copying someone else's painting?'

'I'm as baffled as you are, Mrs Colbeck.'

'How old was this woman?'

'I'd say that she was over fifty, but she seemed to be in excellent health. She would have been about your height, and she held herself well. In fact, I'd go so far as to describe her as being . . . well, almost like an aristocrat.'

'What else can you remember about this woman?' asked Lydia.

'Oh, she was very much more of a lady. That's what fooled me, I suppose. There was more than a whisper of wealth about her. She was not a struggling artist, working in a garret. She painted for the sheer pleasure of it.'

'I'm the same,' confessed Madeleine, 'though I do expect some payment for my work. It makes me feel that my efforts were not in vain.'

'Everything you paint is wonderful,' said Lydia.'

'No, it isn't, I'm afraid. I make mistakes sometimes. But let's go back to this other Madeleine Colbeck. If she was able to win you over,' she went on, turning to the owner of the shop, 'she must be something of an actress.'

'That never occurred to me at the time,' said the other. 'She seemed so plausible – though my husband, Davy, thought there was something strange about her. I ignored his advice because there was the chance of a profit. She was happy to let me have fifty per cent of the asking price. It's one of the main reasons that I accepted her painting – not knowing that it was a copy of someone else's work. I'm sorry, Mrs Colbeck. Foolishly, I believed everything that she told me.'

'Then she is a practised confidence trickster.'

'How can we catch her?' asked Lydia.

'I can think of one way,' said Madeleine before facing the proprietor. 'I don't suppose that you would let me work here as your assistant, would you?'

'Well, I suppose that I could,' replied the other, 'but this woman is unlikely to come back so soon. She told me that she would leave it for a week.'

'That's when I'll be back to confront her,' resolved Madeleine.

CHAPTER TWELVE

A miracle occurred at Scotland Yard. When Robert Colbeck delivered his report, Superintendent Tallis did not once interrupt him. That was highly unusual. Tallis was in the habit of breaking up the inspector's flow with demands for further detail about certain points in the narrative. He was now eerily silent. Colbeck took advantage of the unexpected freedom to talk at length about the murder investigation in Shrewsbury. It was only when the inspector's report was complete that Tallis finally found his voice.

'Are you convinced that the man calling himself Jack Brown was the killer?' he asked.

'I am, sir.'

'And do you have a description of this individual?'

'It was given to me by the stationmaster, the person who first made us aware of what had happened in Shrewsbury.'

'Your telegraphs were full of praise for this man.'

'The praise was well deserved, sir. Mr Biddle has been extremely helpful. But there have been others who deserve a mention – Dr Clement and Archie Reeves, in particular. They gave us invaluable information about the town.'

'Yet there has still been no arrest,' sighed Tallis. 'Thanks to your warning, I was able to put Mr Lockyer's house under surveillance. The suspect did appear, but Detective Constable Hinton was unable to arrest the man.'

'I'm sure that he did his best, sir.'

'There was a violent struggle but Jack Brown – or whatever his real name is – escaped. Hinton did, however, manage to wrest a weapon from him.' He opened a drawer in his desk and took out a large knife. 'This is it.'

'The suspect is clearly a dangerous man,' said Colbeck, studying the knife. 'Hinton did well to disarm him.'

'But he failed to overpower him, Inspector. The killer is still at large.'

'And we still don't know who hired him.'

'Didn't his son give you the names of his father's enemies?'

'No, sir,' said Colbeck. 'Young Mr Lockyer doesn't believe that such enemies exist.'

'Then what was the motive behind the murder?'

'He has no idea. His love for his father verges on hero-worship. He can't understand why anyone would wish to take the life of such a remarkable man. My own view is that the son is in for some very unpleasant surprises. I feel sorry for Pelham Lockyer.'

'My sympathy is reserved for Julian Lockyer's wife. She has lost a man with whom she lived for the best part of forty years.

The one blessing is that she will be unaware of his death. I've met the poor woman, and her mind is no longer functioning.'

'Then she will not be shocked by any revelations that come to light.'

'Quite so,' said Tallis. 'What are your next moves?'

'Firstly, I'd like to speak to Detective Constable Hinton about his brush with the killer.'

'Then I should warn you that he came off worse in the tussle.'

'If he was able to disarm the man,' said Colbeck, indicating the knife, 'then he deserves praise. He will be able to give us some sort of description of the suspect.'

'You'll find him here at Scotland Yard.'

'Then I'll talk to him at once.' Colbeck rose to his feet. 'Unless you have any further questions for me.'

'There is one thing,' said Tallis quietly.

'What is it?'

'When you met him, did the chief constable . . . say anything about me?'

'He indicated that the two of you were not the best of friends, sir.'

'Is that all?'

'No,' replied Colbeck. 'He asked me to pass on a message to you.'

'What was it?'

'"Stay away from Shropshire."'

The superintendent bristled. 'While he is there, it's the last place on earth that I wish to visit.'

'May I ask why, sir?'

'No,' growled Tallis, eyes blazing. 'You may not.'

* * *

Caleb Andrews liked to keep busy in his retirement. He met a group of former employees of the LNWR on a regular basis and – while he enjoyed talking about old times with them over a pint of beer – he was conscious that some of his friends were simply drifting through what was left of their lives. He, on the other hand, kept himself fully occupied. Apart from regular visits to his daughter and granddaughter, there was always an investigation by his son-in-law that exercised his mind. Since it was related to the railways, he felt obliged to offer his expert knowledge of the system, even though it was often politely ignored. His latest preoccupation was with a crime that affected his own daughter.

'Tell me where this shop is, Maddy,' he demanded.

'Why?'

'Because I want to go there and wait for this other Madeleine Colbeck to turn up.'

'It won't happen for a week, Father.'

'That's what she told the woman who owns the shop,' argued Andrews, 'but I don't trust a word that this "artist" said. I bet that she'll keep popping in there to see if anyone has bought her painting. If I'm there, I can grab her.'

'But you have no powers of arrest.'

'She's a criminal and needs to be handed over to the police.'

'I agree,' said Madeleine, 'and I'd love to be able to confront her.'

'One of us should be in that shop every day. Think how annoyed you'll be if this woman comes before the week is up.'

'Mrs Dowling, who owns the shop, promised to get in touch with me at once.'

'What use is that if the bird has flown?' said Andrews.

'Let me handle this, Father.'

'But the woman might slip through your fingers. That won't happen if I'm lurking somewhere in the shop. I can leap out and accuse her.'

'Apart from anything else, I'm not sure that Mrs Dowling would like to have a man hidden away on her premises. It's very kind of you to offer,' said Madeleine, 'but your place is here, playing with your granddaughter. In any case, Robert will be home any day now. He'll know what to do.'

'Why wait for him when I'm ready to help now?'

'It's because you don't know the sort of person you're up against. Mrs Dowling described her as having the skill of an actress, and the woman is obviously a convincing liar. What if she turns up with a man? You can't tackle two of them, Father.'

'I can, if necessary,' he boasted, putting up his fists.

'Be sensible. Your fighting days are over, I'm afraid.' They heard the letterbox click open. 'There's the post,' she said, going into the hall to retrieve some letters from the floor. She sorted through them. 'Yes, here's one from Robert.'

'What does he say?' asked Andrews, who had followed her into the hall.

'You'll have to be patient.'

'I want to know what's in the letter. It could be important.'

Madeleine opened the missive and read its contents. Her face lit up with pleasure.

'Robert is coming home today,' she said with delight. 'It means that we can take his advice about what to do next.'

Inspector Colbeck, meanwhile, was in his office with Detective Constable Hinton, expressing sympathy for the younger man.

'You did well, Alan,' he said, patting him on the shoulder.

'I failed, sir.'

'You gave him a fright and you made him drop that knife he pulled on you. I've seen it. That blade could have inflicted a far more serious wound than a black eye.'

'My only hope is that I get a second chance to arrest him.'

'It will come, I'm sure.'

'Julian Lockyer lived in a beautiful house,' said Hinton. 'We could see it from the attic of a house opposite. Detective Constable Boyce and I were hiding there in wait for the killer.'

'You learnt something important, Alan – that the man is back in London.'

'I also learnt that he fights like a tiger.'

'Only when he is cornered, I daresay. He attacked Mr Lockyer when the poor man was unable to defend himself. Mrs Burrage, the owner of the hotel, described what she saw when they entered the room. The corpse was covered in blood.'

'Perhaps the killer used the same knife he tried to use on me.'

'You were in a position to defend yourself – Julian Lockyer was not.'

'No, I suppose not.'

'How would you describe the man you tried to arrest?'

'He was about the same height as me,' said Hinton, 'but much heavier. And he was very strong. If Eric Boyce hadn't arrived in time, I might have been badly injured – if not killed.'

'What sort of age would the man be?'

'In his twenties, I'd say. It was dark at the time, so I didn't get a good look at him, but he had the strength – and the speed – of a man of that age. We chased him hard, but he was too fast for us.'

'Who is employing him?' asked Colbeck. 'That's the question we need to answer.'

'I'd love the chance to meet him again, sir. I have a score to settle with him – and I'd know what to expect next time.'

'Then we'll be happy to have you as part of the investigative team.'

Hinton was thrilled. 'Thank you, Inspector!' he said, grinning. 'I was hoping you'd say that. What's our next step?'

'That depends on Mr Lockyer's son.'

'I don't follow.'

'Now that he's back in London and has seen the body being transferred to the funeral home, he will go straight to his father's solicitor.'

'Why on earth would he do that?'

'It's because he's desperate to see his father's Last Will and Testament,' explained Colbeck. 'I'm afraid that he may be in for a profound shock.'

'What do you mean? Were father and son close?'

'Extremely close, I'd say – or so young Mr Lockyer believed.'

'And you think he'll be upset by the contents of the Will?'

'My guess is that he may be astounded,' said Colbeck. 'His father's wishes may distress young Mr Lockyer, but they could act as a valuable guide to us.'

Stephen Penhallurick was the senior partner of Penhallurick, Stacey and Greene, a firm of solicitors with offices in central London. Although he was in his early sixties, Penhallurick looked much older with flowing silver locks matching his resplendent beard. Clients had learnt to respect him and loved his soft West Country accent. It had a soothing effect on most of them, but Pelham Lockyer found it rather irritating. When he called at the firm's offices, he was shown straight into Penhallurick's room. The old man was on his feet at once.

'I'm so sorry that we meet at such a trying time,' he said, shaking the hand of his visitor then waving him to a seat. 'I need hardly tell you that I am deeply distressed at what happened to your father. He was not simply a client of ours but a close friend of mine.'

'I know,' said Lockyer, settling into his chair.

'Death is something that none of us can escape, alas, but sudden death is a different matter altogether, especially where violence is involved. Your father was fit and healthy with many years ahead of him. I pray that the police soon catch his killer.'

'I'm sure that they will. I have every faith in Inspector Colbeck.' He cleared his throat. 'I daresay that you can guess why I came here unannounced.'

'You are more than welcome, sir.'

'I wish to see the details of my father's Will.'

'Ordinarily, you would have to wait until the reading of the Will in front of family members and other benefactors. In your case, however, I believe it is right that you should have access immediately to the information you seek. To that end,' continued Penhallurick, indicating the document on his desk, 'I took the liberty of collecting this from our safe.'

'May I read it, please?'

'I thought I would take you through it in detail.'

'My father promised me that he would be leaving the major part of his worldly goods to be divided between my sister and myself. Is that not so?'

'More or less, Mr Lockyer.'

'There's a note of hesitation in your voice, Mr Penhallurick.'

'Yes . . . there is, I'm afraid.'

'Please explain,' snapped Lockyer. 'You will understand that

175

I and the rest of the family have been through a harrowing experience, made more painful because details of my father's murder appeared in the national newspapers. I have just returned from Shrewsbury and accompanied my father's body to the chapel of rest before coming on here.'

'I can understand the ordeal you must have been through.'

'Then please don't make it even more intolerable by trying to conceal something from me.'

'I would never dream of doing so, sir.'

'You're hiding something, aren't you? Please tell me what it is.'

'The bulk of your father's estate has been left to you and your sister but there is a sizeable bequest for someone else.' He picked up the document and offered it to Lockyer. 'Perhaps you would care to peruse the details.'

'I most certainly would,' said his visitor, rising to his feet.

'Before you do so,' cautioned the other, 'you should prepare yourself what may come as an unpleasant surprise.'

'Let me see for myself,' said Lockyer, snatching the Will from his hand.

'I would advise you to sit down before you read it.'

But the advice went unheard. Pelham Lockyer was so eager to read the document in its entirety that he stood there and scanned every line. It was when he reached the last page that the thunderbolt struck him. His voice became a whimper.

'Can this be true?' he asked.

Penhallurick was sympathetic. 'I fear that it is.'

When Colbeck arrived home early that evening, he was given an ecstatic welcome by his daughter, a warm embrace from his wife and a nod of satisfaction from his father-in-law. Since he had brought home a present for Helena Rose, she was delighted and ran upstairs to show it to Nanny Hopkins.

'How is the investigation going?' asked Andrews.

'We've made some progress,' said Colbeck, 'but we still have some way to go.'

'Well, I hope that you soon make an arrest so you can turn your attention to a crime nearer home. Maddy has told you that someone is copying her paintings and we've been trying to find out who this dreadful woman is.'

'Don't jump on Robert the moment he walks through the door,' chided Madeleine.

'But he might be able to help us.'

'And I'll be happy to do so,' said Colbeck. 'What's the latest development?'

'Lydia and I found another shop where the painting has been put on sale,' Madeleine told him. 'The shop is owned by a Mrs Dowling.'

'Did you ask for details of the artist?'

'Of course we did, but the woman hasn't told the owner where she lives or why she decided to copy another artist's work. She promised to come back in a week's time to see if anyone had bought her painting.'

'Then you must wait until the person who painted it turns up again at the shop.'

'Ideally, we need someone who can arrest her. I don't suppose that we could borrow Alan Hinton again, could we?'

'I'm afraid not.'

'He'd be glad to help,' insisted Andrews.

'I'm sure that he would,' said Colbeck, 'but there are two good reasons why he is not available. The first is that he will be working for me on the murder investigation.'

Madeline was disappointed. 'Oh, I see.'

'That's a pity,' sighed Andrews.

'What's the second reason?' she asked.

'Alan Hinton tried to arrest the man who is our prime suspect. Unfortunately, he failed to do so and was injured in the process.'

'Not seriously, I hope,' she cried in alarm.

'No, Madeleine, but he's very conscious about his appearance. He has a black eye and a long scratch down the side of one cheek. Until he starts to look human again, I'd rather keep him out of your way.'

Alan Hinton had come to the end of his shift and was about to leave Scotland Yard when he bumped into Detective Constable Eric Boyce, who was frowning.

'I've been thinking,' he said.

'What about, Eric?'

'That man we tried to catch.'

Hinton winced. 'Don't remind me.'

'You said that he came to let himself into the house with a key.'

'Yes, it was the one he stole from Mr Lockyer after he'd killed him.'

'But what was he expecting to find there?'

'You've seen the house,' said Hinton. 'It's full of things he could steal. There are rich pickings for anyone bold enough to get in there.'

'The man's a killer, not a burglar. I think he went there to get information of some kind. It would probably be in Mr Lockyer's desk.'

'That would be locked, surely.'

'He'd have taken the key from Mr Lockyer.'

'He wouldn't know how to open a safe without the code,' argued Hinton. 'That's where anything of real value would be kept. Mr Lockyer would have bought the very best on the market. That means the latest Chubb safe.'

'I agree.'

'What's put these thoughts into your mind, Eric?'

'He took a real chance when he tried to get into the house that night. That proves there was something inside that he was desperate to find. Luckily, we were there to stop him but that won't put him off, Alan.'

'Why not?'

'He's got nerves of steel,' said Boyce. 'He's a hired killer, remember. He'll know we won't expect him to have a second try at getting inside Mr Lockyer's house so that he can search for whatever it is that he's after. In fact,' he went on, 'I daresay he probably hung around this morning to make sure that we were leaving the area altogether.'

'That never occurred to me,' confessed Hinton.

'Do you see why I've been so worried about him, Alan?'

'Yes, I do.'

'He'll be back there soon. I feel it in my bones.'

Hinton pondered. 'You could be right,' he said eventually.

'We should be there to stop him.'

'I agree, Eric - and I'd hate to miss a second chance to drag him off in handcuffs.'

When he travelled home in a cab, Pelham Lockyer was in a state of confusion. The visit to his father's solicitor had punctured him to the core. All the certainties in his life had suddenly been violently shattered. More importantly, his unquestioning reverence for his father had been shattered. The truth was so painful that he could hardly bear it. How could he tell his wife about her father-in-law's behaviour, and how could he pass on the same searing information to his sister? Both women would be horrified to learn what sort of man Julian Lockyer had really been. In the wake of his untimely death, they had all grieved. What kind of tears would they shed if, and when, his true character was exposed?

His son's instinct was to conceal the darker side of his father's life even though that would be difficult. There was also the ordeal of the funeral to come. Pelham Lockyer wondered if he could bear to shake hands with mourners as they told him of the high regard in which they held his father. How could he listen to the tributes that poured from their lips and maintain his control? The whole event would be agonising. The very thought of it made him bring both hands up to his forehead as if trying to hold in the fears that were pounding away inside his brain. The death of his father meant that he was now the head of the family, the one who set an example, cared for the other members, helped them in every possible way and made them proud of him. It was a role that terrified him. Having patterned himself so closely on his father, he had learnt what a hideous mistake he had made.

Sitting back in the cab, he tried to shake his mind free by escaping into sleep. The steady trot of the horse was a godsend to him, lulling him into a blessed state where all his demons faded away and allowed him to slip into a deep slumber. How long he slept, he would never know. All that he would remember was the indignant voice of the driver, tugging at his sleeve.

'Wake up, sir!' yelled the man. 'You're back home.'

'What's that?' he asked, opening a drowsy eye.

'We're outside your house, sir. Might I trouble you for the fare? I wish that I could nod off when I feel tired, but it's something I can't afford to do. I've hours of work ahead of me, so I'll trouble you for the money that you owe me – if you please.'

'Yes, yes, of course . . .' said Lockyer, reaching for his wallet as he stumbled back into reality.

Alone with his wife, Colbeck held her in his arms and told her how sorry he was that one of her paintings had been copied by a stranger, hoping to sell her version of it.

'I remember that painting well,' he said. 'It was inspired by that lovely holiday we had at a farmhouse with a railway line at the end of the garden.'

'It was magical, Robert. I tried to capture some of that magic on the canvas.'

'And you did so – brilliantly.'

'It's the reason I was so hurt when I learnt that someone had copied it. I had this overwhelming desire to go in search of the artist and confront him or her.'

'I admire your bravery,' he said, 'and I'm glad that you involved Alan Hinton in the search, if only to protect you. But I still think you should have treated the crime as a matter for the police. Let trained officers do the work for you.'

'I was too impatient to do that. It touched a nerve somehow.'

'Understandably, Madeleine. It must have felt like a personal attack on you.'

'It did,' she replied, 'and I felt that this person had to be caught and punished as soon as possible. Otherwise – if she got away with it – she could copy other paintings of mine.'

'We'll find her for you.'

'In time, perhaps, but I wanted the satisfaction of seeing her face to face and telling her how much pain and fear she'd given me. Besides, Alan warned me that, if I reported the theft, the response from Scotland Yard would be slow. Far more serious crimes are taking place every day. I would have to wait in the queue.'

'That's true,' he admitted, shaking his head.

'I want to see this through to the end, Robert.'

'As long as you don't poach Detective Constable Hinton again,' he warned.

'I give you my word that we won't approach him again.'

'He's working for me now. Alan is no longer available.'

'I understand,' she accepted. 'Murder must take priority and Alan will be delighted to work with you. We'll manage on our own somehow.'

The killer took no chances. After being jumped on the previous night, he wanted to make sure that, if he paid a second visit to Julian Lockyer's house, the coast would be clear. Lurking in the bushes that morning, he had seen the two detectives quit the house opposite and drive off in a cab. Everything suggested that they would not be on duty in the area that night. It would be the time to strike. Rain began to fall, gently at first then with more purpose. He was pleased. Bad weather would keep people indoors. Nobody would be out walking that night. He could move at will.

Archibald Reeves was bent over his desk for a long time, polishing the article he had written about the murder at the Station Hotel. It was due to appear in the *Shrewsbury Chronicle* the next day and he wished to check all his facts. He had paid great tribute to Julian Lockyer but said nothing about the man's reason for being in the town on the fateful night. What had fascinated him was the way that Robert Colbeck had gathered evidence, allowing Reeves privileged insights into the investigation and drawing on the reporter's intensive knowledge of the town. When the killer was eventually caught, Reeves knew that Colbeck would thank him in person for his assistance during the earlier stages. He would be able to write an article about that as well.

Earlier that day, Alan Hinton had approached the superintendent's office with some trepidation, conscious that he had news to report. On his second visit, there was more urgency in his tread. He knocked hard on the door and – when invited in – did so with confident strides. Edward Tallis was unwelcoming.

'What do you want?' he demanded.

'Eric Boyce and I have been talking, sir.'

'I'm not interested in your tittle-tattle, man.'

'It was about last night, sir.'

'Don't remind me about that. You and Boyce failed. There's no more to be said.'

'But there is,' persisted Hinton. 'At the time, we felt that we'd frightened the killer off. Because he'd discovered the house was guarded, he would never dare to go near the place again.'

'I agree. Once bitten, twice shy.'

'We could be wrong, sir. Boyce pointed out that he may have returned to the area to see if we were still on duty there. It's even possible that he watched us leave in a cab so he could be certain that we would not leap out of the shadows again tonight. The front door key may not be of any use to him, but he stole the key to Mr Lockyer's desk as well.'

'So?'

'That might give him access to something of importance.'

'Any valuables would be locked away in a safe, surely.'

'I'm thinking about Mr Lockyer's correspondence with other members of the Great Western Railway board. When I spoke to Inspector Colbeck earlier, he told me that some members of the board must be considered as suspects. They stood to gain by his death. What if they'd fallen out with Mr Lockyer and written to tell him that they would not support his bid for the chairmanship?'

Tallis was amazed. 'All this came from Boyce?' he asked. 'I've never heard him thinking something through the way that you have just done.'

'As we all know,' said Hinton, 'he's a man of few words. But he did make me stop and think. Instead of keeping well clear of the Lockyer house, the killer has every reason to go back there and somehow get inside it. Eric Boyce is right. The man may well return tonight. For that reason, I believe that we should be back in Mr Hull's attic so that we can keep an eye on the property opposite.'

'No,' said Tallis firmly.

'Then we may let the killer slip through our fingers a second time.'

'I'd hate that to happen. I agree that Boyce has shown an intelligence I did not realise he had, and we must be grateful to him. There is, however, a better alternative.'

'Is there, sir?'

'Instead of hiding in Mr Hull's attic, you should be concealed in Mr Lockyer's house itself.' He reached for his hat. 'I'll take a cab there this instant and ask for permission to station the pair of you there. Lockyer's office is the obvious hiding place. That's where the killer will go. Two of you should be able to overpower and arrest this man. To ensure your safety, I'll issue both of you with a firearm.'

Hinton was delighted. 'Thank you, sir. I was afraid that you'd dismiss our appeal.'

'I'm not that stupid,' said Tallis pointedly. 'While I'm away, you can pass on my decision to Detective Constable Boyce. Tell him that he has done something useful for once.'

'What about young Mr Lockyer, sir? He should be made aware of our plan.'

'I agree. I'll call at his house and tell him what precautions we've taken.' He peered at Hinton's face. 'That black eye will start to fade soon.'

'I've almost forgotten that it's there,' said Hinton.

The rain was now pelting down, allowing the killer to make another visit to the house he intended to get into that night. Under a large umbrella, he was virtually invisible. He looked up at the attic of the house opposite. No light showed. Evidently, the detectives had not come back. He decided that it was time for him to return to his own home to enjoy an evening meal.

He always worked best with a full stomach.

The first thing that Pelham Lockyer did when he returned home from his visit to his father's solicitor was to pour himself a stiff drink. One glass of whisky, however, did little to still his desperation so he poured a second. It helped to focus his mind on what lay ahead. He told himself that nothing of what he had learnt must reach the ears of his sister. She and her husband would be travelling down from Scotland the next day. Having idolised her father, Henrietta would be suffering enough. Her brother resolved to keep the full truth from her for the time being.

Lockyer was still brooding when his wife, Marion, came into the room. She was a slim, dark-haired, elegant woman who was surprised to see her husband with a glass in his hand.

'You never drink spirits at this time of day,' she chided.

'I needed something to steady myself,' he said.

'Are you feeling unwell, Pelham?'

'No – just utterly confused.'

'But you have always been able to cope with emergencies.'

'This is rather more than an emergency, Marion.'

'Yes, I know. It's changed our family life forever. Your father seemed so indestructible. I thought that he would live until he was a hundred years old.'

'Sadly,' said her husband, 'he died well short of that age.'

'I still can't believe that he is no longer here. He was so full of life.'

'Indeed, he was – an example to us all.'

'I've had the guest room prepared for your sister and her husband,' she told him. 'Everything will be ready for them. Henrietta will be like us – still reeling from the shock.'

'We must comfort her and Angus as best we can.'

'I'll do my best, Pelham.'

'You always do,' he said, taking her hand with a sudden fondness. 'I couldn't have got through the horrors of this week without you.'

'I know my duty.'

'You're always there and it's my one source of comfort.'

She studied his face. 'Do you feel unwell?'

'I'm in a daze, that's all.'

'You seem so different since you came back from Mr Penhallurick.'

'Mr Penhallurick reminded me of all the things I need to do – not least, making the arrangements for the funeral. It's going to be a hectic time for a while, alas.'

'We'll manage somehow.'

'I hope so.'

He fell silent and seemed to have gone off into a trance. All that she could do was to stand there and wait patiently. Then he began to grind his teeth, and his eyes started to glare. His hand gripped hers so tightly that it made her scream in pain.

'What happened?' he asked, releasing her at once.

'You hurt me, Pelham,' she complained, 'and you've never done that before.'

CHAPTER THIRTEEN

The letter was delivered by hand to the Colbeck residence. It was brought into the drawing room by the maidservant who had picked it up in the hall. She handed it to Colbeck then withdrew. Seated opposite him, Madeleine and her father watched him open and read it.

'Is it anything of importance?' asked his wife.

'Yes, it is,' he replied. 'Superintendent Tallis wanted me to know that he is putting two detectives into Mr Lockyer's home in the hope that they can catch the man who tried to get into the property last night.'

'How do they know that the intruder will return?'

'They don't. They're acting on instinct. Since I am leading the investigation, Tallis insisted that I should know what was happening.'

'Is Alan Hinton one of the detectives?' asked Madeleine.

'He is – along with Detective Constable Boyce.'

'Then why didn't they arrest this man when they had the chance last night?' asked Andrews.

'They tried and failed. I daresay that Hinton's already shrugged off what happened yesterday,' said Colbeck. 'My guess is that the superintendent will have gone first to young Mr Lockyer to get his permission to station detectives inside his father's house. Understandably, the son did ask to be kept informed of every stage in the investigation.'

'Quite right, too,' put in Andrews.

'Alan is not in danger, is he?' asked Madeleine anxiously.

'No, my love,' replied Colbeck. 'Hinton and Boyce have two advantages over this man. They will be concealed where he least expects them to be, and they have been issued with firearms.'

'That's a relief.'

'I'm sorry that I can't be involved myself. If this man really is the person who killed Julian Lockyer, I'd love to be there to make the arrest.'

'You'd be better off eating dinner with us,' suggested Andrews.

'Robert thrives on action, Father,' Madeleine pointed out.

'Then he ought to be in that shop where the fake copy of your painting is on sale, Maddy. In my opinion, the woman pretending to be you should serve a life sentence in prison.'

'That's far too harsh a penalty,' said Colbeck reasonably.

'Not in my book.'

'Father!' exclaimed Madeleine.

'I can see the effect it had on you, Maddy. It really hurt you.'

'It's true – but much worse crimes have been committed.'

'That's right,' said Colbeck. 'It's a question of degree. Murder must always carry a heavier penalty than theft. The person Hinton and Boyce are hoping to arrest tonight is a ruthless killer. He needs to pay for his crime – and so does the man who hired him.'

Pelham Lockyer was surprised when Edward Tallis turned up unexpectedly on his doorstep. The sudden appearance of the superintendent jerked Lockyer out of his preoccupation with the contents of his father's Will. He not only gave his permission for the detectives to be concealed in his father's house, but Lockyer also went there in person to suggest possible hiding places. Before he left, he impressed upon the staff the importance of keeping to their own rooms that night with the doors locked.

'Your mother has already retired to bed,' one of the servants told him.

'That's a relief,' he said. 'If anyone does come here at night, she will be fast asleep.'

Before he had left the house, Lockyer had a last word with the detectives.

'Remember what this man did to my father,' he reminded them.

'Yes, sir,' said Hinton.

'Show no mercy. If he tries to escape – shoot to kill.'

'Leave it to us, Mr Lockyer.'

'Oh,' said the other, 'one last thing.'

'What is it, sir?' asked Boyce.

'Good luck to both of you!'

At the Station Hotel in Shrewsbury that night, the bar was full, and the conversation largely confined to the murder that had occurred there earlier in the week. Seated in her office, Molly Burrage was alone with stationmaster and beginning to lose heart.

'Why have we heard nothing from Inspector Colbeck?' she wailed.

'It's because he's too busy searching for the killer,' replied Biddle.

'I hoped that he'd make an arrest here in the town.'

'This murder took place in Shrewsbury, but it was hatched in London. That's where the man who wanted Mr Lockyer killed lives – and so does the assassin himself.'

'Do you think they'll ever be caught, Simon?'

'Of course they will.'

'How can you be so sure?'

'I trust Inspector Colbeck.'

'That's more than our police do,' she pointed out. 'Inspector Crabbe was in here this afternoon. He told me that the trail has gone cold. The murder will never be solved.'

'Crabbe can't bear the thought of someone else arresting the killer.'

'What if the killer is never caught?'

'Keep faith, Molly!' he urged. 'It's not like you to be so downhearted.'

'The murder is hanging over my hotel like a big, black cloud.'

'Better weather is on its way.' He raised his glass. 'Let's drink to it.'

'Yes,' she agreed, brightening, 'let's do just that.' They clinked glasses then sipped their drinks. 'Thank you, Simon. You always know how to cheer me up.'

His eyes twinkled. 'I know other ways of doing that.'

Laughing aloud, she slapped his hand by way of reproach.

* * *

He came on horseback this time so that he could make a hasty exit from the house. Dismounting nearby, he tethered the animal to a tree and walked stealthily through the undergrowth. Having been surprised during his earlier visit, he checked the area around the house to make sure that nobody was on guard. Everything seemed to be in his favour. The rain had stopped but thick clouds remained to block out the light of the moon. The occupants of the house would be deeply asleep. Curtains were drawn in every room. It was time to move in.

He had already decided on the best way to get into the house. There was a storeroom at the back with a window just large enough for him to get through. He had brought a small hammer to give the window a sharp tap to break the glass. After removing the shards with great care, he put them down on the lawn. It was the work of moments for him to climb through the empty gap and lower himself to the floor of the room. Taking no chances, he listened carefully for any sound in the house. To his relief, he heard nothing. No door was opening; no voices were raised. It was time to make his way to the study.

His paymaster had been thorough. He had not only described the interior of the ground floor in great detail, he'd provided a plan of it with arrows to mark the route to the study. In less than a minute from climbing into the house, the interloper could be letting himself into the room he was after. It brought a smile of pleasure to his face.

The detectives, meanwhile, were waiting for him. They had heard the distant tinkle of breaking glass and realised that someone might have broken into the house. Unfinished business had clearly brought the killer back. Hinton and Boyce were poised for action.

The former was standing behind the door while the latter was crouched behind the desk. Between them, they felt, they could surely overpower the man. They listened intently for the approach of the intruder, but no sound came. The man was clearly moving with extreme care. Hearing the doorknob being gently twisted, they tensed for action. Their moment had come.

Maddeningly, they were unable to take advantage of it. With the door half open, the intruder was alerted by a sixth sense. He felt that he was walking into a trap. He responded immediately, pushing open the door with such force that he knocked Hinton backwards. Boyce, meanwhile, took time to get up from behind the desk. The detectives were far too slow to react. The intruder had already taken to his heels, returning to the storeroom and locking the door before clambering headfirst through the gaping window onto the lawn outside.

By the time Hinton and Boyce had broken into the room, they realised that the man had escaped. The sound of galloping hooves meant that he had ridden safely away and made the notion of pursuing him unthinkable. The detectives had failed for the second time. Later that morning, they would both have to face the ire of Superintendent Tallis. The very idea made their blood curdle.

Since he liked to be at his desk in Scotland Yard first thing, Colbeck had an early breakfast with his wife. He could see that Madeleine was uncharacteristically quiet. She ate her meal in comparative silence. Her husband looked up at her.

'Is there something on your mind, my love?' he asked.

'No, not really,' she murmured.

'Then why aren't you chattering away as usual?'

'I've been thinking, Robert.'

'It's about this woman who copied your painting, isn't it?'

'Yes, it is. I keep wondering what possessed her to do such a thing,' she said. 'Father thinks that it's a terrible crime and that she should be hanged, drawn and quartered.'

Colbeck laughed. 'Fortunately, such a punishment no longer exists,' he said. 'Your father always jumps to extremes.'

'I'm beginning to feel sorry for the woman.'

'Why?'

'We're treating her as a criminal.'

'Technically, that's what she is. The woman copied one of your paintings and tried to pass it off as her own work. You have every right to be outraged.'

'I was outraged – at first. But I've been thinking about the effort that must have gone into her work on that painting. She got most of the details right. I'm wondering if she has the urge to be a real artist but not the imagination to conjure up the scene she wishes to paint.'

'Stop making excuses for her.'

'I mean, it's not as if she's copied a famous painting by Titian or Rembrandt. She picked out something of mine instead.'

'Yes, my love, she did,' said Colbeck. 'If she tried to copy one of the Old Masters, it would have been spotted as a fake instantly and she would have been arrested at once. She deliberately chose an artist like yourself who is less famous so the fact that it's a copy would not be noticed.'

'Lydia noticed it,' she reminded him. 'So did I and so did my father. At first glance, it even fooled me. I was throbbing with anger.'

'You had every right to be, Madeleine.'

'Then why do I feel sorry for this woman?'

'I've no idea.'

'I want her caught and punished and yet . . . well, I try to put myself in her position. When I first started painting, I made all sorts of elementary mistakes. Failure spurred me on. It was only by sticking at it that I slowly improved until I reached the point where my work was good enough to be put on sale at the Red Gallery.'

'I remember how thrilled you were when you sold your first painting.'

'I was over the moon, Robert.'

'Since then, you've got better and better.'

'It's all due to you,' she remembered. 'You supported me and paid for me to have lessons from a real artist. I learnt so much from him about the craft.'

'It's evident in all your work, my love.'

'That woman wants to emulate me.'

'Then she must come up with ideas of her own,' said Colbeck. 'I have no pity whatsoever for her. Put simply, she's a common thief and must be arrested.'

'Why did she choose a painting of mine?'

'That's the first question I'll put to her.'

As they headed for the superintendent's office, they consoled themselves with the thought that they had, after all, been right. The suspect had indeed returned during the night and gained entry to the house. Eric Boyce's instinct had been sound. Hinton was ready to give him full credit for insisting that they ought to be inside the house to make an arrest. When they reached the office, however, they knew that they would get no reward for what was, in essence, a failure. As he tapped on the door, Hinton felt like a naughty schoolboy about to face a merciless headmaster.

'Come in!' yelled Tallis.

'Good morning, sir,' said Hinton, opening the door and leading the way in.

'Yes,' added Boyce. 'Good morning, sir.'

'I was hoping for good news,' said Tallis, looking from one to the other, 'but I can see that I did so in vain. What happened?'

The detectives exchanged a glance.

'Well? Speak up, one of you.'

'I'm sorry to report that we were unlucky,' confessed Hinton.

Tallis frowned. 'The suspect didn't turn up?'

'He turned up,' explained Boyce, 'and broke the window of a storeroom to climb into the house. We were in the study, waiting for him.'

'Then why didn't you make an arrest?'

'He sensed danger, sir. After opening the door, he somehow guessed that a trap had been set for him, so he ran quickly back to the storeroom.'

'Didn't you chase him?'

'Of course,' said Hinton, 'but he locked the door of the room. By the time we forced our way in, he had jumped out through the window.'

'Then why the devil didn't you run after him?'

'He had a horse tethered nearby, sir. We heard him galloping away. However,' Hinton pointed out, 'Detective Constable Boyce deserves credit for suggesting that the man would make a second attempt to get into the house.'

Tallis was unimpressed. 'Neither of you deserves one iota of credit,' he snapped. 'I was expecting more of you, I must say. Two armed detectives were in the perfect position to catch the suspect, and you failed abysmally.'

'The man sensed danger, sir,' said Hinton. 'He took no chances and bolted.'

'It does mean that he may return,' argued Boyce. 'There's something of importance in that study that he is desperately keen to steal. What exactly is it, sir?'

'I wish I knew,' said Tallis. 'If you'd caught him, we might have learnt who was paying him and what he was ordered to steal.' He remembered something. 'It was Mr Lockyer's son who gave you permission to hide in his father's house. He deserves to be told that the plan was a failure.'

'Would you like me to explain to him what happened?' volunteered Hinton.

'No, I don't. This is a task for Inspector Colbeck.'

'Is there any particular reason?'

'Yes – unlike you, he doesn't have a black eye and a distinct whiff of failure.'

Colonel Edgell was in his office with Inspector Crabbe, going through the details of their investigation with a fine-toothed comb. Crabbe sounded a defensive note.

'We did everything that needed to be done, sir,' he claimed.

'Then why is there no positive sign of progress?'

'I sense that we are on the verge of a breakthrough.'

'You can't do that by staying here in Shrewsbury,' argued the chief constable. 'I think that you should be in Scotland Yard, demanding to be given the latest information regarding the crime. In fact, I would go so far as to say that—' Edgell broke off as he heard a loud knock on the door. It opened to reveal a uniformed constable, who handed a newspaper to him then left the office.

'That must be this week's *Chronicle*,' said Crabbe.

'It is, indeed – and I don't think it will bring us any cheer.'

'We've worked hard on this investigation.'

'Yes,' said Edgell, reading the front page, 'but we are no nearer catching the killer.'

'That was partly because Inspector Colbeck got in our way.'

'He's back in London, searching for the man. Let's see what Reeves has to say,' he went on, flicking through the pages. 'Ah, here we are. The title of his article is *The Mystery Thickens*.'

'Does he mention us by name?' asked Crabbe.

'Oh, yes,' replied Edgell, starting to read the article. 'He accuses us of moving too slowly and too ineffectively. Any praise is reserved for Colbeck. Reeves is wickedly accurate.' He tossed the newspaper aside. 'You can never trust reporters. When I fought in India, I recognised the enemy at once by their appearance and fought against them accordingly. It's different with reporters. Just when you think that they're on your side, they snipe at you when you least expect it. The *Chronicle* should be supporting the local police, not denigrating us like this.'

'You should exercise your right of reply, sir.'

'Oh, I will,' promised Edgell. 'I'm not letting Reeves attack us like this without returning fire. It's time he realised that he owes us respect.'

Robert Colbeck was puzzled. When he called at the home of Pelham Lockyer, he expected a friendly welcome. Instead of that, he was given the impression that he was intruding. Shown into the drawing room, he sat opposite Lockyer and wondered why the man would not meet his gaze.

'Superintendent Tallis asked me to give you a report of what happened last night at your father's house,' said Colbeck.

'I already know,' said Lockyer crisply. 'When I called there first thing this morning, they told me that an intruder had got into the house but that your officers failed to arrest him.'

'I am sorry about that, sir.'

'Not as much as I am.'

'The man was too experienced to walk into a trap,' explained Colbeck. 'The moment he sensed danger, he fled on horseback. It was impossible to chase him.'

'It's the second time that your officers blundered.'

'I apologise for that.'

'Outside and inside the house, they let the man get away.'

'Detective Constable Hinton did inflict some bruises on him the first night, but he came off worse in the struggle. It's to his credit that he was ready to tackle the suspect a second time.'

'He let my father's killer escape again,' said Lockyer coldly.

'We are as disappointed as you are, sir. Try to look at it from the point of view of the suspect. We believe that he was paid to kill your father. Whoever hired him wanted something else as well, something that was probably locked in the desk in your father's study. As you know,' said Colbeck, 'the killer had stolen the key to that desk. What was in it that he was ordered to steal?'

'I've no idea,' said Lockyer dismissively.

'I find that difficult to believe, sir.'

'Then we must agree to differ, Inspector.'

'You and your father were so close. You must have been in that study a hundred or more times. Surely, you have some idea what he kept locked away in it. Clearly, it was something he wanted to treasure.'

'That's idle speculation.'

'Then perhaps you will explain why an intruder came to the house on two consecutive nights to steal a particular item. He took an enormous risk on both occasions. Why?'

'You're the detective,' said Lockyer.

Colbeck sat back in his chair and studied him for a full minute before speaking.

'Mr Lockyer,' he said, 'you have my deepest sympathy. You've suffered a dreadful loss. When you came to Shrewsbury, you wanted to know all the details of the investigation. Something has now changed. Your attitude towards me is very strange. Instead of helping me, you are doing just the opposite. It's almost as if you're trying to obstruct me.'

'I resent that accusation,' snapped Lockyer.

'Please look me in the eye and answer my questions.'

'I've told you all that I can.'

'Then why do I feel that you are holding something back?'

Lockyer took a deep breath before speaking. 'I am sorry if you believe that, Inspector. The full impact of my father's murder has now hit me. It's devastating and makes me unable to think straight. I'm sorry if you find me evasive. I promise you that I've given you honest answers to your questions.'

'Then there's no more to be said, sir.' Colbeck rose to his feet and looked him in the eye. He was met by a steely gaze.

When she called at the house that morning, Lydia Quayle was told by the maidservant who opened the door that Madeleine was at work in her studio but had asked that the visitor should be sent up there. Glad of the invitation, Lydia trotted upstairs and found the door of the studio open.

Madeleine was holding a palette in one hand and a brush in the other.

'When I heard the doorbell clang,' she said, 'I hoped that it would be you.'

'I hadn't realised that you'd be working up here.'

'I'm just putting the finishing touches to a painting.'

'May I see it?' asked Lydia.

'Yes, please. I'd value your opinion.'

Madeleine stepped back to allow her friend into the room. Resting on the easel was a painting of a steam locomotive emerging at speed from a tunnel. Lydia looked at it approvingly.

'That's wonderful, Madeleine!'

'Do you really think so?'

'Yes, I do. There's a marvellous sense of power as the train escapes the darkness of the tunnel, and the engine itself is so realistic.'

'It's one that my father used to drive. He once sneaked me onto the footplate. I was intrigued.'

'That's what makes you so individual, Madeleine. If I'd seen this painting in the window of an art dealer, I'd have assumed that it had been painted by a male artist. Yet it's the work of a very gifted woman.'

'Railways are in my blood, Lydia. Mind you, they were often in my nostrils as well,' she recalled. 'Whenever my father came home from work, I could smell the stench of smoke he brought into the house. His clothing reeked of it.'

'He is going to love this painting.'

'I hope so. He can be a fierce critic.'

'You're a railway artist par excellence.'

'Don't be silly,' said Madeleine. 'I can't compete with people like Mr Frith. He's a genius. When I first saw his painting called *The Railway Station*, I stared at it in wonder for ages. It's swirling with people. So much is happening. And in the top right-hand corner, there's a detective making an arrest. The figure reminds me so much of Robert.'

'I'd prefer a painting by Madeleine Colbeck any day.'

Madeleine laughed. 'Don't be silly, Lydia.'

Danger was his element. He lived for its challenge and its excitement. Whether he was committing a murder or climbing into another man's house at night, there was a sense of satisfaction that he could not get elsewhere. As he stood outside the front door of the house, it took him minutes to find the courage to ring the bell.

A manservant let him in and took him to the study. As he entered, he saw the warning scowl on the face of the bearded man seated at the desk. Explanation was unnecessary. His paymaster already knew what had happened.

'Last time I came here, you opened the safe and held a gun on me.' He folded his arms. 'You can't reach it now, can you?'

'I don't need to,' said the older man, opening a drawer and taking out the weapon. 'It's right here in my hand. And if you dare to threaten me again, I'll pull the trigger.'

'You can't do that!' said the other, backing away in fear.

'Then remember that you're my creature. I own you. That means you do everything I say at a time of my choosing.'

'Yes, yes, of course you do, sir.'

'And you only get paid for success.'

The visitor gestured an apology. 'I realise that now.'

'Then don't forget it. I'm a successful businessman whereas you have just crawled out of the sewer that is your natural home. When I needed someone to follow and kill a man I loathed, I paid you handsomely and you deserved your money. Since then, you've been of no use to me.'

'Give me one more chance, sir,' pleaded the man.

'Instead of solving a problem for me, you've become one yourself.'

'Let me have another go at getting into Mr Lockyer's house.'

'You'd only fail once again.'

'No, I wouldn't. I swear to you that I'll get what you want. I'll strike when they least expect it – and there'll be no detectives on guard inside the house next time.'

'Why should I ever trust you again?'

'It's because we're partners,' insisted the man. 'Yes, you're a rich man and look down on me as a piece of slime, but I know who and what you really are. You need me to do your dirty work – and there'll always be a lot of that in your life. One more thing – I can be trusted to keep my mouth shut.'

'That's true,' conceded the other.

'Why don't you put that gun down so that we can talk properly? We're two of a kind, sir,' he went on. 'We know how to get what we want – however risky it may be. Because you asked me to do something dangerous, we're forever joined together. You have obligations towards me. We're friends, sir,' he said, manufacturing a smile. 'Let's work together, shall we?'

After studying him carefully, the older man slowly lowered his gun.

* * *

When he had listened to the report, Edward Tallis was as mystified as Colbeck. The two men were in the superintendent's office. Colbeck had just described Pelham Lockyer's behaviour.

'What's brought about this sudden change?' asked Tallis.

'I don't know, sir. When we met in Shrewsbury, he was eager to talk to me about his father. Today, he was evasive and – dare I say it? – telling me patent lies.'

'Why has he done that?'

'Something has happened,' said Colbeck. 'Since he got back home, he's perhaps learnt something that shows his father in a very different light. In the past, he worshipped the man. Now, I suspect, he's far less ready to regard him as an icon.'

'Why did he feel the need to deceive you?'

'I hope to find out, sir.'

'Perhaps I should speak to him next time,' said Tallis.

'No, no, I think that I'm better placed to discuss the case with him, sir. I know him better than you do. That's why, in a matter of seconds, I was aware of his change of mood.'

'In a word, how could you describe his manner?'

'Embarrassment.'

'Was he in mourning wear?'

'Yes, he was.'

'Yet you saw no hint that he was actually mourning his father.'

'None at all,' replied Colbeck. 'He seemed ill at ease as a grieving son. His behaviour was most surprising. I couldn't decide why.'

'Have you had time to think about the meeting with him?'

'Yes, I have, sir.'

'And?'

'I believe that he has had a nasty shock – something that made him question his earlier veneration of his father. He is, after all, the only son and likely to inherit the bulk of his father's wealth. But there was no sense that he had grown into his new role. If anything, he seemed a trifle overwhelmed by it.'

'Where does it leave us?' asked Tallis worriedly.

'We're worse off, sir. Pelham Lockyer is our major source of information about the murder victim. Without his cooperation, we'll struggle to get a three-dimensional view of his father.'

'What the devil is he hiding?'

'We may never find out.'

'But we must – or valuable evidence will slip through our fingers.'

'I agree, sir,' said Colbeck. 'But I do feel sorry for the man.'

'Why?'

'He looked so dazed. Having started to recover from the shock of his father's murder, he sounded as if his mind was elsewhere.'

'Clearly, it was, if he was unable to talk to you properly.'

'He was a different man altogether – uneasy in my company and anxious to get rid of me as soon as possible.'

'How strange!'

'It's worse than that, sir,' decided Colbeck. 'Instead of helping us, he's now turned his back on the investigation. That suggests to me that he may have discovered something that might – in our hands – turn out to be valuable evidence. In short, he doesn't want the full truth about his father to become common knowledge and is therefore ending his cooperation with us.'

Tallis was exasperated. 'Doesn't he want us to solve the murder?'

'I'm not sure that he does – and we need to find out why.'

CHAPTER FOURTEEN

When the doorbell rang, Pelham Lockyer did not even hear it.
He was so overwhelmed by the problems confronting him that
he could think of nothing else. There was a knock on the door
of the drawing room, making him look up in surprise as the
door opened and a servant led in Christopher Prance, a dignified
old man with a face clouded by grief. Lockyer rose at once to
shake his hand then indicated a chair. His visitor lowered himself
carefully into it. The servant left the room and closed the door
behind him.

'How are you, Pelham?' asked the visitor.

'I'm still in a daze,' confessed the other. 'It's so confusing. The
last time I saw my father alive, he told me that he was going to
spend the night with a friend in Kent.'

'He told me the same thing.'

'Then he lied to both of us.'

'That was so unlike Julian. He was endearingly honest. It's one of the reasons we became such close friends.'

'He drew great strength from your friendship, Mr Prance. Father was so grateful when you championed his bid to become the next chairman of the GWR.'

'He was the obvious man to take over. I was happy to support him.'

'Thank you.'

'I take it that you have been in touch with your sister,' said Prance.

'Yes, of course. Henrietta is travelling down from Scotland with her husband today.'

'This dreadful news must have come as a terrible blow.'

'It's shaken both of us.'

'Your father loved his children. He was justly proud of both of you.'

'Yes, he was,' murmured Lockyer. 'He was a family man in every sense.'

'May I ask how the investigation into his murder is proceeding?'

'To be honest, I'd rather forgotten about that. There's so much for me to do that I've had no time to discuss matters with Inspector Colbeck. When I met him, he impressed me very much. I'm sure that he is busy leading the search for the man who . . .' He turned away to control his emotions. When he faced his visitor again, he was apologetic. 'I'm sorry, Mr Prance. I find it very difficult to talk about what happened.'

'I understand,' said Prance softly. 'I simply called to express my sympathy and to tell you that if there is anything I can do – anything at all – please don't hesitate to call on me. I realise that you must be under intense pressure. If I can ease it somehow, you know where to reach me.'

'Thank you. I appreciate your offer.'

'Julian – your father was like a brother to me. We went into business together and, in due course, we invested in the railway system. It was wonderful to have someone in my life on whom I could rely. Such people are very rare. However,' he went on, struggling out of his chair, 'I'll detain you no longer. I know that you must have a thousand things to do.'

'It was good of you to call, Mr Prance.'

'Don't forget my offer of help.'

'I won't, I promise you,' said Lockyer, rising from his chair.

'One last thing . . .'

'Yes?'

'We were both misled,' said Prance sadly. 'Your father told each of us that he was going to Kent for the night.'

'Have you any idea what took him to Shrewsbury instead?'

'No, I don't,' lied Lockyer. 'It remains a mystery to me.'

It was not until they reached the station that Victor Leeming managed to ask a question. Having been whisked into a cab, he and Colbeck had been driven there at speed. The inspector led the way to the ticket office and bought two tickets to Shrewsbury.

'Why are we going there again?' asked Leeming.

'I think that we missed something.'

'What is it?'

'I won't know until we find it,' said Colbeck. 'In any case, it will be good to see the stationmaster again. I need to thank him for a favour he did.'

'What do you mean, sir?'

'Well, if you remember, Archie Reeves promised to send me a copy of the *Shrewsbury Chronicle*. It's published today. I sent a telegraph to Mr Biddle, asking him to send word to the reporter that I will be able to pick up a copy in person so he can forget my request.'

'I'd never have thought of doing that,' admitted Leeming.

'It pays to look ahead, Victor.'

'What about Colonel Edgell? Are we going to be seeing him?'

'Oh, yes. He deserves to know how the investigation is going.'

Leeming grinned. 'Will you pass on the superintendent's best wishes?'

'No,' said Colbeck firmly, 'and you know why not. They loathe each other.'

'I'd pay to see the pair of them in a boxing ring, punching away.'

'It will never happen, Victor.'

'Pity!'

They walked to the platform and waited for their train to arrive. Leeming was curious.

'What about this business with one of your wife's paintings?' he asked.

'I've had to leave Madeleine to cope with that. She won't give up until she finds the woman who dared to copy her work.'

'Why would anyone do such a thing?'

'It was because the woman thought that she could get away with it. Purely by chance, Lydia Quayle spotted the fake copy in a shop window in Soho. It's now turned up in a different shop – at a lower price. Apparently, this other so-called artist is not simply trying to make money.'

'Then why go to all the trouble of copying someone else's work?'

'We'll have to wait and see, Victor. Meanwhile, we have a few mysteries of our own to solve.'

Pelham Lockyer was also in a railway station, waiting for his sister to arrive after the long journey from Scotland. Though she was a redoubtable woman, Henrietta would have been badly shaken by the dreadful news and would want every detail that her brother could provide. He resolved that he would only give her the bare outline, saying nothing about what he had learnt when studying their father's Will. Henrietta would know the hideous truth in due course. As a caring brother, it was his job to protect her from learning it too soon when her spirits would be at their lowest and her defences at their weakest.

Colonel Edgell was alone in his study, reading once again the article written by Archibald Reeves about the failings of the local police force during the murder investigation. He was honest enough to concede that mistakes had been made, but he was irritated by the way that he and his men were portrayed. Readers of the *Chronicle* would start to lose faith in their police, and he hated the idea. Scrunching the newspaper up, he tossed it into the wastepaper basket.

There was a knock on the door then it opened to reveal a uniformed policeman.

'What do you want?' asked Edgell.

'Inspector Colbeck is asking to see you, sir.'

'Damn the fellow! I thought he was in London.' He inhaled deeply. 'Oh, very well.' He flicked a hand. 'Show him in, please.'

The officer disappeared and returned seconds later with Colbeck in tow. The chief constable rose to his feet to extend his hand. Colbeck was given a brisk handshake. He was offered a chair and sat opposite Edgell, who resumed his own seat.

'What brings you back here, Inspector?' asked Edgell.

'What else but an unsolved murder?'

'Yet you believed the killer was not a local man but a Londoner.'

'That's still my opinion,' said Colbeck. 'He used the name of Jack Brown as an alias. When we arrest him, I will tell you what his real name is.'

'Are you close to making an arrest?'

'We are very close, Colonel. My detectives have already had a brush with him and discovered that he fights like a demon. While they continue the search, they are each carrying a firearm.'

'A wise precaution.'

'I know what he did to the murder victim. Evidently, he'll stop at nothing.'

'Inspector Crabbe spoke to the manager of the hotel where this man stayed overnight. The manager described "Jack Brown" as being decidedly unpleasant and was very glad when he left. I look forward to seeing this villain in handcuffs.'

'As, indeed, am I. However, I'm more interested in the name of the man who hired him in the first place. He is at the root of this crime. Who is he and why did his hatred of Julian Lockyer spur him on to find someone to kill the man?'

'Have you spoken to the son since you returned to London?'

'Yes, I have.'

'Couldn't he furnish you with a list of his father's enemies?'

'He still refuses to accept that such people exist.'

'Then he's in for a profound shock.'

'I suspect that he has already had it,' said Colbeck, recalling his conversation with Pelham Lockyer. 'He seems chastened.' He glanced at the wastepaper basket. 'Is that, by chance, a copy of the *Shrewsbury Chronicle*?'

'Yes, it is,' said Edgell angrily. 'It's shown us in a rather unflattering light.'

'Police never get the respect they deserve, Colonel.'

'That's little consolation.'

'I found Archie Reeves a very gifted and conscientious young man.'

'You missed out the streak of venom with which he writes.'

'Is his article that offensive?'

'It's downright objectionable,' said Edgell. 'The very least we hope for is a degree of respect. There's no sign of it in that article by Reeves. He dares to mocks us.'

When he had read the first paragraph in the article, Victor Leeming burst into laughter.

'This is wonderful, Archie. You've got a real gift for words.'

'I had to be careful,' said Reeves. 'There's such a thing as libel.'

'I just wish I could write like this.'

They were in the offices of the *Shrewsbury Chronicle* and Leeming was seated beside the reporter at his desk. The sergeant had just read the beginning of Reeves's article about the murder at the Station Hotel. He turned to the reporter.

'Inspector Colbeck wanted to save you the trouble of sending it.'

'The telegraph arrived just in time,' said Reeves. 'The stationmaster sent one of his porters here with the message. Three cheers for the man who invented the telegraph system!'

'Yes,' agreed Leeming. 'If it didn't exist, the stationmaster wouldn't have been able to send the telegraph that led to our arrival here. We'd have been completely unaware that a murder had taken place, and that the victim was a man linked to the GWR.'

'Did you ever find out what he was doing in the town?'

'Not really – it's one of the things that brought us back here.'

'How is Mr Lockyer's son faring?'

'Not very well, I'm afraid. I think that the full impact of what happened has finally struck home. When Inspector Colbeck spoke to him, the son behaved very strangely.'

'That often happens in the wake of a sudden death. The sense of loss blocks out everything else. I sympathise with the son. It must be horrible to discover that a father you love is murdered on the orders of someone who hates him.'

'All we need to do is to catch the killer,' said Leeming, 'and he will lead us to the person who paid the money for the execution. We won't rest until that happens.'

When the train eventually thundered into the station, Pelham Lockyer walked towards the first-class carriages, knowing that Henrietta would have travelled in one of them. She was one of the first passengers to emerge. Seeing her brother, she ran towards him and flung herself into his arms. Lockyer did his best to calm her down. When Henrietta's husband joined them, he complained bitterly about the slowness of the train. There was no word of sympathy from the burly Scotsman about the murder of Julian Lockyer. After shaking hands with his brother-in-law, Lockyer pointed towards the exit.

'I've got a carriage waiting outside. Let's get away from this pandemonium, shall we?'

Having been to the police station, Colbeck paid a courtesy visit to the Station Hotel to assure its owner that the search for the killer was continuing in London.

'My detectives have already had two encounters with him,' explained Colbeck, 'so he knows that we are on his tail.'

'I won't sleep properly until I hear that you've arrested him,' said Molly. 'I haven't been into the room where it happened for days. It brings back horrible memories.'

'Understandably.'

'But I have some news for you, Inspector. I spoke to Mrs Denning.'

'Who is this lady?'

'She has a house that overlooks the rear of the hotel. We don't get on, I'm afraid. In fact, we haven't spoken to each other for years – but she came here with some information for me.'

'What was it?'

'On the day of the murder, Mrs Denning looked out of her window and saw a man at the rear of the hotel. He was staring up at the rooms above. When she described him, I realised it must have been the person who stayed at a hotel across the road so that he could keep an eye on us.'

'He used the name of Jack Brown while he was there.'

'Mrs Denning didn't know that. What she did tell me was that he looked as if he was up to no good. She said that she was sorry she hadn't warned me at the time, but since we'd fallen out, she kept well clear of me.'

'What changed her mind?'

'Everyone was talking about what happened that night. Mrs Denning felt that it was silly not to tell me what she saw, so she turned up on my doorstep. Seeing how upset I still was, she threw her arms around me.'

'That's how neighbours should behave, Mrs Burrage.'

'Anyway, we're friends again now. We had a cup of tea together.'

'I'm glad that you gained something good from that dreadful night.'

'That's what Simon – Mr Biddle, the stationmaster – said to me.'

'He's been very helpful to us,' said Colbeck.

'He's certain you'll catch the killer before too long.'

'It may take time, I'm afraid. He's now very conscious of the fact that we're searching for him so he will be very careful. But we'll get him eventually.'

'When it happens, I'll start to sleep properly.'

'You could also reopen the room where Mr Lockyer stayed.'

'It might take some time before I do that,' she said, frowning. 'To be honest, I still shudder whenever I walk past it. Mrs Denning told me that I ought to wait a few weeks and then open it to customers. Somehow, she managed to cheer me up. I'm so glad we're friends again.' She chuckled. 'The funny thing is that I can't remember why we fell out in the first place.'

When they reached Pelham Lockyer's house, a servant came out to carry the luggage indoors. Lockyer's wife, Marion, also appeared to welcome her sister-in-law and husband to London. The exchange of platitudes did not last long before the carriage was driven the short distance to the home of the late Julian Lockyer. After looking at the house in which she had been born and brought up, Henrietta had to use a handkerchief to stem her tears. Her brother had a warning for her.

'Mother will not even recognise you, Henrietta.'

'But she must, surely.'

'Since your last visit, she has become even more confused.'

'What does her doctor advise?'

'Mother is beyond the reach of medicine. The best that we can do is to offer her love and understanding. Her mind wanders alarmingly at times.'

'Oh dear! Does Mother know that . . . ?'

'There was no point in telling her that Father had died. It would only have confused her. You wish to see her, of course, but make allowances, please.'

'I will, Pelham.'

A servant had already opened the front door and stood waiting for them. As they entered the house, he explained that their mother was in the garden.

'The doctor advised that she have as much fresh air as possible,' said Lockyer.

He led the way through the house and into the garden. Seated in her chair, his mother was singing quietly to herself. Her son bent over her to kiss her gently on the cheek.

'I've brought Henrietta to see you, Mother.'

'Who?' she croaked.

'I'm your daughter,' said Henrietta, moving forward to kiss her mother and to beam at her. 'You remember me, don't you?'

'I've never seen you before,' said the old lady.

'Pelham and I were born here.'

Her mother was bewildered. 'Who is she talking about?'

'We just came to see how you were,' explained Pelham.

'And to say how much we've missed you,' added Henrietta. 'My husband and I have come all the way from Scotland to be with you. I must say that you look wonderful. How are you?'

The question seemed to upset her mother. Instead of welcoming her daughter, she drew back and turned her face away. Henrietta tried to embrace her, but she was prevented from doing so by her brother. He led his sister gently into the house. Their visit was over.

After the stench and clamour of London, Colbeck was glad to be back in Shrewsbury. When he left Molly Burrage, he walked to the offices of the *Shrewsbury Chronicle* and joined Leeming and Reeves in the latter's office. The reporter was glad to see him again.

'Welcome back, Inspector,' he said, shaking the newcomer's hand. 'Please take a seat. Is there anything I can get you in the way of refreshment?'

'The most refreshing thing I can think of is reading your article in the *Chronicle*.'

'It's wonderful,' declared Leeming, handing a copy of the newspaper to him. 'I've read it three times.'

'That's praise indeed,' said Colbeck. 'Victor hardly ever looks at a newspaper.'

'I tried to be even-handed,' explained Reeves. 'Where credit was due to the local police, I made sure that they got it.'

'But we come out of it the best,' said Leeming. 'Archie has done us proud.'

Colbeck shook his head. 'I can't say that I take pride in our achievement. The killer is still at liberty,' he reminded them, 'and we still have no idea who sent him here. Also, of course,' he went on, 'we've yet to establish what brought Mr Lockyer here in the first place.'

'You must have some idea by now,' suggested Reeves.

'I have dozens of possibilities in mind, Archie, but we need more evidence before we understand what really happened. That's why Victor and I paid a second visit. It's been a delight to come here again and meet those – like yourself – who have been so helpful to us.'

'Read the article,' advised Leeming. 'It's not as wickedly funny as the one about Superintendent Tallis that appeared in *Punch*, but it tickled me.'

'It wasn't meant to be funny,' argued Reeves. 'Murder is a serious business. I just pointed out the way in which Colonel Edgell and Inspector Crabbe had made repeated mistakes. Anyway, I'll let you read it for yourself before I say anything else.'

'Thank you,' said Colbeck, turning his attention to the *Chronicle*. 'There were reports in the national daily newspapers, but I'll vouch that they're not as accurate as your version of events.'

Much as she loved her father, there were times when Madeleine found him exasperating.

'Why on earth did you go to the shop?' she demanded.

'I was curious,' he replied. 'The man who owned that first place was a real bully. I wanted to make sure that this time you had a shopkeeper who was on your side.'

'Mrs Dowling was very understanding, Father.'

'I know that now – but only because I met her face to face.'

'You had no reason to interfere,' she told him.

'You're my daughter, Maddy. I've every right to interfere if someone is trying to take advantage of you. A woman copied a painting of yours and dared to call it her own work. The very least she deserves is a spell in prison.'

'Is that what you told Mrs Dowling?'

'Yes, it is. We had a long chat over a cup of tea.'

'A cup of tea?' echoed Madeleine. 'The woman has a business to run. She can't have strangers calling in and expecting a cup of tea.'

He cackled. 'I had a biscuit as well,' he confided. 'Besides, I'm not a stranger. I'm the father of the artist whose work has been copied and I'm as anxious as you are to catch the woman.'

'I still wish you hadn't gone there.'

'Why? Are you ashamed of me or something?'

'Of course not,' she said. 'I just didn't want interference.'

'You're changing your tune, aren't you? When you went to see your painting in the window of a shop in Soho, you were glad to take me with you. I stood up to that horrible Mr Davies when he tried to browbeat you and Lydia.'

'Yes,' she conceded, 'you did. I was glad to have you there.'

'So was Victoria – that's Mrs Dowling to you. We got on very well.'

'I still wish that you hadn't gone there without telling me.'

'I didn't tell you, Maddy, because I knew you'd try to stop me.'

'I hate the thought that you went there behind my back.'

He spread his arms. 'I was acting in your interest,' he pointed out. 'It's what any father would do. If someone steals something from my daughter, they'll answer to me.'

When he called at the house, the man was immediately shown into the drawing room. The bearded old gentleman was seated in his armchair. His visitor remained on his feet.

'I got your message, sir,' he said.

'Good. A change of plan is indicated.'

'Why?'

'I'm looking ahead to the funeral,' explained the other. 'It's a critical time for us. Everyone from his father's house – including the servants – will be going to Pelham Lockyer's house after the event. And that includes the mother, even though she doesn't understand what's happened.'

The man gave a sly grin. 'In other words, the father's house will be empty.'

'And there'll be no detectives lurking there. It's the ideal time to break in.'

'When is the date of the funeral?'

'It's still to be decided,' said the old man, handing him an envelope. 'There's money for you inside because I want you to hire mourning wear. If anyone does see you near the house, they'll think you're there to pay your respects.'

'It will be a good disguise, sir.'

'Come and go in a cab. If you're on foot, you'd attract attention.'

'Leave it to me. I'll be in and out of that house in a matter of minutes.'

'Don't you dare come to me empty-handed,' warned the other.

'I'll earn my fee this time,' asserted the other. 'Both of us will get what we want, sir. That's a solemn promise.'

'Don't fail me again, or I'll have no further use for you. Do you understand?'

The visitor quailed. 'Yes, I do.'

Summoned to the superintendent's office, Alan Hinton was unsure whether he would receive blame for past failures or instructions about future duties. When he entered the office and saw a rare smile on Tallis's face, he was able to relax. The superintendent held up a letter.

'You are mentioned in dispatches,' he explained.

'I don't understand, sir.'

'Do you remember Mr Hull?'

'How could we forget him?' said Hinton. 'He was so kind to us.'

'Kind and thoughtful. He's written to say that you and Boyce are welcome to stay in his attic whenever necessary. Mr Hull walked his dog past the Lockyer residence yesterday and noticed that there was a workman repairing the window of the storeroom. It will be far less easy to break next time. That should make the occupants feel safe.'

'Surely the intruder won't come back again, will he?'

'It's a possibility we can't dismiss. I suspect that he'll wait some time before making a third attempt to get into the property. Something in Mr Lockyer's study clearly has an attraction for him.'

'Or for the man who is paying him.'

'That's a valid point. The burglar is also a killer, we must remember,' said Tallis, eyes narrowing. 'That's why I was so annoyed that you and Boyce failed to arrest him.'

'We are as annoyed as you, sir.'

Tallis glared at him. 'I very much doubt that.'

'What are our instructions?'

'We must bide our time. According to Mr Hull, friends and relatives are visiting the house to express their condolences. The funeral will be well attended. I daresay that the entire board of the GWR will turn up to show their respect. In the wake of the event, there will certainly be a gathering of some sort for family and friends.' He raised an eyebrow. 'Can you see what I'm thinking?'

'Yes, sir,' said Hinton. 'Mr Lockyer's house will be virtually empty.'

'It's the ideal time to make another attempt at getting into it.'

'Do you want me and Detective Constable Boyce to be lying in wait, sir?'

'No, I don't.'

Hinton was disappointed. 'Why not?'

'It's because you and I will be on duty this time. I've given my word to Mr Lockyer's son that we'll catch his father's killer. When that happens,' said Tallis, tapping his chest, 'I intend to be there.'

Since his sister had arrived, Pelham Lockyer had been unable to spend any time alone with her. When he'd returned home with Henrietta and her husband, therefore, he waited for a moment when he could speak to her in private. Inviting her into his study, he showed her the obituaries of their father that had appeared in various newspapers. Every one of them praised his financial skills and his readiness to take chances.

'Unfortunately,' said Lockyer, 'he took one chance too many.'

'What do you mean?' she asked.

'Father should have been more careful.'

'Are you saying that he was in danger?'

'It appears so, Henrietta.'

'What was he doing in Shrewsbury, anyway?'

'I still have no idea. He told me that he was going to stay with friends in Kent.'

She was appalled. 'He lied to you?'

'I'm afraid that he did.'

'That's dreadful! As a rule, he was such an honest man.'

'I know. Why did he feel the need to deceive me? It really wounded me.'

'Do you think that he was deliberately hiding something from you?'

'No,' he said, 'I can't believe that. Father and I were so close.'

'Then why did he mislead you?'

'We may never know.'

'But we must, Pelham. Didn't the police have any idea what he was doing there?'

'They're as baffled as I am, Henrietta.'

'Do you think that he went there to see someone that we . . . know nothing about?'

'Put such thoughts from your mind,' he said sharply. 'They're an insult to our father. Have you forgotten the work he did for the church? He was a God-fearing man, and we should remember him as such. Well, you read those obituaries. One of them said he was a kind of saint.'

'It's how I'll remember him. He used to read from the Bible when he put me to bed.'

'He did the same to me, Henrietta. I treasure those memories.'

'Father had such a beautiful singing voice. I loved to hear him singing in church.'

Her brother spoke in a whisper. 'Those days are gone, I'm afraid.'

'Pelham,' she said, taking him by the arms and looking up at him, 'I know that you still see me as your little sister, but I'm a grown woman now. I have a husband, two children and I run a sizeable house. Treat me as an adult, please.'

'Yes, of course.'

'Is there something you're not telling me?'

'Of course not,' he said vehemently. 'I'd never deceive you, Henrietta.'

'That's what I hope.'

'I give you my word that I am not hiding anything from you. It would never cross my mind to do so. We've always been so open with each other.'

'It's something that I treasure.'

'If I seem a trifle preoccupied,' he said, 'it's because I am still in shock.'

'I'm the same. Since I heard the news, I've been wandering around in a dream.'

'Reality will set in when we make the funeral arrangements,' he warned her. 'I'd like your help in sending out cards, please.'

'I'll be only too glad to help.'

'Thank you.'

He bent forward to kiss her gently on the cheek then gazed at her. She was still almost startlingly pretty. Motherhood had filled her out slightly, but her black mourning wear concealed the changes. Outwardly calm, Pelham was in fact on tenterhooks. He hated having to lie to his sister and feared the moment when the truth finally came out. For the moment, he was protecting her from a pain that gnawed inside him relentlessly. He even managed a weak smile. Henrietta had to be kept in the dark for the time being – or she would be disgusted by the truth about their father.

'Let's go and find that husband of yours,' he suggested.

'Angus is dying for a chat with you alone. He's brought a bottle of his favourite whisky.'

Pelham managed a weary smile. 'That's just what I need!'

CHAPTER FIFTEEN

When she called at the house later that afternoon, Lydia found that, apart from the servants, Madeleine was on her own. After hugging her friend, the visitor looked around.

'Where is everybody?' she asked.

'My father has taken Helena Rose to the park and Nanny Hopkins has gone with them. I'm all alone and glad to be so.'

'Why?'

'Father is a wonderful support to me,' said Madeleine, 'but he does act on impulse from time to time. It can be unnerving.'

'What has he done now?'

'He went back to the shop where my painting is on display – except that it's not really my painting, of course. It's a forgery.'

'Why did he feel the need to go there?'

'You may well ask, Lydia. I love him dearly, but he drives me to distraction sometimes. He said that he wanted to check that the owner of the shop was honest and reliable.'

'Mrs Dowling was patently both those things.'

'Father wanted to be certain.'

'I'm sure that he meant well, Madeleine.'

'I thought that Mrs Dowling would find him a nuisance, but he obviously charmed her. She gave him a cup of tea.'

Lydia laughed.

'And a biscuit.'

Her friend laughed even louder.

'It's not funny, Lydia. It's . . . embarrassing.'

'Don't take it too seriously.'

'When he told her that he had been an engine driver, Mrs Dowling was very impressed. She also told him that he looked incredibly well for his age. Father lapped up the praise.'

'Did he look at the fake painting?'

'Yes, he did,' said Madeleine, 'and he pointed out the mistakes that the other artist had made with the engine itself. He praised my knowledge of steam engines and told her that I'd never make blunders like that.'

'I can't see why you're so annoyed, Madeleine.'

'It's because he went behind my back. If he'd warned me what he had in mind, I would have stopped him going there. As it is, he's boasting about the free cup of tea and the biscuit.'

'That's more than Mrs Dowling offered us.'

'We were there to ask for a favour. My father was simply being nosey.'

'He was on your side,' Lydia told her. 'I envy you. Parental support was something I never enjoyed. My father and mother were always too busy to bother about me. In their own way, they must have loved me, but they were not very good at showing me affection. And they certainly didn't advise me how to paint a steam engine. Your father is a godsend to you.'

'In many ways, he is,' agreed Madeleine.

'Then he did you a favour by taking the trouble to see Mrs Dowling.'

'I wouldn't go that far.'

They were in the drawing room. Madeleine had ordered tea earlier, and a maid brought it into the room on a tray. Madeleine thanked her and the woman left. Lydia eyed a plate of biscuits.

'Your father will be back for one of those,' she said.

'Oh, no, he won't,' insisted Madeleine, 'because we'll have eaten them all.'

Because Colbeck and Leeming were sharing a compartment with two elderly ladies, they were unable to discuss their latest visit to Shrewsbury. The discussion was postponed to the ride back to Scotland Yard in a cab. Robert Colbeck went immediately to the superintendent's office to give his report. Tallis listened intently to it before showing his disappointment.

'In other words,' he said, 'this expedition of yours was a failure.'

'I beg to differ, sir. I felt it was a success.'

'But we are no nearer an arrest as a result of your outing.'

'I have a theory, sir.' Colbeck outlined his thoughts to the superintendent.

'I don't usually approve of your theories, but this one has a ring of authenticity to it. Wait a moment,' Tallis went on, thinking it through, 'if Mr Lockyer was brought to the town for that reason, why did this "friend" employ an assassin from London?'

'The simple answer is that it's far easier to hire a killer here in the nation's capital than it is in a sleepy market town like Shrewsbury. We may, of course, be making the wrong assumption,' said Colbeck. 'The person Mr Lockyer went to see might be a genuine friend, who is terrified to come forward because they don't want the publicity involved with a murder investigation. If he or she favours a quiet life, they'd prefer to mourn the death of their friend in silence.'

'The least that they could do is to send us anonymous information.'

'Colonel Edgell has already had posters put up, offering a reward to anyone who comes forward with significant information. So far, there's been no response.'

'It's good to hear that Edgell has done something right at last,' sneered Tallis.

'You sound very critical of him, sir.'

'I still carry wounds inflicted by the man.'

'May I ask why?'

'No, you may not.'

'Soldiers who served together in places like India usually view each other as trusted comrades. That is clearly not the case here.'

'No, it isn't,' snapped Tallis. 'It's an unfortunate coincidence that Colonel Edgell and I are leading investigations into the same murder. He is a relative newcomer to law enforcement, so I hold the whip hand over him in that respect. That's why I'm so keen to solve this crime and prove to him that there is something in which he can never equal me.'

Colbeck had never seen him in such a vengeful mood before. It perplexed him.

* * *

Henrietta and her husband were in one of the guest bedrooms at her brother's house. It was the first time since their arrival in London that they had been alone together. Angus Rennie was able to speak freely. He was curious.

'What's wrong with Pelham?' he asked.

'He's been devastated by our father's murder,' she said. 'And so have I.'

'Yes, my love, but you've reacted as I would expect, and I've done my best to support you through this difficult period. Pelham, on the other hand, is behaving strangely.'

'I suppose that he is, Angus.'

'You're too caught up in your own sorrow and that's as it should be. Pelham is different. He is saying all the right words to us, but he doesn't feel the loss as deeply as you do. Frankly, I find his response to the calamity rather odd.'

'In what way?'

'There is no sense that he is really in mourning.'

'That's a cruel thing to say, Angus,' she complained.

'I speak as I find. '

'Think what Father's untimely death will mean for my brother. He's head of the family now and that will bring huge responsibilities. No wonder he seems slightly disorganised.'

'Face facts, Henrietta. He's close to being inhospitable.'

'Angus!' she exclaimed.

'Well, he is. Normally, he and I have a proper conversation when we meet. Not this time, I'm afraid. Pelham is so disengaged. It's almost as if he doesn't want us here.'

'That's an appalling suggestion.'

'Then where is he?' asked Rennie. 'He told me that he had to go out somewhere. People don't go out somewhere when they have guests, especially if one of them is a sister they rarely see. What the devil has got into your brother? And where the hell is he?'

Kneeling at the altar rail in the parish church, Pelham Lockyer poured out his pain and confusion in a silent prayer. He had accepted that his father would die one day and that he would inherit the business, but it had never occurred to him that the death would be so soon and so sudden. The discovery that he had not really known his father had turned fond memories of the older man into so many glaring lies. Unable to change family history, he could at least hide some of its more hideous aspects from his sister. It was his duty to do so.

He remained on his knees until the intense pain forced him to struggle to his feet.

'Working as an artist,' said Madeleine, 'has taught me so much. Whenever I've been to art galleries, most of paintings there are the work of men. Then I discovered that there have been many women artists in the past, some of them good enough to have their paintings hung beside the work of famous male artists.'

'Some of your paintings deserve to be in a gallery,' said Lydia.

'Oh, I don't think so. Such talent as I have pales beside that of the great artists. They had true inspiration. I just have an urge to put paint to canvas and celebrate steam engines.'

'Yes, but you're a woman in what is largely a man's world. You're a pioneer, Madeleine.'

'Oh, no, I'm not.'

'There are hardly any other female artists.'

'That's what I thought when I started out,' said Madeleine. 'Then

Robert brought home a book that showed me how ignorant I was. It was a collection of paintings by women artists over the centuries. They were brilliant. One of them was an Italian artist named Artemisia something and she puts people like me in the shade.'

'I refuse to believe that.'

'Then you should look at her painting of Susannah and the Elders. It's amazing. Its use of shadow is astonishing. The illustration was only in black and white, but I went to the National Gallery to see a painting of hers in full colour. It took my breath away, Lydia. I can't ever compete with someone like her. Artemisia's paintings are so dramatic.'

'I bet that she could never paint a steam engine as well as you do, Madeleine.'

'That's only because she'd never seen one. She lived over two hundred years ago, Lydia, well before railways had come into existence. Looking at her work, I was humbled.'

'You're not in competition with artists like her.'

'Perhaps not, but she does make me realise that I'm just a talented amateur. Artemisia, on the other hand, was a genius. Her paintings could hang in the finest art galleries in the world.'

Colbeck visited Pelham Lockyer the next morning. Hearing his name being announced, Lockyer came quickly to the front door to prevent his visitor from leaving.

'No, no, Inspector,' he said, 'please stay. My sister, Henrietta, would be interested to meet you. Both of us would like to know how the investigation is going.'

'In that case,' said Colbeck, removing his top hat, 'I will come in – but I won't intrude for long, I promise you.'

Stepping into the hall, he handed his hat to the servant who had opened the front door then followed Lockyer into the drawing room. He was introduced to Henrietta and her husband, both of whom rose to their feet to exchange a handshake with him. When everyone sat down again, it was Angus Rennie who spoke first.

'Your name sounds familiar, Inspector,' he said. 'Why is that, I wonder?'

'My work did take me to Scotland on one occasion,' replied Colbeck, 'and my name did appear in newspapers there. Before I joined the Metropolitan Police Force, I worked as a barrister, so I was fascinated by the differences between the English and Scottish legal systems. We have no procurator fiscal, for instance.'

Rennie snapped his fingers. 'I remember you now. You were highly praised.'

'I was lucky enough to be feted by your press,' said Colbeck modestly, 'but I was not the only Scotland Yard detective to be involved. Others deserve a share of the acclaim.'

'What about this latest case?' asked Lockyer.

'We feel quietly confident of making an arrest in due course, sir.'

'It can't come soon enough. The entire domestic staff at my father's house were terrified to realise that the killer had found a way into the house late at night.'

'I sympathise with them.'

'The man somehow evaded two of your detectives.'

'Evidently, he is an experienced burglar. Such people develop instincts that enable them to escape danger. As soon as he sensed it, he fled. But we did anticipate his return to the house,' said Colbeck. 'That's the reason we took precautions.'

'I hope that your officers don't let us down again,' said Lockyer.

'The investigation continues, sir. In fact, it's the reason I'm here. The fact that your sister is visiting you is a bonus to me. I can put the same question to you, Mrs Rennie. Did either of you know what reason your father had to go to Shrewsbury?'

'You asked me that before,' said Lockyer, 'and my answer remains the same – no, I don't.'

Colbeck turned to the sister. 'Mrs Rennie?'

'When I got married,' she explained, 'I moved to Scotland with my husband. That was years ago so I've been unaware of my father's movements since then.'

'Was he in the habit of going away on his own?'

'He did occasionally visit a friend in Kent – a man he has known for years.'

'Are you sure that that's where he went?'

'Of course,' said Lockyer peevishly. 'I've told you before how truthful he was.'

'Until he felt the need to go to Shropshire,' Colbeck reminded him.

'That was a rare example of my father being dishonest.'

'Someone in his circle,' suggested Colbeck, 'was a false friend. My belief is that a person close to him hired a man to follow and kill Mr Lockyer. The man was biding his time. When he followed your father to Shrewsbury, he saw his chance and took it.'

'This is only speculation,' argued Rennie.

'I'm trying to get into the mind of the person who paid for what was, in essence, an assassination. He wanted the crime to be committed far away from London, so his killer waited until he saw his quarry boarding a train. He then followed his target.'

'My father was more than a target,' said Lockyer indignantly. 'He was a remarkable man with an astonishing business career. And he was on the point of achieving something he had coveted for a long time – a key position on the board of the GWR.'

'You told me that he was universally admired by his colleagues on the board.'

'He had no enemies there, Inspector. You'll have to look elsewhere.'

'I'm not so sure about that,' said Colbeck.

'Do you know all the other board members?' asked Rennie.

'Yes, I do,' replied Lockyer. 'To a man, they respected my father. I've had letters of condolence from almost every one of them. My father's closest friend was Christopher Prance. He has a lot of influence on the board. When he proposed my father as the next chairman, he canvassed other members and sought their vote.'

'This gentleman might be worth a visit,' said Colbeck. 'Do you have his address?'

'Had you come earlier,' said Lockyer, 'you could have met him in person because he called here to offer what comfort he could. He's the oldest member of the board and is also the wisest.'

'Then he should be interviewed,' said Colbeck.

'I'll need to consult the address book in my study, Inspector. Please excuse me.'

'Of course, sir.' As Lockyer left the room, Colbeck turned to the others. 'I'm sorry that your visit is overshadowed by a terrible crime. But I am confident that the man who committed the murder will be caught and convicted.'

'What makes you so confident?' asked Rennie.

'Put it down to experience, sir. Once I'm searching for someone, I always find them in the end, however long it takes.'

'That's very reassuring,' said Henrietta.

'And while I am on the trail of the killer here in London, the police in Shrewsbury are still gathering evidence there. Between us, we'll find the man we are after.'

'I sincerely hope so,' said Rennie. 'Her father's death has been a huge blow for my wife. The only thing that will ease her pain is the arrest of the man responsible for his murder.'

'I understand, Mr Rennie, and I assure you that we are working as quickly as we can. Murder investigations, however, often take time. Please try to be patient.'

Madeleine was enjoying a cup of tea with her guest when she remembered something. Quickly putting down her cup, she turned to Lydia.

'I've just remembered her full name,' she said.

'Whose first name?'

'That Italian artist I mentioned. It was Artemisia Gentileschi.'

'Is she the one whose painting was in the National Gallery?'

'It was only there on loan for a short period,' said Madeleine. 'I stared at it for ages. The colours were so vibrant and there was a wonderful sense of drama. Just think of it, Lydia. This woman was rubbing shoulders with a host of famous Italian painters.'

'She sounds like an extraordinary woman – but then, so are you.'

'Don't be ridiculous.'

'You are, Madeleine. You're not only a wife, mother and brilliant painter. You've now turned yourself into a detective to catch this dreadful woman.'

'I'm also a daughter, remember. That means I need to keep an eye on my father. He's far more trouble than Helena Rose.'

'I don't believe that. He's an asset to you.'

'Yes, he is – in his own way.'

'He dotes on his granddaughter. It's wonderful that she has someone from an older generation in her life. By the time I was sixteen, I'd lost all my grandparents. Anyway, let's go back to the problem that's vexing you. Who is this woman copying one of your paintings and why did she choose to do so?'

Madeleine pulled a face. 'I simply don't know, Lydia.'

'Doesn't Robert have a theory about her?'

'He would if he had the time. Unfortunately, he's working around the clock on a murder case so he's unable to help me. Besides, it's my problem so I need to solve myself.'

'With help from me, I hope.'

'Yes, please.'

'And don't forget Mr Andrews.'

Madeleine laughed. 'I'd never be allowed to, I'm afraid.'

Because the address that Colbeck had been given was on the other side of London, he stopped off at Scotland Yard to pick up Victor Leeming. As they got into the cab, the sergeant was curious.

'Where are we going?' he asked.

'We're meeting a man who was a close friend of Julian Lockyer's and who led the campaign to get him elected as the next chairman of the GWR.'

'What's his name?'

'Christopher Prance. I wanted you to be there because you are a good judge of character. I've no doubt that Prance will do all the talking. I need you to take notes of what he tells us.'

'I'll do that gladly,' said Leeming. 'How did you get on at the son's house?'

'His sister and her husband had arrived from Scotland, so I was able to talk to both of Lockyer's children. Like her brother, Mrs Rennie was still shocked by the turn of events.'

'It takes time to adjust to a massive blow like that.'

'The only thing that can bring a sense of relief to the pair of them is the arrest of the killer and of his paymaster. Their relief, however, may be tempered by an uncomfortable discovery.'

'I don't follow.'

'They are about to learn of an aspect of their father's private life,' said Colbeck, 'that may well cause them considerable pain and embarrassment.'

Seated behind his desk at the police station, Colonel Edgell listened to the latest report from Sergeant Crabbe then looked upwards.

'Hear us, oh Lord!' he cried ironically. 'We need help.'

'I think that we're making progress, Colonel.'

'But we're moving too slowly, Inspector. You've gathered mounds of information, but you still have no idea whatsoever who the killer was.'

'He's from London, sir. That much is certain.'

'Then you must extend your search there. An overnight stay may be necessary.'

'My wife won't like that,' warned Crabbe.

'What is more important?' demanded Edgell. 'Helping to track down a killer or keeping Mrs Crabbe in a good mood?'

'Sarah worries a lot.'

'Not as much as I do. I worry that we seem to have been marking time in this investigation. I also worry that national newspapers are blaming us for our failure. Then there is that waspish piece in the *Chronicle*. I'd like to strangle Archibald Reeves with my bare hands. He mocked us cruelly.'

'He gave us no credit for the work we've put into this investigation.'

'London!' said Edgell, rapping on his desk with his knuckles. 'That's where you must go.'

'When?'

'Immediately. I won't have us squeezed out of this investigation. Even if it means working with the loathsome Edward Tallis, you must do it. I'm sorry if your wife is forced to endure a night or two without you beside her, but work comes first, Inspector.'

'Yes, Colonel. Do you have any message for Superintendent Tallis?'

Rage coloured the other man's cheeks.

'No, obviously you don't. In that case, I'll be on my way – as soon as I've broken the bad news to Sarah.'

Crabbe left the room as swiftly as he could.

Pelham Lockyer and his visitors were seated in the drawing room, enjoying a cup of tea. Lost in contemplation for minutes, Lockyer sat up abruptly.

'I do apologise,' he said. 'I was miles away.'

His sister squeezed his arm. 'We understand, Pelham.'

'It is I who should be comforting you, dear sister.'

'That's my job now,' said Rennie, smiling at his wife. 'I'm always here for you, Henrietta.'

'I know,' she replied with a wan smile.

'We were glad to meet Inspector Colbeck,' he added. 'What an elegant man! I've never seen a detective so well dressed. He's a real dandy.'

'It's not his clothing that I admire,' said Lockyer, 'it's his mind. He sees and evaluates things that the rest of us don't even notice. And he has the most extraordinary record of success.'

'He certainly inspires trust.'

There was a protracted silence. It was eventually broken by Henrietta.

'Can you feel it?' she asked, looking at each of them in turn.

'Feel what?' asked her husband.'

'The atmosphere of this house is so different without Father. He visited you here often and was such a presence.'

'I agree, Henrietta,' said her brother. 'When I came in through the front door, I always knew instantly if he was here. He changed the atmosphere of our home somehow.'

'Yes,' recalled Rennie, 'he did have a powerful personality.'

'We'll never be aware of his presence again,' sighed Lockyer. 'I already miss him so much.'

'Then try to recall only fond memories.'

'That's good advice, Angus.'

'Good memories soothe. Bad ones only trouble you.'

'I don't have any bad memories of him,' said Henrietta. 'If I was naughty as a young girl, Father must have been annoyed at my behaviour, but he never let it show. He was so understanding.'

'That's how I remember him,' said her brother.

'I always found him rather intimidating,' confessed Rennie. 'When I sought the hand of his daughter in marriage, I was trembling like a leaf.'

'You never tremble,' said his wife.

'I did on that occasion, my love.'

Her face lit up. 'Looking back, I have the fondest memories of Father.'

'And so do I,' agreed her brother, forcing the words out of his mouth and even managing the semblance of a smile.

* * *

When the cab reached their destination, they alighted and took their first look at the home of Christopher Prance. The house was even more impressive than the one owned by Julian Lockyer. After he had paid the driver, Colbeck led the way to the front door and rang the bell. The door opened almost immediately. A manservant looked from one to the other.

'We've come in the hope of seeing Mr Prance,' said Colbeck. 'We are detectives from Scotland Yard, engaged in the hunt for the killer of Mr Julian Lockyer.'

'Please come in,' said the man, stepping back out of their way. After they had entered, he closed the front door. 'I'll let Mr Prance know that you are here.'

He went into the drawing room and allowed them enough time to look at the paintings on the wall. They were gilt-framed portraits of famous figures from British history. Leeming stared in fascination at Admiral Lord Nelson, but his pleasure was cut short. The manservant came out and led the visitors into the drawing room. Prance was on his feet, ready to shake hands with each of them in turn and saying how grateful he was to meet them.

'Let's sit down,' he suggested. 'I can't wait to hear how the investigation is progressing.'

'We're rather hoping that you can contribute to it, Mr Prance,' said Colbeck, as they all sat down. 'If you have no objection, Sergeant Leeming will record the information you give us.'

Prance beamed. 'I'd be delighted to help in any way that I can,' he said. 'At what stage are you, may I ask?'

'We believe that the murder may be in some way connected to Mr Lockyer's position as a board member of the GWR. You, I believe, were leading his campaign to become chairman.'

'There was nobody else to touch Julian. He would have been a perfect choice.'

'Why was that?'

'He had experience, a gift for leadership and a readiness to work all hours. Also, he had an abiding love of railways.'

'I share that love,' admitted Colbeck.

'I don't,' grumbled Leeming.

'You must forgive my colleague. He has yet to understand the value of the railway system or to appreciate the place that the GWR occupies within it. In essence,' Colbeck went on, 'what happened was this. Mr Lockyer went to Shrewsbury for some reason, having told his son that he was, in fact, going to stay with a friend in Kent.'

'Julian told me the same thing, Inspector. I believed him.'

'Were you shocked to discover that your friend had told you a lie?'

'I was both shocked and saddened. He was always so honest in his dealings with me.'

'Our belief is that he must have been watched by someone hired to kill him. When he set off to Shropshire, he was unaware that he was being followed by an assassin. We know where that man stayed overnight in the town and what train he took out of there. He was using the name of Jack Brown,' said Colbeck, 'but it was certainly an alias.'

'And you believe that he came back to London?'

'We're certain of it, sir. Two of my detectives saw him approaching Mr Lockyer's house in the dead of night.'

'They tried to arrest him,' said Leeming, 'but he managed to get free and outrun them.'

'I'm sorry to hear that,' said Prance. 'Why on earth did he come to the house?'

'That's what I'm hoping you could tell us, sir,' explained Colbeck. 'As it happened, he returned the next night and tried to get into the study. Anticipating his return, detectives were waiting inside the property to arrest him. Unfortunately, he sensed danger and fled.'

'This time,' said Leeming, 'he'd come by horse and galloped away out of their reach.'

'Dear me!' exclaimed Prance. 'This is dreadful! Was it not enough for this individual to murder Julian? Did he have to burgle the man's house as well?'

'He came in search of one item in particular,' said Colbeck. 'At least that is what I believe. Having broken into the house, he went straight to the study. What was he after?'

'There was a safe there, Inspector. Anything of value was kept in it.'

'My detectives tell me that it was a Chubb safe, extremely difficult to break into. Besides,' said Colbeck, 'the intruder had the key to Mr Lockyer's desk. He had stolen it along with other things after he had killed him. I feel that he came to the house in search of something that was in that desk. What could it be?'

Prance shrugged. 'I've no idea, I'm afraid.'

'It was important enough to bring the killer to the house two nights in a row. Could it be a letter that might explain why Mr Lockyer decided to go to Shrewsbury? Or was it something to do with his being almost certain to be elected as the next chairman of the GWR?'

'It could be either, I suppose,' said Prance.

'I'm told that you knew him better than anyone else.'

'It's true. I did. I admired and loved the man.'

'Could you tell us how your friendship with him first started?'

Prance took a deep breath. 'Well, it was years ago when we first met,' he said fondly. 'What brought us together was a chance encounter . . .'

Edward Tallis was seated at his desk, studying a report, when there was a knock on his door.

'Come in!' he shouted. A uniformed policeman entered the room. 'Well?'

'There's a Detective Inspector Crabbe eager to see you, sir,' said the man.

'What the devil does he want?'

'Shall I show him in?'

'If it was left to me,' said Tallis, 'I'd rather you showed him out of the building altogether.' He sat back in his chair. 'Oh, very well. Bring him in – but warn him that I am very busy.'

'Yes, Superintendent.'

The policeman withdrew then reappeared moments later with Crabbe. He went out immediately, leaving the two men to stare at each other in silence. Eventually, Crabbe spoke.

'Colonel Edgell sends his regards.'

'I refuse to believe it,' said Tallis, glowering. 'Why have you come here, Inspector?'

'I have new information regarding the murder to pass on, and I'm hoping to find out what progress has been made by your detectives.'

'My officers are still gathering evidence. The best person to speak to is Inspector Colbeck. Have you time to wait for him?'

'My orders are to stay in London as long as is necessary.'

'Please sit down.' As Crabbe lowered himself into a chair, Tallis studied him. 'How is Colonel Edgell coping with his new position?'

'He is quickly adapting to law enforcement, but there is still a lot for him to learn. As our new chief constable, he has certainly made his mark.'

'That means he is bullying everyone – as usual.'

'Colonel Edgell has never been involved in a murder investigation,' explained Crabbe, 'so he has had to defer to those of us who have done so. Since the crime took place in Shrewsbury, we wish to be involved in catching the person responsible for it.'

'The person or persons,' corrected Tallis. 'Inspector Colbeck is certain that more than one individual is involved.'

'I look forward to hearing his evidence.'

'He will be pleased to be reunited with you. I could wish that you were here at the behest of a different chief constable,' he confessed, 'but that's a personal matter.'

'Colonel Edgell did warn me that you might be . . . uncooperative.'

'Then he was wrong to do so. All that matters to me is solving this murder and handing over those responsible to the hangman. One warning, however. You will find me far more amenable if you do not mention the chief constable's name again in my presence.'

Crabbe nodded. 'He told me you would say that.'

Christopher Prance was a highly successful businessman, living in comparative luxury because of the decisions he had made during his career. Yet he was modest enough to claim that Julian Lockyer had a better grasp of business matters and – had he lived – would have gone on to have even greater achievements than him. For his part, Victor Leeming was relieved when the older man's recitation finally came to an end. There had been so much information to record in his notebook that his hand was aching.

'Thank you, sir,' said Colbeck. 'Your comments about Mr Lockyer have been illuminating.'

'I spoke from the heart.'

'You said very little about Mr Lockyer's son.'

'Pelham is a mirror image of his father – clever, determined and tireless.'

'The murder has had a powerful impact on him.'

'The same goes for all of us – Julian's family and friends.'

'You said earlier that he was entirely without faults,' noted Colbeck.

'Mr Prance's exact words,' said Leeming, reading from his notebook, 'were that Mr Lockyer was close to being a saint.'

'Does that mean,' asked Colbeck, 'that he had no secrets?'

'None at all,' replied Prance. 'What you had with Julian was a man of extraordinary decency. He was not only an outstanding businessman – he was a true gentleman.'

'That's how his son described him. But I have a feeling that he no longer believes that his father was entirely without fault. Why is that?'

'I can only speak for myself, Inspector. Julian was remarkable in every respect.'

'Then why did he lie to you and to his son about his visit to Shrewsbury?'

Prance bit his lip. 'I wish that I knew, Inspector.'

CHAPTER SIXTEEN

Colbeck was extremely glad to have met Christopher Prance and wished that he had done so earlier. Leeming, by contrast, wished that the man had not been quite so verbose. He had filled page after page of Prance's comments. On the other hand, he realised, they now had a much fuller account of Lockyer's business activities than his son had given them.

'Thank you, Mr Prance,' said Colbeck. 'Our conversation has been illuminating.'

'It's been a delight, Inspector. I've long wished to meet you.'

'Why?'

'One of my closest friends on the board is Stephen Rydall.'

'Ah, yes,' said Leeming. 'He turned to us after that terrible crash in the Sapperton Tunnel.'

'It was an interesting case,' added Colbeck, 'even though it had its distressing moments, one of which involved my having to go underwater in the nearby canal.'

'Stephen mentioned the incident,' said Prance. 'He admired your bravery.'

'Looking back, I tend to see it as an act of folly. I was soaked to the skin.'

'It was for a good cause, sir,' Leeming reminded him.

'Quite right, Sergeant.'

'I don't think that this case will require you to swim in a canal,' said Prance. 'But it's heartening to hear of the extremes to which you will go in pursuit of the killer.'

'A killer and the man who hired him,' said Colbeck. 'The latter must be someone with a burning hatred of Mr Lockyer, so much so that he had him watched carefully by the assassin. Since you were so close to Mr Lockyer, you will almost certainly have met the man who contrived his death.'

'Everyone in our circle admired Julian,' claimed Prance.

Colbeck raised an eyebrow. 'Or pretended to do so.'

'You didn't know him, Inspector. I did and I'll vouch for his honesty.'

'Everyone has some defects, sir.'

'He was the exception to the rule.'

'I wouldn't advise you to place a wager on that,' warned Colbeck.

After listening to Inspector Crabbe's report, Tallis had to concede that the police investigation in Shrewsbury had been as thorough as it should have been. The superintendent was inclined to give praise to Crabbe rather than to the chief constable.

'I will pass on this new information to Inspector Colbeck,' said

Tallis. 'Thank you for taking the trouble to come here. You have clearly worked hard on this case.'

'Thank you for recognising it,' said Crabbe. 'We've had scant praise in the newspapers.'

'It's a problem that we face as well. Reporters have a nasty habit of getting under our feet during an investigation, then blaming us for not making an instant arrest.'

'We've been traduced in national newspapers and ridiculed in the *Shrewsbury Chronicle*.'

'Mockery of police activity should be made an arrestable offence.'

'Sergeant Leeming mentioned that you were once lampooned in the magazine *Punch*.'

'It was cruel and undeserved,' said Tallis angrily. 'I was even featured in a cartoon.'

'A reporter for the *Chronicle* had the gall to sneer at our efforts,' said Crabbe. 'The chief constable was outraged. He expected more support from the press.'

'That shows his ignorance.'

'He is learning very quickly.'

'Does he ever . . . mention me?'

Crabbe was honest. 'I'd rather not answer that question, Superintendent.'

Having retrieved it from her studio, Madeleine opened the sketchbook and showed her visitor an earlier version of the painting. Lydia recognised it at once.

'I remember it now,' she said. 'You narrowed the focus so that you only showed a small section of the train, and you only gave a back view of the family as they scrambled into their compartment.'

'Figures are my weak point,' confessed Madeleine. 'It's the reason I include so few of them in my paintings. As you can see, this is a train belonging to the LNWR. If I dared to feature any of the other railway companies, Father would go berserk.'

'Did he give you any help?'

'It was advice rather than help, Lydia. I thanked him for some of suggestions and quietly forgot the ones that were no use to me.'

'Are you going to tell him that a second print of yours has been bought by the same woman?'

'No,' said Madeleine defiantly. 'There are times when he's best kept in the dark.'

'He's as keen to catch the woman as you are.'

'I know and I'm grateful. But I hate it when he acts without warning.'

'Why did the woman choose that particular painting?'

'When we finally track her down, we'll find out.'

'How do you think she'll react?'

'I hope that she's honest enough to confess that she committed a crime. If she's so interested in paintings of railways, why doesn't she use an idea of her own?'

'It's because she doesn't have your creative ability, Madeleine.'

'These things are relative.'

'What do you mean?'

'Well, this woman chooses to steal my ideas because she's just beginning as a painter. She's not confident enough to invent a scene of her own. I like to think of myself as an artist but, when I saw that painting by Artemisia Gentileschi in the National Gallery, I realised I could never match her sheer brilliance. It took my breath away,' she confessed. 'That will never happen to anyone looking at a railway scene of mine.'

'A painting of yours may one day be on display in the National Gallery.'

'There's not a chance of that happening,' said Madeleine with a laugh. 'Besides, they already have a brilliant painting of a steam engine. It's called *Rain, Steam and Speed* and was painted by no less an artist than Turner. I have the greatest admiration for that painting.'

'Yes, I remember it well. When it was stolen, Robert managed to recover it – with a lot of help from you, Madeleine.'

'It happened to be a favourite of mine.'

'I know. When you saw a fake version of it, you realised it was the work of a forger.'

'Only because I knew and loved every detail of it.'

'Then you and Mr Turner have something in common,' said Lydia. 'You both had your work copied. I wonder how Turner reacted when he realised what had happened.'

'Unfortunately,' said Madeleine, 'it's too late to ask him. He died years ago.'

When he went to the superintendent's office to deliver his report, Colbeck sensed at once that something had happened. Edward Tallis was moody and preoccupied.

'Do you feel unwell, sir?' asked Colbeck.

'I'm never unwell,' snarled Tallis. 'I'm as fit and healthy as you.'

'I'm relieved to hear it.'

'If my manner mystifies you, I apologise. I had a visit from Detective Inspector Crabbe. He'd been sent here by a man whose name I have no wish to mention.'

'I understand.'

'I don't think you do,' said Tallis darkly. 'But enough of me.

Tell me what you've learnt.'

'My discussion with Mr Prance was illuminating. He provided me with valuable information about Mr Lockyer's role on the GWR board. Passions sometimes run high at board meetings, he admitted, but he refused to believe that any of his colleagues might plot the murder of Julian Lockyer. I choose to disagree.'

'Why is that?'

'I have this feeling, sir.'

'Oh dear!' sighed Tallis. 'We need more than one of your stray feelings. Hard evidence is the only thing that interests me.'

'It will come in due course, I promise you.'

'I sincerely hope so.'

'Did Inspector Crabbe bring any new information with him?' asked Colbeck.

'Leave Crabbe until we've dealt with Christopher Prance,' ordered Tallis. 'I want to hear exactly what he told you – word for word.'

Molly Burrage had hoped that the publicity about the murder at her hotel would gradually ease off but, if anything, the opposite had occurred. Reporters from national newspapers had descended on the town, some of them even booking a room at the Station Hotel so that they could interview its owner and staff. People from neighbouring towns and villages also poured into Shrewsbury, ostensibly to visit its market but also there to gape at the place. The impact on Molly began to tell on her nerves. She confided in her barman.

'I can't take much more of this, Wilf,' she confessed.

'It's getting you down, isn't it?'

'I'd hoped that the killer had been caught by now.'

'That may not happen for weeks,' said Harris, 'months, even. We need to brace ourselves for a long wait. And besides, people are still ready to stay here.'

'Yes, but for the wrong reasons. We're not a hotel now. We're a murder scene. People seem to get a thrill out of that.'

'Interest in us will slowly die down.'

'That means business will collapse altogether,' she complained.

'We'll just have to hope that things eventually pick up.'

'I need regular money coming in.'

'Try not to let it prey on you.'

She rolled her eyes. 'If only I could, Wilf!'

'At least all those reporters have gone.'

'But they've been replaced by guests asking to be shown the room where it happened. How can people be so ghoulish? A gentleman was killed here. What sort of pleasure can anyone get from looking at the place where it happened?'

'Some people have warped minds.'

'That's what Simon keeps saying.'

He pulled a face. 'It's not all the stationmaster has to say.'

'What do you mean?'

'I don't need to tell you why he's in here so often.'

'Simon is just a friend,' she said defensively.

'He'd love to be much more than that, and you know it.'

'Well, it's not going to happen, Wilf, I can assure you of that. I've no wish to be married again. I treasure my independence. At least, I did until this calamity happened,' she confided. 'I'm starting to believe that things will never be the way they used to be.'

'That's why Biddle keeps sniffing around here. Be warned.'

'He's a friend I can rely on.'

'Well, I find him a damned nuisance. He nurses a glass of stout all evening and only comes to life when you step into the bar. My wife has no time for him.'

'That's because she doesn't really know him. I do and I like him. Simon has done lots of favours for me and, in sending for Inspector Colbeck, he did me the best favour of all.'

Hubert Crabbe's visit to Scotland Yard had been at once illuminating and sobering. The nation's capital was beset by a rising tide of crime. The Metropolitan Police Force was working at full stretch to cope with the endless demands on it. Simply being inside its headquarters had been a source of pride for Crabbe. There was a buzz of excitement about the place. At the same time, however, it reminded him that he had few of the resources enjoyed by Scotland Yard. Working in Shropshire seemed hopelessly parochial by comparison. He found his visit overwhelming at first.

Since Crabbe had been told that Colbeck would be at Scotland Yard later that day, he returned there in the hope of seeing him. Crabbe was given disappointing news by Superintendent Tallis.

'I'm afraid that the inspector decided to go to Maidstone.'

'Oh dear!' said Crabbe.

'He is following a line of enquiry.'

'I'd be interested to hear what it was.'

'That makes two of us,' said Tallis. 'He interviewed a man named Christopher Prance, a close friend of Julian Lockyer's. Copious notes were taken. When he read through them, the inspector decided that he simply had to go to Kent as a matter of urgency.'

'I see. I'd hate to miss him. Is he likely to be here tomorrow?'

'Who knows?'

'Didn't he tell you?'

No,' said Tallis with a dry laugh. 'Inspector Colbeck is a law unto himself.'

As soon as he met Lockyer's old friend in Maidstone, Colbeck knew that he had made a wise decision. Desmond Villiers was delighted to meet the detective leading the investigation into the murder of Julian Lockyer. He gave his visitor a warm handshake and waved him to a chair. They were in the drawing room of a large and impressive house standing close to the river. Villiers was a handsome man of middle years and medium height. There was an almost boyish enthusiasm about him. Colbeck noticed that the man had an excellent tailor and that his hair had no trace whatsoever of grey in it. He looked remarkably healthy.

'I'm sorry to come without any warning,' Colbeck apologised.

'I could not be more delighted, Inspector. I was horrified to hear of Julian's murder. He was my closest friend, you know. We were at Rugby together. I was honoured when he asked me to be best man at his wedding and he, in due course, performed the same role at my wedding. There was a time when the four of us – husbands and wives – were inseparable. It was idyllic,' said Villiers. 'We had such wonderful times together.' His face fell. 'Then, of course . . . Julian's wife was taken ill . . .'

'How old would Mrs Lockyer have been at the time?'

'She was barely into her forties. It was so sudden and dramatic. She went from being perfectly healthy to becoming an invalid in a twilight world. My own wife, Cecilia, had been very close to her but Frances no longer recognised her. It was very distressing.'

'It must have been a terrible blow to Mr Lockyer.'

'Indeed, it was,' agreed Villiers, 'but you would never have known it. Julian was so devoted to his wife that he helped her in every way, acting at times as an auxiliary nurse. Most husbands would have behaved very differently towards a wife in such a predicament.'

'Did they ever visit you here?'

'No, they didn't. Julian came on his own a few times and stayed the night here. He and I always finished up reminiscing about the past with a bottle of whisky to jog our memories. The last communication I had from him was a fortnight ago. He promised to come here again very soon. We were so disappointed that he'd been unable to find the time to visit us.'

'You were still in his mind, Mr Villiers,' said Colbeck. 'He told both his son and Mr Prance that he was coming to Maidstone for the night. Instead, he went to Shrewsbury.'

'Did he say why?'

'He told the owner of the hotel where he stayed that he was in the town to see a friend.'

'Julian never mentioned a friend in Shrewsbury to me,' said Villiers, puzzled, 'but he talked freely about everyone else in his life. He and I were like brothers, Inspector. Julian hid nothing from me. Do you have any idea who this "friend" might be?'

'I don't, I'm afraid – and neither does his son, Pelham.'

'Will you be able to track this person down?'

'We're determined to do so, sir. To that end, I've already asked someone to begin a search for this friend. What puzzles me is why this friend of Lockyer's has not come forward himself to help our investigation. Only hours after they met,' recalled Colbeck, 'Julian Lockyer was murdered. You'd have thought that this individual would be as anxious as we are to find the killer.'

* * *

Archibald Reeves loved the town in which he lived and where he was employed as a reporter. Having been involved in writing about Shrewsbury and its county for so long, he flattered himself that he knew both as well as anyone. Colbeck had asked him to see if he could find out where Julian Lockyer had gone on the night before he was murdered. Having only a rough idea of where the man might have been, Reeves hired a horse so that he could get around more easily. When he mounted the animal, he did so with qualms. Because he was an indifferent horseman, he hoped that his mount would be obedient and responsive. Unfortunately, the animal was in a skittish mood, kicking its back heels from time to time and making Reeves hang on for dear life.

They trotted along the High Street, continued into Wyle Cop and came to a halt at a point where the English Bridge spanned the River Severn. The horse looked dubiously into the water below. It had grave doubts about going over it on the bridge. Reeves was simply grateful that they were stationary at last. It gave him an opportunity to look at some of the dwellings on the opposite bank. Most had land attached to them but there was the odd cottage standing alone in a small patch of land among the smallholdings. He wondered what sort of people lived in the cottages. What kind of existence did they have and how did they support themselves?

Now that the horse was at last comparatively passive, Reeves had the courage to dismount and take hold of the bridle. He gave the animal a pat of gratitude then, in the interests of research, he led the horse slowly over the bridge towards Abbey Foregate.

Although he and Julian Lockyer were a mere three or four years apart, Villiers seemed much younger than his friend. He was clearly fit, healthy and buoyant. Part of the reason for this,

Colbeck guessed, was that he had a wife some years younger than him. When he was introduced to Cecilia Villiers, the inspector was surprised by her appearance. She was an attractive woman in her early forties with a hint of vivacity about her. When she was introduced to Colbeck, her face lit up.

'I'm so pleased to meet you, Inspector,' she said, eyes alight. 'We've seen your name in the newspapers. It's such a relief to us that you are leading this investigation. Aren't we, Desmond?'

'Yes, my love,' said her husband. 'After talking with the inspector, I feel certain that it is only a question of time before the killer is arrested.'

'Be patient, please,' said Colbeck. 'We still have a long way to go.' He turned to Cecilia. 'Your husband has been telling me how close you and he were to Mr and Mrs Lockyer.'

'Julian and Frances were among our closest friends,' Cecilia told him. 'At one time, I was hoping that they might become even closer to us – but it was not to be.'

'My wife is referring to our daughter, Emily,' explained Villiers. 'She and Pelham Lockyer were fond of each in their early twenties. We hoped that marriage would bring the two families closer, but it was not to be. Pelham found Emily a little too lively for his taste and she, in turn, thought him rather dull.'

'They were clearly not suited,' said Colbeck.

'Emily was simply not ready for marriage,' Villiers told him. 'Do you have children, Inspector?'

'We have a young daughter who is an absolute delight.'

'Wait until she gets old enough to catch the eye of a young gentleman.'

'There are several years before that happens,' said Colbeck, turning to Cecilia. 'I'm told that you and Frances Lockyer were very close.'

'We had such wonderful times together,' she replied with a nostalgic smile, 'then she was struck down by this beastly illness. It was terrible to watch her decline. I still visit her whenever I can, but Frances no longer recognises who I am.'

'That must be very painful for you, Mrs Villiers.'

'It's agonising, Inspector.'

'In some ways,' noted Villiers, 'it's a relief. She is blissfully ignorant of what happened to Julian.' He turned to Colbeck. 'We are deeply grateful for your visit, Inspector.'

'It's been a pleasure to meet you,' added his wife.

'I hope that meeting us has been of some value to you.'

'Indeed, it has, Mr Villiers,' said Colbeck. 'What you have told me about your best friend has been extremely helpful. And it has been a delight to make your acquaintance,' he went on, turning to Cecilia. 'Thanks to this meeting with both of you, I now have considerably more insight into the life of and character of Julian Lockyer.'

Pelham Lockyer was seated at the desk in his office, staring at a photograph of his parents. It had been taken at a time when his mother had been healthy and active. To see her looking so bright and cheerful made him remember her as a young mother. That person, he told himself, no longer existed. The same, alas, could be said of his father, beaming happily in the photograph but now lying on a slab in the premises of a funeral director. Sweeping the photograph up, he put it away in a drawer and resolved never to take it out again. It brought back too many painful memories.

There was a tap on the door then Angus Rennie stepped into the study.

'I'm sorry to interrupt you, Pelham,' said his brother-in-law.

'I wondered if I might have a word.'

'Yes, of course. Take a seat, Angus.'

'I won't beat about the bush,' said the other, lowering himself onto a chair. 'What exactly is going on?'

Lockyer shrugged. 'I don't follow.'

'Oh, I think you do. Henrietta didn't notice it because she is still too stunned by your father's sudden death. But I have been very much aware of it.'

'Aware of what?'

'Your total lack of hospitality. We might as well have been complete strangers, not members of the same family. What on earth is going on?'

'Nothing is going on,' retorted Pelham.

'I'm not blind, man. You'd rather we were not here.'

'That's not true at all. It's a time when Henrietta and I need to be together, and I was grateful that you were able to bring her here so swiftly. If I've been a poor host, put it down to the fact that Father's death was like a hammer blow. I'm still in a complete daze.'

'It doesn't mean that you have to ignore us.'

'No, of course it doesn't, and I apologise. I'll be more considerate from now on.'

Rennie studied him closely. 'What's the problem, Pelham?'

'Father was murdered. I can't get that horrifying fact out of my head. Henrietta deals with the news her way and is supported by you. I am still struggling to work out how on earth we can manage without him. He was everything to me, Angus.'

'That's as it should be.'

'I was so proud of all that Father achieved.'

'And are you still equally proud?' asked Rennie, watching him carefully.

'Yes, I am,' declared Pelham. 'Father taught me everything I know, and I'm indebted to him for that. He was a remarkable man without faults. I revere his memory.' He took a deep breath. 'But he would be horrified to hear that I was forgetting the laws of hospitality. You and Henrietta have every right to expect my constant attention. I promise you that is what you will get from now on.' He contrived an apologetic smile. 'Will that content you?'

'It will please us both very much,' said Rennie, hiding his anxieties.

As soon as Colbeck returned to Scotland Yard, he gave the superintendent a report of his visit to the Villiers house. Tallis listened intently then passed on his own news.

'Inspector Crabbe paid us another visit,' he said.

'I'm sorry that I missed him.'

'He was anxious to see you. Crabbe is staying the night in London in the hopes of meeting you tomorrow.'

'I'll make a point of seeing him today,' said Colbeck. 'Do you have the name of his hotel?'

'Yes, I do.'

'Crabbe is not the most prepossessing individual, but he has the right to learn of any developments in the case. How did you find him, sir?'

'I'd never dream of employing the fellow,' said Tallis.

'In his own way, he's very conscientious. The chief constable has a higher opinion of him than we do.'

'Colonel Edgell, as usual, is a poor judge of character.'

'Might I ask if he sent his regards to you?'

'No, you may not,' snapped Tallis. 'I've indicated before that

I'd be grateful if you didn't mention his accursed name again. Please obey me for once.'

'But the colonel is directly involved in this investigation.' Seeing the look in the other man's eyes, Colbeck quickly changed tack. 'Perhaps we should put him aside and pretend that he does not exist.'

'I'd prefer it that way,' grunted the superintendent. 'Remember that.'

'I will, sir. Now, might I have the name of the hotel where Sergeant Crabbe is staying?'

Tallis reached for a piece of paper and handed it to him in silence.

When Caleb Andrews came in from the garden with his granddaughter, he was clearly out of breath. He sank down on a seat in the hall. Having listened to Helena Rose's description of the game she had played with her grandfather, Madeleine sent her off to the nursery and turned her attention to her father. His face was covered in perspiration. He used a handkerchief to wipe it away.

'You should remember your age,' she told him. 'There are limits to your energy.'

'I'm fine,' he croaked.

'Well, you don't look fine.'

'I love playing with her, Maddy.'

'Then you must make sure that she doesn't run the legs off you.'

'You may be right,' he conceded.

'While you were out, a message came.'

'Was it for me?'

'No, it was addressed to me. Mrs Dowling wanted me to know that the woman posing as "Madeleine Colbeck" called at the shop.'

'Did she get her real name?'

'There's only one way to find out. I'll have to go there at once.'

'I'll come with you, Maddy.'

'I'm going to the shop for information. There'll be no cup of tea and a biscuit this time.'

'I can manage without those. It will be nice to see Victoria – Mrs Dowling – again.'

'You can come if you promise to be on your best behaviour.'

Andrews was affronted. 'I'm always on my best behaviour!'

The hotel was in a side-street within easy walking distance of Scotland Yard. When Colbeck reached it, he asked the receptionist if Inspector Crabbe was there. The man was quickly summoned from his room and adjourned to the lounge with Colbeck. They settled into chairs in a quiet corner.

'It's very good of you to come looking for me,' said Crabbe.

'I have news about the investigation to pass on and I would rather do it face to face.'

'Colonel Edgell sent me here.'

'I can understand why he had no wish to come here himself,' said Colbeck, 'and why he preferred to dispatch you. How did you find Superintendent Tallis?'

'A bit daunting, to be honest.'

'He has his virtues.'

'Well, he kept them well hidden from me.'

'Did the chief constable send his regards?'

Crabbe laughed. 'He pretended to do so.'

'I'd be interested to know why.'

'So would I,' admitted Crabbe. 'But when I asked the colonel why he and Superintendent Tallis hated each other, I was told in no uncertain terms to mind my own business.'

'Then let's forget the pair of them,' suggested Colbeck, 'and address our minds to the case in which we are both involved. The main development is this . . .'

On the journey to Victoria Dowling's shop, Madeleine sat quietly in the cab and nursed her hopes. Her father, by contrast, was convinced that the mystery was finally solved. Seated on the edge of his seat, he slapped his knee and cackled.

'We've caught her at last!' he said.

'We've done nothing of the kind,' Madeleine reminded him. 'All we know is that the woman came to the shop to see if anyone had shown an interest in her painting.'

'Mrs Dowling would have got the truth out of her.'

'I doubt that very much.'

'Victoria is clever. It was the first thing I noticed about her. She will have found a way to get the truth out of this woman pretending to be you.'

'Then why didn't she say so in the message she sent me?'

Andrews was deflated. 'I never thought of that.'

'You always jump to conclusions.'

'I'm your father, Maddy. I'm entitled to defend you.'

'Yes, of course,' she agreed, 'but we must face facts. This so-called artist is committing a crime. She will tell any lie to protect her identity. All we can expect to hear is what she said to Mrs Dowling. Don't expect miracles.'

'Why not?' he said, a hand on her knee. 'I'm sitting next to one. You're the biggest miracle in my life – closely followed by Helena Rose, of course – so I'm doubly blessed.'

'Thank you,' she replied. 'When we get there, let me do the talking.'

'But Victoria and I are friends.' He saw the look in her eyes. 'Oh, all right, I'll hold my tongue.'

'Please remember that promise,' she said.

When the cab arrived at their destination, they asked the driver to wait so that he could drive them back home. They then climbed out and went towards the shop, passing another waiting cab as they did so. Victoria Dowling gave them a warm welcome.

'Oh, I'm so glad to see you both again,' she said effusively. 'If you'd been here earlier, you could have confronted "Madeleine Colbeck". She was standing right where you are.'

'I'd have done more than confront her!' said Andrews to himself.

'Why did she come?' asked Madeleine.

'She wanted to know if anyone had shown an interest in her painting,' said the woman. 'I told her the truth. More than a few people had noticed it and obviously liked it – but not enough to buy it, unfortunately. The truth is that I'd hate to sell what is, in fact, a fake.'

'Did you find out where this woman lived?'

'I asked her directly and told her that, if I had her address, I could send word if someone was interested in buying her work.'

'But it's not hers,' insisted Andrews. 'It's a copy of one of my daughter's paintings.'

'Father,' reminded Madeleine, 'you promised to hold your tongue.'

'Sorry, Maddy.'

'How long was she here, Mrs Dowling?' asked Madeleine.

'Long enough for my husband to talk to her cab driver. Davy wandered out and chatted to the man to win his confidence. Then he asked the driver how far he'd come.'

'What was his answer?'

'All the way from Regent's Park,' said Victoria. 'I'd realised that she had money. There's no such thing as a cheap house in that part of the city.'

CHAPTER SEVENTEEN

With half a pint of beer inside him, Hubert Crabbe was a much more amenable companion – friendly, relaxed and talkative. While he could never bring himself to like the man, Colbeck warmed to him slightly while taking an occasional sip of his own drink.

'What did you think of Scotland Yard?' he asked.

'It was impressive,' replied Crabbe. 'In a capital city, it needs to be. Frankly, I was a bit overwhelmed at first. I'd never be able to find my way around a place so huge.'

'You'd soon find somewhere to hide from Superintendent Tallis.'

Crabbe laughed. 'No thanks. I feel at home in Shrewsbury. And I'd rather be someone important in a small police station than a faceless nobody in Scotland Yard.'

'Do you think that I'm a faceless nobody?' asked Colbeck.

'You're an exception to the rule. You'd stand out anywhere.'

'I'm not sure if that's a compliment or a complaint.'

'Everybody knows your worth, Inspector. You've earnt respect.'

'That's reassuring,' said Colbeck with a smile. 'It must have taken time for your constabulary to adjust to a new man in charge, especially as the newcomer had no experience of police work.'

'Colonel Edgell picks things up very quickly. You only need to tell him something once and it's lodged in his brain immediately.'

'That's to his credit.'

'We're lucky to have a man of his quality.'

'Does that mean he has no faults?'

'No, it doesn't,' said Crabbe. 'It means that he ought to stop treating police officers as if they are soldiers in an army. It's the thing that our constables hate the most.'

'Once a soldier, always a soldier – just like Superintendent Tallis.'

'They speak the same language and behave in the same way.'

'I admire men who fight to protect this country,' said Colbeck. 'They put their life on the line and, if they serve in places like India, they risk catching dreadful diseases.'

'Our chief constable is as fit as a fiddle.'

'Will he be pleased with the information I've confided in you?'

'Oh, yes. He'll feel justified in having sent me to London.'

'Are you glad that you came?' asked Colbeck.

'Let me finish this pint,' said Crabbe, lifting his glass to his lips, 'and I'll tell you.'

They were delighted by what they had learnt during their visit to Victoria Dowling's shop. It was as if they'd taken a giant step forward towards learning the real name of the bogus artist. One thing puzzled them. On their return journey, Caleb Andrews was the first to ask the question.

'Why on earth does this woman bother to paint?' he wondered.

'It's because she has an urge to do so,' replied Madeleine.

'No, she doesn't. She can't bring an idea of her own to life on a canvas. She copies you, Maddy. And why ask so little for the painting she's put on sale?'

'Mrs Dowling had the answer to that. The woman has no need of money. Look how well dressed she was, according to Victoria. And remember where she lives. There are no paupers in the Regent's Park area.'

'I still can't see why this woman does it.'

'What she's after is the satisfaction of being regarded as a real artist.'

'But she's not an artist,' he insisted. 'She's just a copycat.'

'If truth be told,' confessed Madeleine, 'we all are to some extent. We learn from the great artists and pinch ideas from them here and there. Gradually, we develop a style of our own and, if we're lucky, we eventually start to produce work that an art gallery can sell.'

'Then someone like this crook comes along and steals your painting.'

'We don't know that she's a crook, Father.'

'What else is she?'

'I wish I knew,' said Madeleine, 'but, after what we've learnt about her today, I'm even more determined to meet her face to face.'

'And I want to be there when you do it,' insisted her father.

No matter how early Colbeck arrived at Scotland Yard in the morning, he could guarantee that Superintendent Tallis would be there before him. He put it down to their differing domestic situations. Colbeck was a family man whereas Tallis was a bachelor who lived alone. When he arrived that morning, the inspector had to pass the door of his superior's office. Curling under it were wisps of smoke from Tallis's first cigar of the day. Colbeck walked on past the door to his own office, only to find a summons that sent him straight back to the superintendent's office. After knocking, he entered the room.

'You're late,' said Tallis, half-hidden by cigar smoke. 'Why is that?'

'I'm here thirty minutes before the time when I'm due to arrive.'

'That's nothing. I've been here an hour.'

'Were you that desperate for a cigar, sir?' teased Colbeck before continuing quickly. 'You're an example to us all, sir. You set formidable targets of punctuality.'

'Someone has to set standards.'

'Quite so, Superintendent.'

'How did you get on with that appalling man from Shrewsbury?'

'He improved on acquaintance, sir.'

'Inspector Crabbe had a distinct smell of failure about him.'

'That's unfair,' argued Colbeck. 'After a few drinks together, he became much more like a human being. Crabbe can't be blamed for working in a provincial police force.'

'He's one of Edgell's minions,' said Tallis, wrinkling his nose.

'I daresay that he thinks I'm one of yours. Alone together, he and I put our differences aside and talked seriously about the case in hand.'

'What's the next step?'

'I'd like to speak to Pelham Lockyer again, sir.'

'For any particular reason?'

'Yes,' said Colbeck. 'He's not been entirely honest with me.'

'You have to allow for the immense pressure he is suddenly under.'

'He's concealing something from us, sir, and I intend to find out what it is. I'm convinced that it has a bearing on this case. As well as Mr Lockyer, I'd like to speak to his brother-in-law, Mr Rennie. Because of his position, he's not consumed by the same grief as the family members. He'll take a more realistic view of recent events.'

'Will you take Leeming with you?'

'No, I think I can work better on my own in this instance.'

'I've been reading his account of your visit to Mr Prance. It's impressively comprehensive.'

'The sergeant likes to record every shred of evidence.'

There was a long pause before Tallis asked his next question. 'Did you and Crabbe talk about my relationship with Colonel Edgell?'

'No, sir.'

'Are you certain of that?'

'Absolutely certain,' said Colbeck smoothly. 'The truth is that your names simply never came up in the conversation.'

Tallis gave a snort of disbelief.

When she heard about the latest visit to the shop that had the painting of a steam engine on sale, Lydia Quayle wished that she had been there at the time. Having called at the house that morning, she was now sitting in the drawing room with Madeleine.

'How kind of Mrs Dowling to get in touch!' she exclaimed.

'It's her husband, Davy, who deserves equal thanks,' said Madeleine. 'He was the person who discovered where the other artist lives. She hails from Regent's Park.'

'We were told that she was rather grand.'

'That's what puzzled me, Lydia. I don't wish to go into details but being an artist means that you can sometimes make a terrible mess. I often end up with oil paint over my hands and forearms. It takes me ages to get it off. If this woman is as well dressed and well-groomed as we are told, I can't imagine her getting her hands dirty in a studio.'

'Yet she must do just that, Madeleine.'

'I suppose so.'

'In which part of Regent's Park does she live?'

'The only way to find out is to have her followed to her home.'

'Is that possible?'

'Mrs Dowling assures me that it is. Next time she turns up, Mr Dowling is going to find out from the cab driver where exactly he picked the woman up. If we discover the address in Regent's Park where this woman lives, we will be able to confront her.'

'This sounds like work for Alan Hinton.'

'Oh, I wouldn't tackle her on my own.'

'What about your father?'

'I'm not sure that he's the right person, Lydia. Father is too vengeful. I need someone who is not at the mercy of his emotions.'

'Then Alan is the ideal person.'

'He may not be available. My own choice would be you, Lydia.'

'Why?'

'But for you seeing the painting in a shop window, I'd be completely ignorant of the act that someone is copying my work. When I confront this woman,' said Madeleine, 'I'd love you to be there.'

Lydia was practical. 'Alan Hinton would be more use.'

* * *

Colbeck was disappointed to call at Pelham Lockyer's house and find that he was not at home. There was, however, a consolation. Hearing the inspector's voice, the man's sister came rushing into the hall to invite him into the house. Colbeck was glad to accept the invitation. He was soon seated in the drawing room with Henrietta and Angus Rennie.

'Is there something to report?' asked Rennie hopefully.

'I feel that we have made a degree of progress,' said Colbeck, 'but I'd rather wait until Mr Lockyer returns so that you can all hear my report together.'

'That's only fair to my brother,' said Henrietta.

'How do you think he is coping with the situation?' asked Colbeck.

'Pelham is coping very well.'

'That's not true at all,' said her husband. 'He's been so preoccupied since we arrived that I tackled him about it.'

'How did he react?' asked Colbeck.

'Well, he was annoyed at first at being challenged, but he came to see it from our point of view. In difficult times, I told him, families come together. They don't ignore each other in the way that he ignored us. In fairness to him,' he went on, 'Pelham eventually accepted that he had been a very indifferent host and apologised.'

'Did he give any reason for his behaviour?'

'He said that he was bewildered by recent events. His father was like a god to him. The murder deprived Pelham of all the certainties in his life. He confessed that he was floundering and had been to church to pray for help.'

'Since then,' said Henrietta, 'he's been much more attentive to us.'

'But he still keeps us at arm's length, my love.'

'Angus!'

'You may not notice it, Henrietta, but I'm very much aware of it. He's . . . preoccupied.'

'In view of the situation,' Colbeck reminded them, 'that's only to be expected.'

Rennie was blunt. 'He's hiding something!'

'Have you any idea what it is, sir?'

'I'm afraid that I don't.'

'We mustn't pester him,' argued Henrietta. 'He's under intense pressure.'

'Then why doesn't he confide in us, my love? I feel I'm deliberately shut out.'

'In times of stress,' Colbeck pointed out, 'people often behave strangely. Mr Lockyer seems to be driven by a desire to be like his father while realising that it's a feat beyond him.'

'He used to be such a friendly chap,' complained Rennie. 'Didn't he, Henrietta?'

'I think he's the best brother in the world,' she said loyally, 'and I hate the fact that we're talking about him like this. It's so unfair of us.'

'Then perhaps we should move the conversation in another direction,' suggested Colbeck. Have the arrangements for the funeral been finalised?'

'You'll have to ask Pelham,' said Rennie. 'He's in charge of that.'

Pelham Lockyer had sat in front of his father's desk for the best part of twenty minutes, certain that it might contain an explanation of why the man had been killed. Lacking a key, however, he had no means of opening the desk. He could easily pay a locksmith to open it, but he was too afraid of what he might find if he did that. The tension was agonising. He knew that the contents of the desk might change his opinion of the man he had loved and copied throughout his life. Pelham lacked the courage to find out the truth. Opening the desk seemed like a terrible thing to do. The very idea made his stomach heave. After staring at the desk for another fifteen minutes, he decided to leave it alone until after the funeral. In his opinion, the man they buried was a paragon of virtue.

The truth about Julian Lockyer could be confronted when he was safely in his grave.

Archibald Reeves could not decide if his search the previous night had been a waste of time or if it had yielded something of value. What it had confirmed was his lack of confidence astride a horse. His mount had been so temperamental that he had elected to dismount and lead it most of the way. When he had returned the animal to the stables from which he had hired it, he'd voiced his complaint. The surly man on duty had given him short shrift.

'Before you ride a horse again,' he'd suggested, 'learn to how to control it.'

When he had dealt with his morning appointments, Reeves found time to visit one the estate agents in the town. The offices of Parke and Jenkins Ltd stood in the High Street. He was lucky enough to have arrived there when Robertson Parke was available. It meant that the reporter was shown into the room occupied by the senior partner. Sensing a possible sale, Parker got to his feet, shook the newcomer's hand and assessed how much money his potential client would be able to spend on a property. Reeves sat down beside the desk. Parke resumed his seat and studied him for a moment. He was a short, fleshy, watchful, middle-aged man wearing a dark suit and a routine smile.

'How can I help you, Mr Reeves?' he asked. 'What sort of property are you after?'

'I'm not here to buy anything,' said the other. 'I just wanted information.'

'Of what nature, may I ask?'

'There's a pretty cottage on the other side of the English Bridge. I understand that you were responsible for selling it.'

'How do you know that?'

'There was a noticeboard of yours tucked away on its side in the garden. Evidently, you haven't had it removed yet. The house was locked and there was nobody at home.'

'May I ask why that property has aroused your interest?'

'It was only one of the cottages that caught my eye,' said Reeves. 'It happened to be the prettiest. I'm a reporter with the *Shrewsbury Chronicle* and I've been trying to interest my editor in an article about properties of real character in the town.'

'Oh, I see,' said Parke, brightening at the thought of free publicity. 'We have several other properties you may wish to include.'

'Let's talk about the one I mentioned. It's utterly charming and has a delightful garden. The place would be ideal for a young couple or indeed for much older inhabitants who are moving towards the end of their lives. Who owns it and why is your noticeboard still there if the property is sold?'

'It was an oversight on someone's part,' said Parker, wincing. 'I'll have it removed today.'

'And the name of the new owner is . . . ?'

The estate agent suddenly began to look uncomfortable.

* * *

As soon as Colbeck got back to Scotland Yard, he summoned Victor Leeming and told him in detail about his visit to Pelham Lockyer's home. Leeming was interested to hear what man's brother-in-law had claimed.

'Lockyer is in a world of his own,' said Colbeck. 'He's so shaken by what he learnt about his father that he can't even manage to be civil to his sister and brother-in-law.'

'We need to find out why, Inspector.'

'I've tried to do so but Lockyer refuses to confide in anyone.'

'There is another way of getting the information we need,' suggested Leeming.

'Is there?'

'You believe that Pelham Lockyer must have had access to his father's Will. Its contents upset him. Why don't we go to his solicitor and demand to read the Will as a matter of urgency?'

'No solicitor would allow us to do so. They're duty bound to protect their clients.'

'You said that the son must have had access to the Will.'

'He's family but we are not,' said Colbeck. 'The fact that Pelham Lockyer's behaviour is so odd confirms my feeling that he has already seen details of his father's wishes. They must have come as a thunderbolt, hence his strange behaviour.'

'Can't we persuade him to confide in us?'

'I fancy that he's too horrified to do so.'

'But he's hiding valuable evidence from us,' said Leeming.

'Then we'll have to find another way of getting hold of it,' said Colbeck thoughtfully. 'By the way, I had a meeting with Sergeant Crabbe earlier today.'

'Better you than me. I've no time for the man.'

'When we had a drink together, he became almost human. They

are still working hard to find fresh evidence about the murder, and I commended him for that. He did admit that having to work with an inexperienced chief constable was a handicap.'

'Did you ask him about Colonel Edgell's obvious hatred of the superintendent?'

'Yes, I did.'

'And?'

'Crabbe has no idea how it came about.'

'Didn't he ask the chief constable?'

'Of course – but he was told so forcefully to mind his own business that he hasn't dared to raise the subject again.'

'But Edgell and the superintendent were comrades-in-arms.'

'Both of them seem to have forgotten that, Victor.'

Alone in his office, Edward Tallis opened a drawer in his desk and took out a framed photograph. It had been taken shortly before he had left the army, and it featured a group of senior officers in Her Majesty's Bengal Army. Tallis could not believe how young he looked. The photograph brought back memories of fierce combat and intense heat. His gaze fell on Colonel Richard John Edgell, the officer at the centre of the photograph. The very sight of the man refreshed old wounds.

Opening the drawer, he put the photograph away then slammed the drawer shut.

'Solve this damned case, Colbeck!' he hissed. 'Get that bastard off my back.'

Now that the date for Julian Lockyer's funeral had been settled, notices needed to appear in the newspapers, and family members and friends had to be informed. Anxious to share the burden of contacting them, Henrietta was in her brother's office to do her share. When she saw the list of names of those to be contacted, she was amazed at its length. She looked up at her brother.

'I hadn't realised there would be so many,' she said.

'Father had a wide circle of friends,' he told her.

'I've never even heard of some of these people.'

'Leave them to me, Henrietta, and concentrate on our relatives.'

'Very well . . .'

She began to write names on the black-edged cards before slipping them into envelopes. After a while, she looked up at her brother.

'May I ask you something?' she said tentatively.

'Yes, of course.'

'It's a question that Angus put to you.'

Pelham bridled. 'Then don't waste your breath.'

'We're worried about you. Something has upset you deeply, hasn't it?'

'Nothing upsets me more than being badgered,' he snapped.

'I'm your sister, Pelham. I have a duty to offer you help.'

'Well, I don't need it. I'm grateful that you helped me with this chore but I'd rather we carried on in silence. I am coping with the horror of Father's murder in my own way. Allow me to grieve, Henrietta. Is that too much to ask?'

'No, of course not. I'm sorry to upset you.'

'Please pass on the same message to your husband,' he said sharply. 'The last thing I need at a time like this is someone firing hurtful questions at me. I just want to be left alone so that I can grit my teeth and get through this nightmare.' He glared at her. 'Do you understand?'

* * *

Madeleine Colbeck was just descending the stairs when she heard the doorbell. She waved a hand at the maid who appeared from the kitchen.

'It's all right,' she said. 'I'll see who it is.'

The maid withdrew at once, leaving Madeleine to open the door and find Alan Hinton standing outside. The couple exchanged greetings then she invited him into the house.

'I got your message,' he said.

'Thank you for coming so promptly.'

'I'm off duty now, Madeleine.'

'Come into the drawing room. I need to ask you a favour.'

'I've got a feeling that I know what it is,' he said, following her.

When they had sat down, she explained the situation regarding the bogus painting. Hinton was impressed by the fact that they at least had some idea where the woman who had painted it lived.

'It sounds to me as if Mrs Dowling's husband is a born detective.'

'He winkled the information out of the cab driver,' Madeleine explained. 'The next time she turns up at the shop, Davy is going to follow the cab to her home. During the day, he's keeping his horse saddled in readiness.'

'Excellent!'

'Once we have her address, I can confront this woman. I just wondered if you could find the time to come with me.'

'I'd be delighted,' he said, 'but shouldn't Lydia be with you? But for her, you'd never have found out that someone was copying your work and passing it off as her own.'

'Lydia agreed that I needed someone with the power of arrest.'

'Then I'd be pleased to assisr you.'

'That will at least stop her from copying my paintings,' she said.

* * *

Alone in his office, Colbeck was delighted when a uniformed constable brought a letter for him.

'It was delivered by hand,' said the man.

'Where is it from?' asked Colbeck.

'The House of Commons.'

Masking his surprise, Colbeck dismissed the man and opened the envelope. He was delighted to find a short note inside from Dr William James Clement, Member of Parliament. It appeared that Clement was in London for a few days and wondered if they might meet because he had brought information for Colbeck. Realising what the information must be, Colbeck left the building at once and hailed a cab.

'Where to, sir?' asked the cab driver.

'The House of Commons – as quick as you can, please.'

'Very good, sir.'

The driver obeyed his request, using his whip to get the horse moving at speed and overtaking other cabs in his way. His passenger, meanwhile, was delighted by the summons from Clement. It boded well. When they eventually arrived, Colbeck paid the driver and headed for the main entrance. The two policemen on duty outside the building recognised him immediately and stood back to let him enter. After speaking to a porter, Colbeck learnt where Clement's office was then picked his way through a positive warren. When he reached the office that he was after, he rapped on the door and was pleased to hear a familiar voice invite him in.

'What a lovely surprise!' said Clement, getting up from his desk to shake his hand. 'I wasn't expecting such a prompt response to my letter.'

'I came as soon as I could, Dr Clement. But I thought parliament was in recess.'

'It is. I came to take part in an important committee meeting. Since I had information to pass on to you, I hoped to do it in person – and here you are. But how did you find me without a guide?' he asked. 'This place is honeycombed with passages.'

'I have been here before,' explained Colbeck. 'In fact, I once had the pleasure of arresting a Member of Parliament.'

'Heavens – who was that?'

'Sir Humphrey Gilzean. The arrest didn't take place here, but I had visited the place beforehand when doing the research that identified him as a criminal. I learnt my way around the endless passages.'

'It took me months to do that. Anyway,' said Clement, indicating a chair, 'do please sit down.' They both took a seat. 'May I ask how the investigation is going?'

'As someone who was involved in it, you have every right to do so. My answer is that we are making steady progress. An arrest is not too far away.'

'Excellent. I hope that I can make a small contribution to your work.'

'In what way?'

'You may remember that we had no precise idea of the drugs found inside Mr Lockyer. The body has since been examined by an expert toxicologist and this is what he found.' Picking up a sheet of paper, he handed it to Colbeck. 'The killer did not believe in half measures. Don't worry if you can't recognise some of those drugs. I had difficulty identifying all of them. My special area in medicine was intestinal obstruction.'

'Good heavens!' exclaimed Colbeck, seeing the list of names. 'Was all this necessary?'

'No, Inspector. The first two drugs on the list would have been enough to send him off into a deep sleep. The rest would have accelerated the process – but, if had been allowed to live, he would eventually have woken up with no more than a bad headache and a queasy sensation.'

'Instead of which, he was killed while under the effect of this compound.'

'I hope that information may be of use to you.'

'It is extremely useful,' said Colbeck, 'and it explains something that was puzzling me.'

'What was that?'

'Why did the murder victim put up no resistance? The answer must be that he was already asleep. Mrs Burrage, the owner of the hotel, told me that Mr Lockyer had bought a bottle of whisky from her, and he had clearly tasted it before he left the hotel that night. She remembers the smell of it on his breath.'

'So?'

'The killer must have got into his room and poured some of the drug into the bottle. He then left the room by way of the window,' said Colbeck, thinking it through, 'and returned by the same means hours later. Mr Lockyer was deeply asleep, having had a glass of whisky before getting into bed. Killing him would have taken no time at all.'

'Poor man! He was a sitting duck.'

'The killer was ruthless. He gathered up everything of value – including the whisky bottle, I daresay – climbed out of the window and vanished into the night.'

'Heartless rogue!'

'Thank you for providing vital evidence,' said Colbeck, holding up the sheet of paper. 'This has been a great help, Dr Clement. I'm so grateful that you came to London today.'

'It's been a pleasure to help you. But tell me about this Member of Parliament whom you arrested. It must have happened before I was elected. What on earth was the man's crime?'

'Amongst other things, he was responsible for a murder, and for ordering the kidnap of the young woman who now happens to be my wife.'

Pelham Lockyer was making an extra effort to be more hospitable to his sister and her husband. As they enjoyed tea together at his home, he was very attentive towards them. Henrietta was duly grateful, but Angus Rennie was suspicious.

'What is all this pretence for?' he asked bluntly.

'It's not pretence, Angus. I'm genuinely happy to have you here.'

'Well, it's nice to be noticed at last.'

'Pelham has a lot of his mind,' said Henrietta.

'Families take priority in my book,' insisted her husband.

'And in mine,' said his brother-in-law. 'I am rightly criticised for being abstracted. Both of you deserve my deepest apology. It won't happen again, I promise you.'

'Does that mean you'll tell us what has been weighing on your mind?'

'It's the devastating shock arising from Father's death. I've been left with all sorts of problems to address. But that doesn't excuse my behaviour when you first arrived.'

'We find ourselves very welcome now,' said Henrietta. 'Thank you, Pelham.'

'Isn't there some way that we can help?' suggested Rennie.

'Simply having you here helps to lifts my spirits. When Father was killed, I felt horribly alone. He was such an important figure in my life – and he's gone. I still struggle to believe it.'

'So do I,' admitted Henrietta.

'My life suddenly came to a dead halt,' said her brother. 'I felt paralysed. It was only when I met Inspector Colbeck that I was able to confront reality. His help has been crucial. I'm just praying that he will have arrested the killer before we have the funeral. When the man is behind bars, I will shed a huge burden.'

'About time, too!' said Rennie under his breath.

After leaving the House of Commons, Colbeck went straight back to Scotland Yard. Colbeck then handed the superintendent the list of drugs he'd been given. After studying them for a few minutes, Tallis put the piece of paper aside.

'What does this tell you?' he asked.

'It tells me that the person who prepared the mixture made doubly sure that it would be strong enough to send the victim into a deep sleep.' Colbeck gritted his teeth. 'Mr Lockyer was utterly defenceless.'

'Did Dr Clement find traces of these drugs during the postmortem?'

'No, sir. He needed the help of an expert toxicologist. The doctor's main interest has been in another area of medicine.'

'What area is that?'

'Well, it seems that, in his younger days, he won a gold medal for a publication of his. Dr Clement is an expert on the anatomy, physiology and pathology of urinary organs.'

Tallis gulped. 'Oh, I see.'

'He's taken a close interest in the murder of Julian Lockyer.'

'And so have I,' said the other forcefully. 'I need signs of progress, Inspector.'

'You've just had one in your hands,' said Colbeck. 'That list proves that the victim was drugged before the attack so that he was unable to hold off his killer.'

'Yes, but we have no idea who that killer is.'

'We have a very clear idea of his identity. Detective Constables Hinton and Boyce got close to the man on two separate occasions. They described his size and shape, and the fact that he can run faster than either of them.'

'Who employed him?'

My belief is that it someone on the board of the GWR – a rival of Lockyer's perhaps, or an enemy who has a grudge.'

'I thought you told me that Lockyer was admired by his colleagues on the board.'

'That's what his son told me, and Christopher Prance said the same thing. But I have a strong feeling that they are both wrong. Someone close to Lockyer has been waiting for a chance to strike. He had the man followed to Shrewsbury and killed during the night.'

'Who is the person behind the murder?' demanded Tallis.

'I feel that we're getting ever closer to him, sir – and that's a promise.'

The moment he saw the man through the window, approaching the house, he was annoyed. He reached for his walking stick and levered himself to his feet. When his unwanted visitor was eventually shown into his office, the old man was livid.

'What the devil are you doing here?' he demanded.

'I've been thinking,' said his visitor.

'You were told to stay away and lie low. As for thinking, it's something I do before I give you orders.' He pointed an accusatory finger. 'Orders I expect you to obey.'

'I needed to speak to you because I'm fed up with being kept in the dark. You hired me to follow then kill a man, but you didn't tell me why he deserved to be killed.'

'You don't need to know.'

'Yes, I do,' said the other. 'I also deserve to be told what's in Mr Lockyer's desk. I've taken risks on two occasions to get into that house and had to fight off detectives the first time. What is so precious in that desk?'

'Paperwork.'

'What sort of paperwork?'

'Correspondence,' said the old man irritably. 'Letters that are very precious to me because they contain information I've been after for years.'

'What's to stop Lockyer's son from getting a locksmith to open the desk?'

'My guess is that he is afraid of what he might find. Unlike his father, the son doesn't have the guts to know the truth. I do. It's vital that I see some of the letters hidden away there.'

'Are they the reason you wanted Lockyer killed?'

'That's no business of yours.'

'Oh, yes, it is,' insisted the visitor. 'I took huge risks to kill someone. It means that I've got Inspector Colbeck and his detectives on my tail, and they got too bleeding close to me – twice in a row. They're not looking for you, are they? Oh, no. I'm the one with a target on my back. You're in the clear. Unless . . .'

'Are you daring to threaten me?' yelled the old man.

'I'm just reminding you that you were the one who ordered the murder. If I get caught for it, you'll hang beside me.'

'If you obey orders, neither of us will be arrested.'

'I need more money.'

'You've already been paid handsomely.'

'That was before I knew that the police would be on my tail. I thought I'd committed the perfect crime. I made it look as if Lockyer had killed himself. I stole everything worth having, including the whisky bottle in which I put that potion you gave me. Then I caught an early train back to London next day, thinking that the police would never catch me.'

'And they still haven't,' the old man reminded him.

'It's not for want of trying. My instincts saved me,' he recalled. 'On your orders, I broke into that house and what did I find? Detectives were waiting for me in that office. Luckily, I caught their stink. That's why I had to make a run for it.'

'You did well,' conceded the other.

'Then I'd like a bonus to prove that you appreciate what I did for you. And I want something else as well.'

'What is it?'

'An explanation of why you hated Lockyer so much that he had to be killed.' He folded his arms defiantly. 'I'm not leaving here until you tell me.'

The old man began to squirm.

CHAPTER EIGHTEEN

Colbeck was pleased to see Lydia Quayle arrive so early at the house. He was grateful for the help that she had given his wife in the search for the artist who had copied one of Madeleine's paintings. Colbeck was further delighted to hear about the initiative shown by Victoria Dowling's husband.

'It was very clever of him to chat to the woman's cab driver,' said Madeleine.

'I agree,' replied Colbeck, 'but he doesn't have to wait until the next time this self-styled "artist" appears so that he can follow her cab on horseback.'

'Doesn't he?'

'No, Madeleine. There's a much easier way to trace the woman.'

'What is it?' asked Lydia.

'Use the resources of the Metropolitan Police Force. We have constables who patrol that area every day. They will know exactly where the cab ranks are. I can give them a description of this other Madeleine Colbeck, and each of them can then talk to cab drivers in their area. Sooner or later, she will be traced.'

'That's wonderful!' said Madeleine. 'Why didn't I think of that?'

'It's because you're not a detective, my love.'

'Will you organise a search for the cab driver?'

'I'll be happy to set it in motion.'

'There's an additional favour to ask,' said Lydia. 'When we confront this woman, we'll need someone able to arrest her. We need the help of a detective, Robert. This woman needs to be stopped. I know how much hard work goes into Madeleine's paintings – not to mention the amazing talent she has.'

'It was Robert who encouraged me to develop that talent,' Madeleine reminded her.

'I did indeed,' said Colbeck, 'and I've been justly proud of your achievements. Nobody else has the right to copy paintings of yours and the gall to steal your name. It's high time that this other Madeleine Colbeck was taught a lesson.'

Long after his visitor had left, the old man was still seething with rage. The person he had employed as an assassin was now daring to make demands on him, asking for more money and threatening to cease working for him unless it was paid. It put the old man in an awkward position. While he hated having to agree to his demands, he had handed over the money, first getting the man's promise to steal something important from Julian Lockyer's house. Until he had the correspondence in his own hands, he could not even think about getting rid of a man on whom he relied.

But one thing was certain. The assassin had to die for daring to threaten him. The old man would not need to hire someone to kill him. He resolved to shoot the man himself. It would give him the satisfaction he needed and rid him of someone who had become a danger to him.

Later that evening, Colbeck had a pleasant surprise. Having enjoyed a leisurely dinner with his wife and Lydia Quayle, he was joined by Archibald Reeves. The reporter had come in the hope of catching him at home. Colbeck gave him a warm welcome and waved away his apologies for disturbing him at home. He introduced his visitor to the two women then took Reeves into his study so that they could talk in private.

'It's obviously my day for having unexpected visitors from Shrewsbury,' said Colbeck.

'Oh?' said Reeves. 'Who else has come here?'

'It was Dr Clement – but he didn't come to my home. He told me that he was in the House of Commons on political business but had something of interest to tell me. I took a cab there immediately.'

'I think I can guess what information he had brought. Dr Clement must have had a toxicologist's report on Julian Lockyer.'

'He did indeed, Archie. It was good to meet him again, though I did manage to startle him.'

'How on earth did you do that?'

'I told him that I had once arrested a Member of Parliament.'

'A lot of them deserve arrest!' said Reeves.

'It was not my only connection with the political world,' said

Colbeck. 'During one investigation, I had valuable help from Lord Palmerston himself when he was Prime Minister.'

'I can't compete with him, but I'm hoping that I can supply some useful information.'

'We're in need of every scrap we can get, Archie.'

'You'll remember that you asked me to keep my eyes open.'

'As a reporter, that's second nature to you.'

'What isn't second nature is riding a horse,' confessed Reeves. 'The one I hired was the most difficult animal to ride. In the end, I dismounted and led him over the English Bridge.'

'What did you find on the other side?'

'All sorts of interesting things. The most arresting one concerned a property that had been sold less than a month ago. It had been occupied by a family of three – husband, wife and child – and two servants. But they were not there at the time.'

'Why not?'

'Nobody knew, Inspector. A few days earlier, they had simply left the town and caught a train. I'm wondering if they had good reason to do so.'

'A connection to Julian Lockyer, perhaps?' asked Colbeck hopefully.

'It's possible. Neighbours told me that they were nice people but that they guarded their privacy. Their names were Mr and Mrs Nash. I decided to dig a little deeper, so I approached the estate agent who had sold the property to them. To win him over, I pretended that I was hoping to write an article about properties in the area. But he remained evasive and refused to give me the name of the person who actually paid for the house.' Reeves grinned. 'That set me wondering.'

'I've already started to wonder myself. Could that have been the house that Mr Lockyer had gone to on the evening of his murder?'

'If so, it would explain why they left the property so suddenly. The town was suddenly alive with rumours about the murder. When they realised that the police might conduct house-to-house searches, they decided to leave at once – because they had a connection to the murder victim.'

'Then again,' warned Colbeck, 'their departure could have been a coincidence.'

'Simon Biddle disagrees,' said Reeves. 'When I asked him about four adults and a child catching a train not long after the murder, he remembered them. They had a lot of luggage and seemed to be in a desperate hurry. Mind you,' he warned, 'lots of other passengers were also anxious to catch a train so the family didn't stand out that much.'

'I know the estate agent didn't tell you who bought the house, but I wonder if it was Julian Lockyer.'

'It was the first name I thought about.'

Colbeck sat back in his chair and brooded for a few minutes. Having come to a decision, he snapped his fingers. 'I may have to go to Shrewsbury once again.'

Having shared an excellent meal with his sister and his brother-in-law, Pelham Lockyer was in a more relaxed mood. He asked them about their life in Scotland and wondered if it were noticeably colder that far north. Pleasant conversation continued for a couple of hours. Henrietta then excused herself from the table and left the room. The mood changed instantly. Rounding on his host, Angus Rennie directed an angry question at him.

'How much longer can you keep this up, Pelham?' he demanded.

'I've no idea what you mean,' replied the other, shaken by the Scotsman's tone.

'The truth is bound to come out sooner or later.'

'I prefer not to talk about it, Angus.'

'My wife is set to inherit something from her father. That means she will be present at the reading of the Will. She will hear every detail of your father's bequests.'

'So?'

'Henrietta will be as shocked as you clearly are.'

Lockyer flicked a hand. 'I'm sorry but I refuse to have this discussion.'

'All that you're doing is to postpone the horror of discovery.'

'You're jumping to ridiculous conclusions.'

'Then why, in God's name, can't you tell us the truth about your father?'

'The truth is that he was a wonderful man,' insisted the other, puce with anger. 'I prefer to remember him for his many excellent qualities and not for any . . . minor weaknesses.' He rose to his feet. 'Good night, Angus.'

Leaving the room abruptly, he slammed the door shut.

Though he arrived early at Scotland Yard next morning, Edward Tallis found that someone had got there even earlier. On his desk was a letter from Colbeck, explaining that there had been a development in the case and that it was taking him back to Shrewsbury. Tallis tossed the letter aside in anger.

'Why didn't you give me some details?' he howled.

A message from Colbeck was also awaiting Alan Hinton. He was told that he had to contact police officers based in the Regent's

Park area and ask them to question cab drivers about a woman one of them may have driven recently. Details of her appearance and destination were given. Hinton was thrilled to take part in the search for the person who had not only dared to copy one of Madeleine's paintings but had even stolen her name.

'How many more times must we go back there?' complained Leeming, as the train set off.

'I thought that you liked the place, Victor,' said Colbeck. 'It has great charm and is free of the abiding stink and never-ending tumult of London.'

'I'd still rather stay in the capital.'

'We go where the evidence takes us.'

'Did it have to be so early in the morning?'

'I believe that Archie Reeves has given us a new source of evidence.'

'Well, I'm not convinced,' said Leeming, stifling a yawn with his hand.

'Have faith.'

They were seated in an otherwise empty compartment of a train that was steaming along at speed. While Colbeck enjoyed looking at the passing countryside, Leeming was bemoaning the fact that he had not been able to have breakfast.

'Don't worry, Victor,' said Colbeck. 'We'll have something to eat at the railway station.'

'I may have starved to death before then.'

His companion chuckled. 'It's good to find you in such a positive mood.'

'Did the superintendent send us back to Shrewsbury?'

'No,' admitted Colbeck. 'Sometimes we must act on our own

initiative. And that is exactly what we are doing.'

Leeming sighed. 'He won't be happy about this.'

'If we find new evidence, he'll be absolutely delighted.'

As he stacked some bottles on a shelf in the bar, Wilfred Harris was starting to lose heart. His earlier confidence had evaporated.

'I'm worried that the murder will never be solved,' he said.

'Then we'll go on losing customers,' complained Molly Burrage. 'We have to put our trust in Inspector Colbeck.'

'My trust is beginning to weaken.'

'Well, mine isn't. He promised to arrest the killer, and I believe that's what he'll do.'

'I think he's still floundering.'

'That's a terrible thing to say, Wilf! You should be ashamed.'

'I'm just facing facts.'

'The inspector warned us that it might take time.'

'How can he find the killer in a city as big as London?'

'I don't know – but I'm sure that he will.'

'Remember what Annie Garrow told us,' said the barman. 'When she first met Mr Lockyer, he stared at her so hard that she was frightened.

There was something very unpleasant about him.'

'He didn't deserve to be murdered, Wilf.'

'Somebody believed that he did.'

'Then we must rely on Inspector Colbeck to find that person,' she said firmly.

When they arrived at their destination, they had to wait several minutes before the stationmaster was free to talk to them. Pleased to see the detectives, Simon Biddle invited them into his office.

'I was hoping that we'd see you again,' he said.

'Archie Reeves supplied new information,' explained Colbeck.

'Yes, he told me about that young family who left the town in a hurry.'

'You remembered them, apparently.'

'All I remembered was that they were in a great hurry and had a lot of luggage.'

'Which train did they catch?' asked Leeming.

'It was one that would take them into Wales,' said Biddle. 'The station was crowded so I only got a glimpse of them.'

'Thank you for your help, Mr Biddle.'

Colonel Edgell was alone in his office when there was a tap on his door. It opened to admit Hubert Crabbe, who apologised for disturbing him.

'Has something happened?' asked the chief constable.

'Yes, sir. I had a message from Constable Marklew.'

'Who is he?'

'One of the police officers on duty at the railway station.'

'What was the message?'

'Inspector Colbeck and Sergeant Leeming have just arrived there.'

Edgell sat up with interest. 'What the devil has brought them back?'

When they reached the offices of Parke and Jenkins Ltd, they were grateful that Robertson Parke was available. He got to his feet to shake their hands in turn then all three of them sat down. Parke gave them his broadest smile.

'Welcome to Shrewsbury, gentlemen,' he said. 'What sort of property did you have in mind?'

'The one that Archibald Reeves talked to you about, sir.'

The estate agent's face fell. 'Oh, I see.'

'My name is Inspector Colbeck, and this is Sergeant Leeming. As you may know, we are detectives from Scotland Yard, investigating the murder of a man named Julian Lockyer.'

'What's brought you to me?' asked Parke.

'Your refusal to provide information. When Mr Reeves asked who owned a house on the other side of the English Bridge, you told him that the information was confidential.'

'It is, Inspector.'

'Concealing it from us,' warned Leeming, 'is an offence.'

'I can't tell you what I don't know,' explained Parke. 'The house was bought on behalf of the present occupants by a London solicitor acting for them. He paid the asking price on their behalf and Mr and Mrs Nash moved in. They are not short of money,' he confided. 'They have already spent a lot on improving the house. Mr Nash seems to work from home. That's all I can tell you.'

'When did they move in?' asked Colbeck.

'Months ago – when the renovation was finished.'

'Might I see the contract for the sale of the house, please?'

'Yes, of course,' replied Parke, opening a drawer in his desk and taking out a pile of documents to sift through. 'Everything was legitimate,' he went on. 'I handled the sale myself.'

He found the contract and handed it to Colbeck. 'Here it is, Inspector.'

After reading through it carefully, Colbeck made a note of the solicitor acting for the anonymous buyer. He then returned the contract to Parke.

'Thank you, sir. You've been very helpful.'

'Yes,' added Leeming. 'Archie Reeves told us you refused to show him the contract.'

'Discretion is vital in our trade, Sergeant,' said Parke.

'The London solicitor will say the same thing to us,' predicted Colbeck. 'If he'd had the sense to come forward earlier, we could have solved the murder in a matter of days. I'll have some stern questions to put to him.' He looked at Parke. 'What sort of person was he?'

'Secretive.'

'Well, he won't be able to keep any secrets from us, I promise you.'

Molly Burrage was in her office, studying the bookings for the week ahead. There would be several empty rooms at the Station Hotel. Her income was steadily dwindling. When there was a tap on the door, it opened for Colbeck to step into the room.

'Good heavens!' she exclaimed, getting to her feet. 'Wilf and I were talking about you earlier today.'

'This is a flying visit, Mrs Burrage.'

'Do you have any news about the investigation?'

'I have the best news possible,' he told her. 'Unless I'm mistaken, we've just picked up information that will lead in due course to the arrest of the killer – and to the person who hired him to commit murder.'

'That's wonderful!'

'We're taking the next train back to London to continue our work. But I felt that you deserved to know that – with luck – the curse on your hotel will soon be lifted.'

Tears of joy filled her eyes, and she threw her arms around him.

* * *

Colonel Edgell came out of his office and saw Inspector Crabbe walking towards him.

'I was just coming in search of you,' said Edgell. 'Have you any idea what Colbeck and Leeming are doing here?'

'Whatever it was,' explained Crabbe, 'it didn't take them long.'

'What do you mean?'

'I've had another message from the railway station, sir.'

'And?'

'Colbeck and Leeming are on their way back to London.'

Edgell was astounded. 'Why did the pair of them come here in the first place?'

It was a question that Edward Tallis had asked himself many times. Colbeck had left him with insufficient information, and he vowed to discipline the inspector when the latter returned. At the same time, however, experience had taught him that Colbeck had an extraordinary knack of getting good results by acting on his own initiative. Perhaps it was better to rein in his anger until he was face to face with the man responsible for it.

The first thing that Colbeck did when he returned to Scotland Yard was to tell the superintendent about the visit to Shrewsbury and the discovery at the estate agent's office. Tallis was grateful for the new information and waited until the recitation had finished before he asked a question.

'Did you get in touch with the local police?' he asked.

'There was no need for that, sir. It was a flying visit.'

'Then you made no contact with Colonel Edgell?'

'No, sir.'

'I'm grateful. He and I have loathed each other since our days

299

in the army together.'

'That's a matter between yourself and the colonel,' said Colbeck.

'It is and it isn't,' decided Tallis. 'I believe that you deserve to know the root of our mutual hatred – as long as you do not voice it abroad.'

'You can rely on my discretion.'

'Then the explanation is simple. When we served in the army in India together, we got along well – or so I thought. When he was awarded the Kabul Medal in 1842 for service in Afghanistan, so was I. When he was awarded the Punjab Medal, so was I. Because of my record, I was in line for promotion to the rank of major. At the last moment, it was blocked. I was reliably informed that Edgell had been responsible.'

'Yet you went on to get promotion, sir.'

'Almost a year later,' said Tallis. 'Edgell couldn't stop me that time. I've hated the man ever since and he has despised me.'

'I suspect that envy is involved,' Colbeck pointed out. 'But you've had your revenge. Colonel Edgell must have been angered when he saw you being promoted to a high rank in the Metropolitan Police Force. His own attempt to move into law enforcement was rebuffed at first.'

'Hearing of his rejection gave me a feeling of great contentment.'

'I'm sure that it did. Thank you for confiding in me.'

'I felt that I had to get it off my chest,' said Tallis. 'I know that I can rely on you to keep a secret. It's been a source of great discomfort to me over the years. Right,' he went on, rising to his feet, 'that's enough of my problems. You and Sergeant Leeming can tackle this solicitor together. What was his name?'

'Penhallurick – Stephen Penhallurick.'

* * *

Caleb Andrews was delighted to hear that the woman would almost certainly be arrested later that day. He rubbed his hands together with relish.

'I want to be there when it happens, Maddy!' he insisted.

'It's a job for the police, Father.'

'Can't I at least watch her being handcuffed?'

'It's unlikely that she will need to be restrained,' his daughter pointed out.

'If it were left to me, I'd drag her off in chains. Yes,' he went on, 'and I'll wait outside the court when she's been sentenced. As she comes out, I'll throw rotten apples at her.'

'Don't be ridiculous!' she said, laughing. 'We're not talking about someone who has committed a heinous crime. I'm not even thinking about her punishment. All that interests me is what drove this woman to copy one of my paintings? It's a complete mystery.'

When they left Scotland Yard, they hailed a cab and gave him an address. The journey was not long. After they'd reached their destination, Colbeck paid the driver. He and Leeming then looked at the offices of Penhallurick, Stacey and Greene. The solicitors occupied a large house in a cloistered part of the city. Colbeck led the way to the front door and rang the bell. They were soon let into the building and taken to the office occupied by Stephen Penhallurick. Surprised to see them, the solicitor offered them seats.

'We prefer to stand,' warned Colbeck. 'My colleague is Sergeant Leeming, and he has been taking part in the investigation into the murder of one of your former clients. I am Inspector Colbeck, charged with leading the investigation.'

'What brings you here?' asked Penhallurick.

'We've not long returned from Shrewsbury,' explained Colbeck. 'I was able to question an estate agent by the name of Robertson Parke.' He smiled. 'I can see from your startled expression that you know the gentleman.'

'It's true,' admitted Penhallurick.

'Indeed, you bought a house from him.'

'I was acting on a client's instructions.'

'A client by the name of Julian Lockyer,' said Colbeck. 'We were shown the contract for the sale. Your signature was on it.'

'I was simply doing what I was told to do,' bleated the solicitor.

'Unfortunately,' Colbeck reminded him, 'Mr Lockyer was killed on the night after he had visited that house. I have been on the trail of his assassin. Why didn't you feel obliged to help me?'

The man shrugged. 'What could I have done?'

'You could have saved us a lot of time, sir. If you had told us what had taken your client to the town, we'd have understood why he was there. He went to see the people who lived in the house you bought for them, didn't he?'

Penhallurick nodded.

'Who were they?'

'I'd rather not say.'

'You have no choice,' said Colbeck. 'We're talking about a murder investigation. Isn't it time that you started helping us instead of trying to keep secrets?'

'What happens in my dealings with a respected client is confidential.'

'You broke that rule for the sake of Pelham Lockyer,' said Colbeck. 'You let him see his father's guilty secret, didn't you? It's shaken him to the core. I spoke to his sister and brother-in-law. All three of us agreed that his behaviour is strange. I think that he's in a daze because he made a bruising discovery.'

'He demanded the truth, and I gave it to him.'

'What is this truth that you've been hiding?' asked Leeming.

'I think that I can tell you that, Sergeant,' said Colbeck. 'The reason that a house was bought in Shrewsbury is that it was a gift for the young woman who gave birth to Mr Lockyer's daughter.' He turned to the solicitor. 'Am I right, sir?'

There was a lengthy pause before Penhallurick was able to speak.

'Yes, Inspector,' he mumbled. 'You are.'

Information came back to Scotland Yard far earlier than expected. Two cab drivers who operated from a rank in Regent's Park recognised the woman in question from the description of her. Each of them had taken her to and from the shop owned by Victoria Dowling. Alan Hinton acted swiftly. He went by cab to the Colbeck residence to pick up Madeleine. She was thrilled that the address had been found and keen to confront the woman who had caused her such pain and vexation. They set off for Regent's Park with high hopes.

Alan Hinton had forgotten what a beautiful, well-planned area it was with trees in abundance and rows of delightful villas. But there was little time to admire the scenic delights. Madeleine was clearly on edge, keen to challenge the woman who had copied her work and tried to sell it. When they reached the house, they saw that it was screened by a row of trees. After asking the driver to wait, the two passengers got out. Emboldened by the opportunity to bring a stop to the woman's behaviour, Madeleine went up the drive first and used the knocker with force. Hinton stood beside her. The door was opened by a maidservant, who looked at them in surprise.

'I am Detective Constable Hinton,' he said, 'and this is Mrs Colbeck. We need to see the lady of the house.'

'Is Mrs Sanderson expecting you?' asked the maidservant nervously.

'No, she isn't. May we come in?'

Without waiting for her to respond, he eased the young woman gently aside then led Madeleine into the hall. The maidservant was horrified.

'You can't come in like that!' she cried.

The door of the drawing room opened, and a handsome, middle-aged woman swept into view. Her voice was stern.

'What's going on?' she demanded. 'Who are these people?'

'My name is Madeleine Colbeck,' said Madeleine, stepping forward to confront her. 'You stole both my name and one of my paintings, Mrs Sanderson.'

The woman was too shocked to reply. She had to steady herself with a hand against a wall.

'Detective Constable Hinton is here to arrest you,' added Madeleine, indicating him.

'I did nothing wrong,' wailed the woman.

'I'm afraid that you will have to come with us,' said Hinton.

'But you don't understand. I meant no harm.'

'Well, you certainly caused it.'

'All I was doing was trying to keep my husband alive.'

'What do you mean?' asked Madeleine, seeing her distress.

The woman took a deep breath. 'Follow me . . .'

On the cab ride back to Scotland Yard, they were able to review their visit to the solicitor.

'The fellow deliberately delayed our investigation,' said Leeming ruefully.

'He would argue that he was acting in the best interests of his client,' said Colbeck. 'Mr Penhallurick was concealing a secret that could create a lot of pain and dismay if it became common knowledge.'

'Quite right, too! A man of that age, seducing an innocent young woman.'

'It does explain why Mr Lockyer attended church so often and gave such generous donations. It was his penance. In his own way, he tried to do his best for the young woman involved. I daresay that he helped to find her a young man prepared to marry her.'

'Scandalous!'

'It was something I had never suspected,' said Colbeck. 'To be honest, I had the feeling that Lockyer was closely involved with a man with whom he had been at Rugby School – Desmond Villiers. I met the fellow. Even though he is himself now married, there was clearly a deep and lasting affection between the two men. Villiers idolised him.'

'What will he think of his friend when he hears that Lockyer slept with a girl who was barely into her twenties?'

'Hopefully it's a secret that will be kept from him.'

'We've certainly learnt something important,' said Leeming, 'but it's brought us no closer to the person who arranged Lockyer's murder.'

'I disagree. I fancy that he sits on the board of directors of the GWR.'

'Are you sure?'

'I feel it in my bones. He's a man of means and I guarantee that he will have recently discovered what happened to a young female member of his wider family. Enraged by the information, he would have been moved to strike.'

'But we have no idea who this man is, sir.'

Colbeck smiled. 'I know someone who does.'

Before she could lead them out of the hallway, Mrs Sanderson needed to get her breath back. She was clearly in distress. Even though she had cause to despise the woman, Madeleine felt sympathy welling up. Alan Hinton was firm.

'You have been breaking the law, Mrs Sanderson,' he told her. 'And I believe that you know it.'

'We meant no harm,' said the woman.

'Well, you certainly caused plenty of it. Mrs Colbeck was extremely upset.'

'What made you copy my work?' asked Madeleine.

'I didn't,' replied Mrs Sanderson. 'My husband is the artist in the family. Come and meet him, please. I must warn you that he's very fragile. Please treat him gently.'

'He hasn't treated Mrs Colbeck gently,' observed Hinton.

'No,' agreed Madeleine. 'He's given me sleepless nights.'

'I'm so sorry about that,' said the woman. 'We intended no harm. Nigel is the kindest man in the world. At least, he was before he became ill. Follow me.'

She led them upstairs and along a corridor to a room at the far end.

'This is his studio,' she explained. 'I must ask you to wait here while I prepare him for what will be a terrible shock.'

'I had one of those,' said Madeleine to herself.

Entering the studio, the woman was gone for several minutes. Hinton became restive. Before he could go into the room himself, the door opened, and Mrs Sanderson stood back.

'Please come in,' she invited. 'Nigel is ready for you now.'

Hinton gestured that Madeleine should go first. He was not far behind her. The first thing they noticed was an elderly man in his pyjamas propped up on pillows in a chair. His welcoming smile failed to conceal the hollow cheeks and the dark circles beneath his eyes. His scalp was a mass of wrinkles. Evidently, he was very old and very sick. Madeleine's gaze went to the canvas on the low table in front of him. On it was a rough outline of another painting of hers. She felt a combination of shock and pain.

'Don't say anything,' warned Mrs Sanderson. 'Nigel won't be able to understand you. His mind is in a far worse condition than his body. But there's one thing that's making him cling to life. It's the paintings of Madeleine Colbeck.'

'Why them?' asked Hinton.

'He spent his working life as an architect. It was his passion. That was years ago when he always had a pencil in his hand and dozens of ideas in his head. Then came his illness,' she said with a hand on her husband's shoulder. 'It affected his mind more than his body. For years, he spent most of the day asleep. Then out of the blue, he asked for paper and pencil – and the first thing he drew was a steam engine. He had a childish passion for them. That was how we came to discover your paintings, Mrs Colbeck. I bought a print of one from the Red Gallery. My husband was delighted.'

'That's no reason why he copied the painting and signed it with my name,' said Madeleine. 'It was an act of downright theft.'

'But it wasn't, I assure you,' said Mrs Sanderson. 'Nigel insisted on using your name because the painting was, in every sense, your property. We never sought to profit from the sale. We hoped that it might gain more attention for someone who is such a talented and unusual painter.'

'Are you claiming that you were helping me?' asked Madeleine, aghast. 'Don't you realise that you were committing a crime?'

The old man began to gabble, and his wife bent down close to him to pick up what he was saying. Neither of the visitors could make sense of the words that dribbled out of his mouth. What they did grasp was a genuine sense of apology. Nigel Sanderson had intended no harm.

Madeleine was chastened. When she worked on a painting, she stood at an easel and dabbed oil paint on the canvas. Since the old man was unable to stand, he worked on a table like an architect at a drawing board. In becoming an artist, he had found something that made him wake up every day and occupy his mind. Copying Madeleine's painting had given him some purpose in life. His apologetic smile acknowledged that he could never be as good an artist as she was. He had simply wanted to find a wider audience for her.

'You have real talent, Mr Sanderson,' Madeleine told him. 'You've no need to copy me.'

'It's an act of homage,' explained the man's wife. 'He is grateful for the way that your work opened his eyes. In that sense, you've helped to keep my husband alive. And there's another thing. It may seem strange that a man who was a successful architect should turn to painting, but he's not an architect anymore. That world has disappeared from his memory. When he saw a painting of yours, it inspired him somehow. He begged me to buy oil paints. He spent many long, happy hours at his easel. It was a joy to see him so busy and so involved. When I told him that someone wanted to offer his work for sale, he was thrilled. It gave him a sense of validation as an artist - even though he was only copying a painting by someone else. It brought him alive again and it has given me time with my darling husband that is so precious to me. I can't thank you enough for that.'

Madeleine was touched. Having come to challenge the woman, she had discovered that Mrs Sanderson had not been the artist. It was her husband who had created copies of her work, doing so extremely slowly yet deriving great satisfaction from the exercise.

'He has a real gift for drawing figures,' she said. 'It's my weakness. I can conjure up a steam engine or a railway station with ease but creating real people is more difficult. Advise your husband to paint portraits. That's where he would be at his best.'

'Does that mean he has to stop copying you?' asked the woman sadly.

'It's in his best interests.'

'I agree,' said Hinton. 'What you call an act of homage can be seen as a case of theft. That would make you and your husband liable to arrest.'

'Surely not!' she exclaimed.

'I'll press no charges,' said Madeleine. 'Now that I've seen what your husband is doing, I'm pleased that my work has a positive value. But I'd much rather he kept any copies of my work for himself instead of trying to sell them. Thank you for explaining how and why he became so interested in a painting of mine.' She turned to the old man. 'You signed my name so cleverly on the canvas that you made me blink.' He laughed. 'We're sorry to have disturbed you, Mrs Sanderson. Now that I know the truth, I feel duly flattered.'

'Does that mean no arrest is necessary?' asked Hinton.

'It means just that,' replied Madeleine. 'It's time for us to go . . .'

* * *

After a hard day's work, Edward Tallis sat back in his chair and eyed his box of cigars. Before he could reach for one, there as a knock on the door and Colbeck came into the office. The superintendent glared at him.

'I expected you back earlier,' he rasped.

'We were held up, sir.'

'Did you learn anything from Lockyer's solicitor?'

'We learnt a great deal,' said Colbeck. 'Because of information we gleaned from him, we went to the home of Christopher Prance, the oldest member of the GWR board.'

'What was the point of that?'

'He knows all the members intimately and, during my earlier meeting with him, assured me that none of his colleagues was in any way involved in Mr Lockyer's murder. I felt at the time that he was too quick to absolve them all of blame. I remembered a photograph of board members he had on his wall.'

'Did someone catch your eye?' asked Tallis.

'Yes, sir. There was a man with his arm around Lockyer's shoulders. It was a gesture of support for a friend – but his eyes told a different story. Something that the solicitor told us made me think of that individual, so we went back to Mr Prance's home to view the photograph again.'

'What came of your visit?'

'A desire to arrest the man responsible for Lockyer's death,' said Colbeck. 'I felt that you might wish to be present.'

After a pleasant afternoon in the company of his daughter and his grandchildren, Douglas Noble waved them off from the house and retired to his study. Five minutes later, he heard the doorbell ring. It was followed by the sound of the front door being opened. Noble was unable to hear the muffled conversation on the doorstep. What he did hear soon afterwards was a knock on his door.

'Come in!' he called.

The door opened to reveal two male visitors.

'Mr Noble?' asked Tallis politely.

'Yes. Who might you be?'

'I am Superintendent Tallis from Scotland Yard and this Inspector Colbeck. We have been involved in the search for the man who was responsible for the murder of Julian Lockyer.'

'Why come to me?' asked Noble.

'We believe that you are the person we need,' said Colbeck levelly. 'I've not long come from the home of Christopher Prance. He showed me a photograph in which you appeared next to Mr Lockyer with your arm around his shoulders.'

'He was a good friend of mine,' argued Noble. 'I was congratulating him.'

Colbeck frowned. 'Arranging someone's murder is hardly an example of friendship. Since you are disabled, you obviously could not commit the crime yourself. You would have had to hire someone to act on your behalf.'

'Someone who used the alias of Jack Brown,' said Tallis.

'I've no idea what you're talking about,' claimed Noble with a dismissive laugh, getting up from his chair with the aid of his walking stick. 'I've never heard such nonsense.'

'We'd like you to come with us, sir,' said Tallis.

'I'll do nothing of the kind!' retorted Noble.

'Then we will have to arrest you and drag you out in handcuffs. Surely, you wish to avoid that humiliation?'

Noble looked from one to the other. 'Who put you up to this?' he asked.

'We reached you by a simple process of elimination,' explained Colbeck. 'I saw Mr Prance earlier on and I saw that photograph.'

'I'd just agreed to support his bid to become chairman.'

'Your gesture was an example of true friendship – but your eyes were full of malice.'

'It's in your interests to come quietly, Mr Noble,' said Tallis.

'I'm innocent, I tell you!'

'The court will decide your fate, sir,' said Colbeck, eyeing the desk. 'In which drawer do you keep your address book?'

Noble was alarmed. 'Why do you wish to see that?'

'Because it is likely to contain the name and address of the man you engaged to follow and kill Julian Lockyer. At your age, memory is less reliable. You need to write everything down.' Colbeck moved to the desk. 'Is it in this drawer?' he asked, pulling one open.

'No,' cried Noble, waving him back. 'If you want the address book, I'll get it for you.'

Opening another drawer, he thrust in a hand and pulled out a gun. He aimed it first at Colbeck and then at Tallis. Neither of them blenched.

'Thank you for admitting your guilt, sir,' said Colbeck quietly. 'It will help to shorten your trial.'

'Put that weapon down!' ordered Tallis, moving towards him.

'Stop right there!' snapped Noble, turning the gun on him.

'I spent most of my career in India, sir, fighting in the army against people who had no scruples about taking a human life. Guns were trained on me time after time but, as you see, I survived to tell the tale. Give me the weapon,' he invited, extending a palm. 'You know that it's the sensible thing to do.'

Noble began to weaken. As he took a few steps backwards, his eyes glared.

'Lockyer deserved to die,' he howled. 'Do you know what that animal did?'

'Yes,' said Colbeck, 'but he did his best to make amends.'

'Make amends! How can you make amends for ruining a young woman's life?'

'Mr Lockyer did everything in his power to atone for what he did. Thanks to him, the young woman is happily married and making a new life for herself and her child.'

'He violated my niece,' said Noble, trembling. 'When I finally learnt the truth, I had to make him pay for the shame he brought on my whole family. If I'd been fit enough, I'd have murdered that evil man myself. As it was, I had to hire an assassin.'

'Is his name in your address book?' asked Colbeck.

'Yes, it is.'

'Then I'll search for it, if you don't mind.'

'I do mind!' yelled Noble. 'I did what I felt I had to do, and I have no sense of shame. Lockyer is dead and the world is a better place as a result. You said that my confession of guilt will make for a shorter trial. Well, there's a way of avoiding the trial altogether.'

Before either of them could stop him, Noble put the gun to his head and pulled the trigger.

When he was given his orders, Victor Leeming was told to take Detective Constable Eric Boyce with him. The two of them climbed into a cab.

'Where are we going?' asked Boyce.

'The inspector is giving you a third chance to catch the man who slipped through your fingers twice. Somehow, Inspector Colbeck found out where the killer lives. We'll stop in the adjacent road then move in on foot.'

'How on earth did he get hold of the address?'

'It doesn't matter,' said Leeming. 'He also discovered the man's name – Aaron Peake. We know how slippery he can be so we must take no risks.'

'Very good, Sergeant.'

The cab eventually turned in to an area that featured rows of small, dirty, identical houses. Ragged children played in the streets. Because the sight of a hansom cab was so unusual, some of them ran behind the vehicle. When it finally stopped, Leeming got out and sent them on their way. After asking the cab to wait for them, he led the way to the next street. The killer's address was in the middle of the row, next to a lane that led to the rear of the dwellings.

'Give me time to get in position,' said Leeming, 'then knock on his door. One glance at you and Peake will make a run for it. I'll be waiting.'

'Be careful, Sergeant. He's a cunning devil.'

'Join me as soon as you can.'

Obeying his orders, Boyce waited a few minutes then he marched to the house where their quarry was living. He used the door knocker forcibly. There was an immediate response.

'You don't need to make such a bloody noise,' said a woman's voice from within the house.

The door was flung open to reveal a scrawny woman in her twenties with straggly hair and a tattered dress. After taking one look at Boyce, she turned around and yelled aloud.

'It's trouble, Aaron! Run for it!'

Victor Leeming was ready for him. Crouching in the lane at the rear of the house, he heard the woman's yell followed by the sound of a door opening and being slammed shut. Footsteps were fast approaching. Standing back from the gate, he waited until it was unlocked then stuck out his leg to trip up the man who came racing out. Peake hit the ground with a resounding thud. Before he could move, he felt someone dive on top of him, pull his arms behind his back and expertly handcuff him. A stream of foul language came out of the prisoner's mouth, and he did all he could to shake Leeming off. It was to no avail. Boyce came out through the door and helped Leeming to haul the man to his feet. When the prisoner tried to spit at him, he ducked.

'Got you at last!' said Boyce. 'Third time lucky.'

Edward Tallis took Colbeck's advice on how much information to release to the newspapers. The superintendent wanted lavish praise but limited scrutiny. He lauded the work of his detectives in solving the murder of Julian Lockyer and acknowledged valuable help in Shrewsbury from Colonel Edgell and his constabulary. The name of the killer was plastered over the front pages and the suicide of the man who employed him was also given maximum space. Professional jealousy on the part of Douglas Noble was assumed to be the motive for Lockyer's murder. At all events, the case was solved and the killer sentenced to death by hanging.

Because of Colbeck's adroit handling of reporters, the young couple who had recently moved into a house in Shrewsbury were not even mentioned. They would be able to return to the town in due course to live there in peace. The Station Hotel was the main beneficiary. The great black cloud over it had disappeared completely, and guests began to pour in once again.

As Tallis glanced at the newspapers spread out on his desk, he gave a sigh of satisfaction and turned to Colbeck.

'It's good to be praised by the press and not vilified,' he said.

'Enjoy the experience while you can, sir,' advised Colbeck. 'It's a rare event.'

'You did all the hard work.'

'Under your direction, it should be made clear. You deserve to wallow in adulation.'

'What pleases me most,' said Tallis, taking a letter from a drawer, 'is this. Colonel Edgell has been in touch. He not only congratulated me on the way that my detectives solved a perplexing murder, he took the opportunity to assure me that he did not block my promotion to the rank of major. Indeed, he recommended it.'

'I am glad that you no longer need to brood about what you perceived as a personal attack on you. Your hatred of the man has no basis.'

'Quite true,' said Tallis, smiling. 'When the dust has finally settled on this case, I may even decide to visit Shrewsbury in person.' He handed the letter to Colbeck. 'Read it for yourself. Between the lines, I fancy, is an invitation to visit an old soldier beside whom I was once proud to fight.'

'Both of you will gain an immense benefit from a meeting, Superintendent.'

'I hope so.'

'As a newcomer to law enforcement,' said Colbeck, 'he may well ask your advice.'

'Yes,' agreed Tallis. 'It's highly likely. I'll be happy to give him wise counsel. I know the first thing he must do.'

'Do you, sir?'

'Yes, he must find his own version of a brilliant Detective Inspector like you. That will make his life as a Chief Constable immeasurably easier.'

'Are you suggesting that I am transferred to Shropshire,' teased Colbeck.

'Heavens above - no!' howled Tallis. Your place is here and I'll fight anyone who dares to try to take you away.'

'Even though he once held a senior rank in the Bengal Army?'

'Even then, Inspector. Where would Scotland Yard be without you? The notion is unthinkable!'

Colbeck smiled. 'I appreciate your faith in my limited abilities, sir.'

EDWARD MARSTON has written well over a hundred books, including some non-fiction. He is best known for his hugely successful Railway Detective series and he also writes the Bow Street Rivals series featuring twin detectives set during the Regency; the Home Front Detective novels set during the First World War; and the Ocean Liner mysteries.

edwardmarston.com